SWEET

Christina

man she l

seen him f

alone on a … see his father – with murder in his heart.

Now she returns to the little village of Berghmere and the lovely old house, Sweetcrab, standing on the edge of the marsh. But time has done nothing to blur the edges of that dreadful night and once more she finds herself surrounded by suspicious hatred in an atmosphere charged with menace.

Available in Fontana by the same author

The Sand Rose
The Sea House
Nightingale at Noon

MARGARET SUMMERTON

Sweetcrab

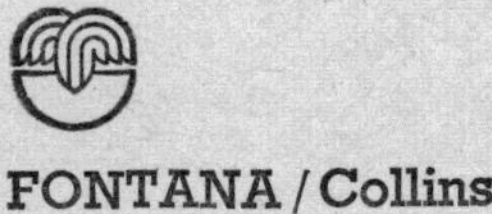

FONTANA / Collins

First published by Wm. Collins 1971
First issued in Fontana Books 1974

Printed in Great Britain
Collins Clear-Type Press London and Glasgow

CHAPTER ONE

On the plane from Kennedy to Heathrow I was fortified by a belief that the six months' self-discipline I'd exercised over my spasmodically deranged mind had paid off. Pride in my victory, release from the recurring bouts of hysterical fantasies in which my eyes played vile tricks on me amounted to a sense of personal salvation.

Until the outcome of that hard-won battle was certain I had not dared return to England after a two and a half year spell working in New York. If I'd lost I'd have had no alternative but to turn a deaf ear to Tim Woodham's plea. To have submitted myself to the scrutiny of a tightly-knit village community where eyes were primed with knowledge, memories keen-edged and merciless would have been insupportable. Though it had never happened, my most terrorizing fear was that one day someone who knew Christina Graham would witness one of her mad-woman acts.

But for over six months now I'd been free of the hallucinations that persuaded me it was Cary disappearing round a street corner, leaping into a cab, striding into a store. Twenty times or more in two years I'd run the breath out of my lungs to catch up with him, only to stand stuttering apologies to a stranger who'd plainly doubted my sanity or my morals.

The last time had been seven months ago, coming out of Macy's. I'd clutched what my deluded mind had misled me into believing was Cary's coat-sleeve, found myself staring into a scowling, affronted face before, sick with disappointment, I'd turned and run. It had been then that, under my breath, I'd sworn an oath to myself: that was the final act of self-torture, an end to the haunting. Never again would I be transformed into a demented woman chasing a Will-of-the-wisp man.

But the mind doesn't take orders. The senses aren't subject to reason. Cary was standing a few yards ahead of me in the line to the immigration desk. I *was* looking at the back of his head, at the silky ash-brown hairline that could belong to no man on earth but him; at his delicately pointed ear-lobes, at the proud set of his shoulders. Even his tweed jacket was a replica of the one he'd worn that last night in the Bird Hut.

Once I would have run forward, grabbed his arm, hung on. Now, though the oath to myself was erased from memory by a flood-tide of joy, I retained a few dregs of reasoning power that calculated for me, dictated that I was not in a city street where, with the speed of a conjuring trick, he could melt from sight in a crowd. There was no public or private transport at hand to whisk him away. He was a captive of officialdom which could not be bypassed – my captive. Three British passport holders were ahead of him, six between us. When his passport was stamped he could only move in one direction: obliquely to the Customs Hall, which would automatically turn his profile towards me. Only then would I step out of line, walk fast – not run – across the space dividing us.

It *was* Cary. This time it was no devil trick of mind or eye. The coincidence amounting to a small miracle, that we should return to England on the same day, that he was actually within a few yards of me, obliterated the dark and crucifying past, and left me with a sense of standing in blinding sunlight. I'd call his name: he'd cry mine. Beyond that point imagination did not function, but it was enough that within a minute I'd touch the warm, living flesh of his hand.

With patience born of certitude I kept check of the sequence of movements that could only follow a prescribed order. The queue ahead of Cary had shrunk to two. The man at the desk was tucking his passport into his pocket, making towards the Customs Hall, and a woman had taken his place. When she moved away, Cary put his passport on the counter. The last seconds of waiting were timeless, the absolute quality of my belief that it was Cary making an area of lightness in the top of my head. Now! I foresaw the pattern of the next half-minute as precisely as though it had already happened. But the pattern slipped into a grotesque distortion of my imagination. Instead of aiming directly for the Customs Hall, after a couple of steps he paused, and as though the intensity of my concentrated stare exerted a physical pull, looked round at me, baffled, uneasy. For perhaps the length of two seconds the eyes, the mouth, the shape and skin texture of a face I'd never seen were blown up monstrously to over-life size, then my vision blurred producing a semi-blindness. He could only have walked to the Customs Hall, but I didn't see him go.

When the blindness passed, it left a wake of vicious self-loathing for the pitiful creature afflicted with a recurring sickness of the mind that every little while burst the bounds of sanity. The effect of this ice-cold exposure of myself was physical nausea. I had to press hard on the counter to keep upright as the Customs officer asked his parrot questions, prodded fingers into the corners of my suitcases. When he'd chalked my baggage I went and leaned against a wall, postponing the moment when I must pass through the barrier, meet Sue waiting on the other side.

I'd known her as far back as I could remember. We'd lived in the same East Anglian village, shared Hester's nursery lessons under Addy, gone to the same school, left Berghmere to work in London in the same month, and when my world exploded in the narrow margin of a single night, Sue, on the point of leaving for a job in New York, had master-minded the formalities of one for me. We'd shared an apartment there until Sue had returned to England three months ahead of me. Also, as we were both only children, we served as substitute sisters, holding no secrets from one another, except that I was subject to spasms of lunacy that set me pursuing strange men down streets, round corners. I'd never confided that haunting sickness to a living soul. And I never would.

For Sue, Cary was a horror-figure, self-damned for ever. I accepted that verdict in relation to herself. Murderers are pariahs, obscenely marked with the stain of the human blood they have shed. For sensible people, and Sue was an eminently sensible girl, if you've had the ill-fortune to have counted one as friend, you smartly set about the surgical operation of cutting him out of memory. It was comparatively easy for her: she hadn't loved Cary; she hadn't been his forever love.

It was a porter inquiring: 'Are you all right, Miss?' that reminded me I couldn't cower against a wall all night. Anyway, I was over the worst: there remained only the shivering inside me that no one could see, plus a pin-sized blink of suspicion that I'd made a fatal misjudgment in coming home. But it was too late to revoke that.

Sue came running towards me, arms outflung. 'I was beginning to think you'd missed the plane. What did you have in your luggage, a gold bar or a lump of cannabis?' She slotted her arm through mine. 'Come and meet Jerry. You did once, ages ago, but he's changed out of all recognition. He's come along to drive us home.'

Jerry struck no chord in my memory. He might have been the dumb, two left-footed youth who'd worshipped Sue and whom we'd treated as a hilarious joke; alternatively any one of the small regiment of boy-friends she'd kept on tap when we'd shared the Chelsea flat. Heavily built, he loomed giant-fashion over Sue who was tiny. He had upstanding jet black hair, sideburns and eyebrows to match, and a smile he didn't over-use. He hardly spoke on the journey into town, not that he'd overmuch chance with Sue twittering away non-stop.

When we reached Sloane Avenue she leapt out, held open the car door. 'Remember the old slummy flat! That geyser that nearly blew us up! Wait till you see this one. Leave all that, Jerry will cope with the luggage.' She pulled me across the forecourt, chanting: 'It's warm! Cross my heart. It's got a garbage disposal unit and oceans of cupboards.' Waiting for the lift, her flow of chatter suddenly dried up, and the dizzy gad-fly image was temporarily eclipsed behind one with a sternly quizzing regard. 'I'm always so exhausted when I get off a plane, I could sleep for a week. That's what you look like, flaked out, and a bit green round the edges. You are okay, aren't you, Christy, not wishing you were still on the other side of the Atlantic?'

'I'm fine. Just dying on my feet after the rush of getting away.'

'I can imagine.' To my relief she stopped looking anxious. 'Don't worry about Jerry being underfoot. He's been warned he's only getting one drink and then Exit!'

'Hard lines on him!'

'He'll bear up. We've got a date for tomorrow night.'

I admired the flat that was streamlined, shining and designed to suggest space where, in fact, little existed. Jerry was allowed two drinks before Sue confiscated his glass. He held out a hand to me. 'It's been nice meeting you again, Christina.'

'Nice for me too.' I wondered if he remembered where, and added because he deserved it: 'I'll be gone in the morning. Thanks for chauffeuring me.'

It was ten minutes before Sue came back wearing an absent expression that suggested, though Jerry was fast speeding into the distance, he still remained the pivot of her attention, and that didn't happen often with Sue.

'Nice,' I murmured. 'Very.'

She nodded, then flashed me what was for her an uncharacteristically shy smile. 'It might be for real . . . I don't know yet. But it just might.' She tapped the table as if touching wood. 'I'm nowhere near committing myself, but if it is, it won't make any difference about the flat. We'd move into Jerry's, and you could have this to yourself, or share it. I wouldn't leave you stranded.'

'As if that would matter!'

'But it does,' she insisted. 'Comfortable roosts in inner London for non-millionaires are hard to come by. Is the job all fixed up?'

'Yes. Gordon joins Creath & Howson a month from Monday, and his assistant along with him.'

She chewed her lip, looked doubtful. 'You know best, but Creath & Howson are pretty small fry in the P.R. business.'

'Which is why they made a bid for Gordon. I met their managing director when he was in New York in January, a couple of months after he'd taken over from his father, so it amounts to three infusions of new blood, one young, one pure Madison Avenue, plus me. Financially they're sound and they have terrific plans for expansion.'

'Um! You as a smart executive type! I hate to think that's to be your line for evermore.' Her face took on its bossy expression signalling she was about to lecture me for my own good. 'A month. And how long are you proposing to stay with Aunt Edith?'

'About three weeks.'

'Less if you can,' she ordered. 'And don't get tangled up. Don't start going broody. Christy, you wouldn't dare, not after all this time?'

'Not likely.'

'I wish Mummy and Dad still lived in Berghmere. They'd keep an eye on you.' Her mother suffered from chronic bronchitis, for which reason six months ago, Major and Mrs Duncan had bought a café with living quarters above it in Malta.

'I wish they were. How are they?'

'Slaving away selling pots of tea and Chelsea buns to homesick English tourists. Which puts me off going there for a holiday. Holiday! Dad would have me lashed to the sink washing up.'

She insisted on giving me my supper in bed, while she sat on its twin daring me to leave a mouthful of her mushroom omelette which tasted like egg-flavoured rubber. Normally she dreamed up the menus, I vetted them and cooked what was likely to be edible.

As, thankfully, I put down my fork, with nourishment inside me, she reverted to the Sue by the lift, anxious and stern-eyed. 'Christy, you swear now you're actually here you've not got the jitters about going back to Berghmere?'

'Of course I haven't. I'm suffering from a perfectly natural sense of disorientation at being whipped from the New World back to the Old in a matter of hours. Everyone gets it.'

'Um!' She gave me a maddening sceptical look. 'Well, if you say so. I should have thought a fortnight would have been long enough to get your aunt sorted out. It's not as though she's ill, tied to her bed, is it?'

I summarized Tim Woodham's letter – he was her doctor, as his father had been before him. 'Not ill, but she's become much deafer, and the arthritis in her right hand and both knees is worse, and . . .'

'And,' she finished for me, 'she's more bloody-minded than ever. How old is she?'

'Seventy.'

'Granny's eighty-one and gets highly insulted if you dare suggest she's more than middle-aged.' She paused for a moment, then remarked censoriously: 'Miss Graham should have moved, put a hundred miles between her and Berghmere, then you could have gone and sorted her out without having to face the lot of them.' She stared broodingly at me. 'You might as well know it, Christy, I'm agin it.'

A second uprooting in Aunt Edith's life! When her only brother's wife had died at my birth she'd resigned her headmistress-ship of a primary school in Derbyshire, sold up her home to take on both of us. I considered it unlikely that a move from the house where she'd lived for over twenty years because the man her niece was going to marry had run amok crossed her mind. She wasn't the type to kow-tow to the bludgeoning of fate. To by-pass a pointless wrangle I murmured: 'Oh, I don't know. She was a bit old to find a new home.'

Hours later, when the room was dark, she whispered from the other twin bed: 'Christy, are you awake?'

'More or less.'

She went on in a breathily urgent voice: 'I've never talked about Cary, have I? Plagued you about him?'

'No.'

'But I've got to, just this once. Christy, what you never saw was that he wasn't good enough for you, not by a mile. I cried my eyes out the evening you told me you and he were engaged.'

My flesh seemed to stiffen on my bones with shock. It was as though she had raked dirty fingers over a memory of a golden day that had been ashimmer with happiness. I *remembered* Sue being glad, rejoicing with me. It couldn't have been an act; it followed she must be speaking from hindsight. It was a small betrayal that took a little forgiving, and before I could find the right words, she ploughed on: 'The awful part is that you pretend you've let him go, but I know darned well you haven't. You bottle it up inside you, but sometimes it shows, at least with me. Oh, I know you collected more than your quota of boy-friends in New York, but none of them ever stuck.' She drew in her breath. 'Sometimes I get the idea that you're existing on two levels simultaneously, half of you not only buried in the past but actually living it, as though it was before your eyes sixteen hours a day. Wasting them on Cary Leighton!' She choked on her indignation, rushed on: 'And like as not he married the first girl that took his fancy and they're living happily on the other side of the world. Either that . . . or he's dead. He could be, Christy.'

'He's not dead.'

'How can you be sure?'

'If he were dead I'd know.' Married? That possibility had never occurred to me, and I found it so unlikely that it struck no fear in me.

She sighed, pushed herself on. 'But you've got to admit you're still hung up on him. You do think about him, don't you?'

I lied to comfort her, though what she'd said about my living on two levels bothered me – it cut too near the truth, made a rent in my belief that I'd kept that part of myself locked out of sight: 'Only very rarely.'

There was a silence in which I could sense her racking her brains for words that would quench hope and act as instant therapy in a couple of sentences. It was beyond her. In the end, inspiration failing, she made a flat, emphatic statement. 'Even you must admit that he'd never dare to set foot in England. The moment he did he'd be arrested.'

'Of course I know.' It was a half-lie. My head knew, but not my heart. It should have meant that in England there'd be no basis for the spasms of dementia that shaped a strange man into the image of Cary, set me running. It hadn't worked at Heathrow.

She said sleepily: 'I wish I knew more about what's going on in Berghmere now, but with Mummy and Dad in Malta, I haven't heard any local news for ages. Since Liz got that new teaching job in Gloucestershire, she rarely scrawls more than half a page every six months. Does your aunt write?'

'Not much since the arthritis got into the joints of her right hand.'

'Markham . . .' She spoke his name suddenly, very distinctly. 'I wonder . . .' and then fell asleep before she could put what she wondered into words.

In the darkness, to the background sound of her muted, even breathing, I had for company the memory of the first man I'd loved: Markham Drake, who had obsessed me awake and asleep during the six months that spanned the end of my seventeenth year and the beginning of my eighteenth. At this distance there was no thread of pain, not even a twinge of embarrassment in recalling a period when I'd swung frenziedly between delirious happiness and near suicidal despair, while everyone with my good at heart had tried to induce me to come to my senses; vainly. In the end I'd wrought my own self-destruction. Now, made remote by time, I saw it as a schoolgirl's fantasy of love, naïve, slightly comic. And yet, before I fell asleep, there hummed through my head two lines that Liz, who'd had a shameful tendency at eighteen to quote lush poetry, had used to describe Markham Drake. 'A prince, clothed in light and crowned with stars.' I smiled at my lost love-sick self who in some wasted crevice of memory had stored up that sugar sweet epitaph. For epitaph it was. The stars about Markham Drake's head must have faded, the light in which he walked become dimmed to near darkness when Ophelia died.

CHAPTER TWO

Sue left for her City office at nine, and we shared a taxi as far as Cheapside. Eyeing me with near-approval, she remarked: 'Last night you had me worried, but thank heaven you don't look such a dreary little waif this morning. You are going to take it all in your stride, aren't you? Go on, cross your heart, and maybe I'll believe you.'

I reassured her twice over that was exactly what I was proposing to do, and meant it. The sick tremors of panic had mercifully died out in the night, and I had toppled the shaming picture of that delusion-struck hysteria at Heathrow over the edge of my mind; all right, I'd suffered a relapse, but one that wouldn't be repeated. By now, I'd hammered into my heart as well as into my head one irrefutable fact: Unless he was prepared to risk arrest, a life-sentence of imprisonment, Cary must remain forever an exile from his homeland, and it followed, unless I was crazed past redemption, that my hauntings were at an end.

At Liverpool Street Station, to fill in the twenty minutes before my train came in, I was running my eye over the magazines at the bookstall when my attention was trapped by a pyramid of brightly jacketed novels advertising themselves a Book Society Choice. The author's name was unfamiliar but not the publisher: the Canlet Press.

I picked up the top copy and holding it I was catapulted out of my hard-won calm, overwhelmed by a violent explosion of bitterness that in two and a half years the cup of ambition had been filled to overflowing for two young men, left bone-dry for the third. A couple of callow, get-rich-quick boys operating on a shoestring from a basement in a back street was how Magnus Leighton had summed up Nathan Canley and Eric Sivers – doomed to early bankruptcy if they were fools enough to pit themselves against established publishing houses armed with know-how, capital and a fleet of accountants. Positive of the infallibility of his judgment, he'd airily wafted aside Cary's pleas.

Nathan and Eric, as hard-headed in their youth as Magnus in middle-age, had been equally adamant. A partnership was on offer. It was Cary's, but it must be bought and the asking price was £5,000. Surely, they suggested, a comparatively modest sum for Magnus to advance to his son, if not as a gift, then as a short-term loan yielding interest. As far as they were concerned, the ball was in Cary's court. His dilemma was that he couldn't get it back into play.

For two months Cary had fought a one-sided battle with his father; one-sided because Magnus had refused to fight back, to take seriously a wild-cat scheme designed to rob him of £5,000 which would either go down the drain or mysteriously find its way into the pockets of two young crooks who'd have fled the country before the bailiffs hammered on the door. He knew what he was talking about; he'd met their ilk before. An all-knowing smile, a nod that commended his foresight, or a warm self-congratulatory chuckle. The manner of dismissal varied, but not its effect on Cary: a rage that consumed him, became in the end a life force.

As the deadline Nathan and Eric had set advanced upon us, I'd frantically dredged up alternative sources of money. His mother? His elder brother Wellesley? But as we might have guessed if we hadn't been dizzily spinning in circles, Magnus had primed them. Encourage Cary to leave Berghmere, forfeit his privileged position as a third-generation Leighton in one of the soundest, most esteemed printing firms in East Anglia! Throw away his heritage in exchange for a catch-penny enterprise that would collapse inside twelve months! Mother and brother formed a united front self-righteously determined to save Cary from recklessly laying waste his career.

Markham? I'd queried, and Cary had jeered back: 'Brainwashed months ago . . . by Father.'

We were reduced to our last source, one from which I'd repeatedly shied from tapping. Now Cary thrust me ruthlessly towards it. My father had left me £7,000 held in a Trust

Fund which I could not touch until my twenty-fifth birthday, but some time in my early teens Aunt Edith had inherited money from a distant cousin. I did not know the amount – I'd known better than to commit the cardinal sin of poking my nose into what did not concern me – but I'd gained the impression from her visits to a solicitor in Helsby, the documents flowing through the house at the time of the bequest, that it was a sizeable sum.

'You're not asking her to give you the money, merely to lend it to you until you're twenty-five, when you can pay her back, plus a whopping rate of interest. She can't refuse; why the hell should she? She's got no use for it; I bet she's got no use for it; I bet she's never touched a penny of it, and who else has she got to leave it to but you? Christy, we need the money now if I'm not to remain Father's lackey and Wellesley's little brother for life. We can't afford to wait till you're twenty-five. It's the end for us unless you get to work on her.'

Wretchedly I'd obeyed, but Aunt Edith had refused as emphatically, as unequivocally as Magnus. Had he primed her too. or had she been obeying the dictates of her Puritan conscience? Money to Aunt Edith – who thought in pence and shillings, only grudgingly in pounds – was a sacred trust, accumulated by honest toil, never to be squandered, to be put at risk.

When I gave him her answer the rain had been drumming on the roof tiles of the Bird Hut, and under the circle of light thrown by the old-fashioned oil lamp, I'd stared at the bone-white hate-clenched fists, filled and running over with love and pity plus a dark trembling foreboding that was only a hair's breadth from fear. Defeat was too bitter an experience for Cary to acknowledge aloud; to abandon hope of the only future open to him free from servitude to his father, was like being doomed to walk forever through an unending dark tunnel. For a long while he stared, silent and blank-eyed into a shadow-filled corner of the Bird Hut. When, at last, he opened his mouth it was to speak with the slow emphatic malevolence of one uttering a curse.

'As long as I can remember Father's been bent on cutting

me down to size, the size that suits him, and he'll go on doing it as long as he lives.' Suddenly he smiled, not at me, but into space, as though what he saw afforded him intense pleasure. 'Curious, isn't it, it never dawns on him that he's mortal, that one day the great Magnus Leighton will be a lump of cold, mouldering flesh. I, on the other hand, get a kick out of picturing him buried under a two hundredweight slab of granite, slowly rotting away, his silver tongue silent, the flesh falling away from his fingers, and not a lip left to smile with. That magic smile that charms birds off trees, wins friends and influences everyone who's never been privileged to glimpse his ice-cold heart. Rotted away and in its place a skull's hideous grin!'

A darkness of the heart that robbed me of speech, even coherent thought, made me cry aloud in horror. I would not believe that he wished his father, whom I loved, dead.

The choking sound brought his gaze instantly back from space to me. 'Silly little love, I didn't mean it. You know me better than that.' He pulled me into his arms, cradled me against his shoulder. 'A joke, maybe in poor taste, but that's all it was, a joke. I hope the old boy lives to be a hundred, and he probably will.' He crooned as if I'd been a hurt child. 'There, there . . . just a sick joke, darling. Forget it.'

Magnus Leighton, Lord of Sweetcrab, hadn't been witched to death by his younger son, but one week later, shot through the heart by his own revolver fired by Cary before he had fled, a murderer on the run, from Sweetcrab.

A crackling voice from a loud-speaker informed me that the 10.05 train to Helsby would be leaving from Platform 5. I returned the novel to its place on top of the pyramid, picked up the single suit-case I was taking to Berghmere, and went on my way.

A mile out of Helsby station, the single-storey buildings of the Leighton Printing Works stretched alongside the railway line. The train even slowed down to allow me to spell out the lettering. I was surprised that the name Leighton was still there. From a cutting out of the local paper Mrs Duncan had sent Sue I'd learned that Leighton's had been taken over by a giant London printing consortium, one that had been making overtures for years. Magnus had taken a mischevious pleasure in encouraging the ground-sounding men and then, when success glimmered tantalizing on their horizon, slamming the door in their faces, shooing them off the premises.

But Wellesley had negotiated the sale within twelve months of his father's death and for five years reserved for himself the managing directorship to provide financial cover and status until he was one or two rungs up the ladder of the political career he'd mapped out for himself. A couple of months before I'd left Berghmere the sitting member of Parliament had announced he wouldn't be standing at the next election, and Wellesley had been adopted as the Prospective Conservative Candidate. So in eighteen months or thereabouts, with a majority of 20,000 in his favour, Wellesley Leighton should be taking his seat in Parliament. Thereafter, all he needed was a minimum of good luck and a presentable wife with political know-how and the right family connections . . . he'd probably had her lined up for years. For the last fast-dwindling moments of the train journey I pondered on the wicked vagaries of fortune that, in a family of three children, gilded the future of one, blackened those of the other two.

Tim Woodham was at the ticket barrier, head craned forward, glance peering right and left to pick me out the instant I was in sight, not wasting a second because Tim never had one to spare. If you've known someone since childhood you don't have to guess their age; you know it, and their reaction to any given situation. I'd been in a primary class when Tim had gone to Edinburgh Medical School, and in my last year as Head Girl of Helsby High School when his father had died and he'd taken over the practice. That made him thirty-four.

Physically he had no redeeming feature: a lank, ungainly body, stooping shoulders, uneven features, round brown eyes that mostly peered under or over his spectacles, and straight, lustreless dark hair that barbers were shanghaied into trimming on the run. Yet whenever I heard the words a heart of gold I instantly thought of Tim. Of all men he had been in desperate need of a domesticated, well-organized wife. Instead he'd picked Maureen Turner – or she'd picked him – a sweet-natured butterball who never managed to extricate herself from one crisis before she fell headlong into the next. There were dog-hairs and a smear of jam on his jacket, his shirt was frayed at the cuffs, but a mighty welcoming grin split his face.

'Christina!' he yelled. 'Am I glad to see you!' He picked up my case with one hand, grabbed my elbow with the other and hustled me through the exit. 'I planned on having lunch at the Bull. That way I can brief you before you get home. All right with you?'

'Anything you say.'

He ordered two halves of light ale at the bar. After one swallow he loped off to the telephone to get the latest bulletin on Mollie Prentice who was having her second baby at home. Two minutes later he loped back with the news that the district nurse had arrived, and she judged it would be another hour before his services would be required.

Food, maybe because of Maureen's hit-and-miss catering – rumour had it she fed him on cans of baby food – was a matter of indifference to him. 'If we have the *table d'hôte,*' he said, giving me no opinion, 'it will save all the bother of choosing.'

As the anaemic ox-tail soup was put before us, he set briskly about the task he'd taken on, for which he'd allotted himself a time-ration of one hour.

'As I told you in my letter, there's no cause for alarm. I'm convinced that the root of the problem is that the old girl has entrenched herself behind her disabilities, walled herself in against help. Her worst handicap is increasing deafness. I'm pretty certain a hearing-aid would help. But will she consider one! She acts as though I were dragging her along to a witch-doctor! The arthritis in her knees and right hand troubles her; I laid on a physiotherapist but after two treatments she refused to have her back in the house. She resents being seen in public using a stick and as far as I can make out hasn't been outside since December.' He gave me a rueful but wholly compassionate grin. 'She slipped on a streak of ice coming out of the Post Office, shook herself up so badly she had to be helped home by Lenny Fardon and a mate of his. You can imagine how she reacted to that indignity!'

I could. Lenny Fardon was the village drunk who was only driven to work when he ran out of dole benefit. Aunt Edith not only regarded him as a human parasite but was given to saying so loud and clear.

And, Tim went on, it didn't help that during the last year she'd lost her only two close friends: Minnie Bishop who'd died in October, and Gladys Tugg who had moved to Devon in January to share a house with her widowed sister. Another stroke of bad luck was that Mrs Mays, the charwoman who'd cleaned at South View since I was a child, had developed a faulty heart and had been ordered to retire. Her replacement was Mrs Curtis who had abysmally low standards of cleanliness and, worse, no knowledge of or desire to learn the respectful mien Aunt Edith expected from an employee. The house was urgently in need of basic repairs, but she made do, refused to countenance what she called an army of workmen forever brewing themselves tea at her expense. And, as I knew, Meg, the Jack Russell terrier who had been her shadow for fifteen years, had died.

'Meg had been failing for months,' Tim said, wolfing his soggy golden suet roll. 'She couldn't expect to keep her for ever, but Meg's death hit her hard.'

I nodded. I, too, would miss Meg.

He wiped his mouth with his napkin, stuck his fingers up in the air to act as an abacus: 'One, persuade her to be examined for a hearing-aid; two, bully Mrs Curtis into minding her manners or fire her and dig up a replacement; three, organize a few essential repairs to the house, and, four, rent a television. Oh, I know all about her withering scorn of the goggle-box, but don't ask her permission, just lay one on. Maybe, in time, the habit will creep up on her and stick. They're heaven-sent for the old living alone.'

'Tim!' I exploded. 'You're asking me to perform a series of miracles in three weeks!'

He flashed me his most beguiling smile, consolingly patted my hand. 'Nothing that's beyond you. You're a clever, practical young woman. And don't start panicking, you won't have to start from scratch, I've already put in some groundwork. Keeping my fingers crossed that you'll persuade her into keeping it, I've made an appointment with Charles Sessler, the ear, nose and throat specialist at Helsby General for next Tuesday morning at eleven o'clock, and I looked in at the garage. Joe has a Ford Anglia he's prepared to hire out to you until you get around to buying a car.'

'Probably some old banger with 15,000 miles on the clock instead of the 75,000 it's done!'

'What's the odds! It'll get you about for three weeks.' He gave me a look that was deadly serious, said quietly: 'I've got faith in you, Christina, so don't let me down. She's a game old girl.' He flicked his eye over his watch, beckoned the waiter for the bill.

Game but not lovable, not even comfortable to live with. To me she'd always been an iron woman, the stuff of which martyrs are made. The canons by which she directed her life – abstinence, duty, rectitude, a consuming passion for honesty – were beyond most ordinary mortals. She'd inherited sole guardianship of me when I'd been three years old, the day my father, who'd been afflicted with chronic absent-mindedness after my mother's death, had walked into the path of a speeding lorry. I didn't know whether within any definition of the word she loved me; what I did know was that she'd have gone to the stake rather than fail in her duty towards me.

On the way to the car, Tim quipped: 'Don't look so glum. You'll be able to do what no one else could simply because you're family. The last piece she's got.'

He had a point. In Aunt Edith's rigid code of Victorian morality direct kinship absolved you from a fate she quite literally counted worse than death: that of being beholden to outsiders.

There were three routes from Helsby to Berghmere. Eight miles by the ruler-straight main road, nine by side roads, seven if you used short-cuts that were only navigable at non-flood seasons. Tim, naturally, to cut seconds, took the main road, braced himself behind the wheel of his ancient Austin like a rally driver.

'Be prepared for changes,' he shouted to make himself heard above the engine. 'Campers, caravans and chalet-renters have moved in in droves. And cheers, I say. Does them a damn sight more good than flying to Spain for sun and scampi and gippy tummies. More important, they fill the tills of the local tradesmen. In a small way, we're a boom area now instead of a picturesque backwater.' He gave a snort of scorn. 'I've no patience with the old-worlde preservation brigade who prefer roses dripping over walls with no damp courses to inside sanitation. Campers and caravans spell baths, flush toilets, and meat three times a week instead of once.'

Belatedly he remembered a lapse of manners – not that it would worry him unduly. 'You never told me about America. Was it a success? What sort of work did you do over there?'

'As far as I was concerned it was a huge success. I worked in a public relations firm.'

He wrinkled his nose. 'What do they do?'

'They promote a person or a product. My boss in New York is coming to London for a three-year spell as top consultant and ideas man with a P.R. firm over here. I've been signed up as his assistant.'

'Good for you.' He'd done his duty. His job made such mental and physical demands that he had precious little of himself left over for anyone who wasn't either sick or pregnant. I was surprised, therefore, when he took his glance from the road for a split second, fixed it on me. 'Whatever you were up to, it suited you. You look rare and bonny, Christina. I mean it. Hair's different though. What have you done to it?'

'Nothing except I put it up this morning.'

He indulged himself in a rare flight of nostalgia. 'When she was a kid, you could spot Christina Graham a mile off with that great mane of black hair flying behind her. Grey eyes, but not the same. No girl's eyes are these days.'

'Liners and shadow and long, bewitching false lashes.'

'Making most of them look like bush-babies.'

I didn't argue. We were half-way to Berghmere. I hadn't kept watch on the landscape, rather let myself slide blind-eyed through it. I'd never suffered a single pang of home-sickness for a village or a countryside, only an incurable sickness of heart for one man and one house. From my mid-teens my goal had been a short cut to escape from Berghmere and independence. No three years at University for me; instead a six months' secretarial course in Norwich with a job in London at the end of it. Sweetcrab, the home of my heart I'd come back to visit often. In those days it would have been beyond belief that a time would come when its doors would be slammed against me.

What overcame me was an insidious creeping awareness, a process of osmosis in which I played no conscious part, as individual notes and scenes thrust themselves forward, demanded attention. The immense arc of sky into which ancient church towers as far as twenty miles distant prodded stubby fingers. Lines of whip-branched alders, expanses of flat, heavy chestnut-brown earth, pockets of rushes and reeds as high as my head. And everywhere the eye could reach, the glint and silver flash of water: broad, river, pool and drainage ditch. As nearly as I can describe it, the stark low-toned landscape not only reclaimed me, but exerted a response in me that I had no particular wish to give.

We were silent until we crossed the bridge over the river on the eastern rim of Berghmere, where in two and a half years the number of moored dinghies, yachts and cruisers had trebled. 'Surely,' I pressed, beginning to need reassurance, 'Aunt Edith can't have lost all her friends?' Though when I came to count them up I realized she'd never had many. There was a stiff rod of pride in her that fiercely protected her social status sandwiched between what she archaically termed 'gentry and villagers': a narrow stratum of retired and active professional folk – school-teachers, doctors, bank managers and the clergy.

'She's of an age when friends have a nasty habit of dying off. Younger people have moved in, but she finds it difficult to come to terms with them. Doesn't want to, would be my guess. The new vicar, for instance, is a good enough fellow, but he called on her dressed in a sweater and gum-boots. Consequently he got short shrift and hasn't been back since.' He considered for a moment. 'I'd say about the only real friend she's got is Markham. He seems to keep an eye on her.'

Markham's name dropped casually into such a context startled me, presenting a baffling realignment of personalities.

Granted he'd known her since boyhood but the relationship had been formal: on his side scrupulous courtesy towards an elderly woman; on hers a watchful eye for mud on his shoes. Markham visiting an old house-bound woman! Why? Out of kindness of heart, a sort of errand of mercy? Hardly! I worried round it until, without warning, there flashed across my inner vision his brilliant deep blue glance, the smile that could beguile or cruelly mock according to his mood, and I thought with absolute conviction, he must be getting something out of it, though what, I hadn't a clue.

'He's back at Holland Court then?'

'Yes. He's been back there permanently oh . . . getting on for two years now.'

Alone. Driven back to the vast silent rooms, or not driven, there voluntarily to lick his wounds, wait for grief to subside and die.

'How is he?'

'He seems to have weathered it, at least to outward appearances. Work's a great balm, of course, and he's been at full stretch trying to pull the place into some sort of order, reorganize it on modern lines, and from all accounts he seems to be making a fine job of it. Even so, you don't come through an experience like that the same man as you went in.'

The experience he meant was the death of Ophelia, Markham's wife, who, the first Christmas I'd been in New York, had been suffocated to death under an avalanche of snow when they'd been ski-ing in Austria.

He continued in a grieving, outraged tone: 'She was three months pregnant.'

If I'd known what questions I wanted to ask, there would have been no time to put them. We were at the end of the village High Street, turning off into a narrow by-road that ran away from it at a sharp angle. A couple of hundred yards and South View was in sight, a modest square house without adornment or pretension, as solidly unimaginative as its name. My father had bought it on his marriage to my mother, rightly judging it a suitable residence for a master printer who was the works manager of Leighton's.

Tim leapt out, carried my suitcase up the front path, deposited it on the top of the flight of railed steps that ended at the door, loped back. I saw the question coming, braced myself. Down to the last half-minute, some reference had to be made; after all, he'd been one of Cary's friends.

Acute embarrassment coupled with desperate concern contorted his plain face. 'Christina, all this, coming back to Berghmere, it hasn't been too hard on you, has it?'

'No. It's all too long ago and far away. It's all right, Tim. No need to worry.'

'I'm glad. After I'd written to you, I suffered a few pangs of guilt . . .' He grinned relief. 'But if you say it's all right, then it is.' His conscience clear, he squeezed my shoulder. 'I better be haring back to the Prentices', see how Mollie's coming on. You know where to find me, and Maureen will be bringing the kids along to see you. Oh, and mind and keep me posted about Tuesday's appointment with Sessler.'

When the sound of his car died away, I turned and looked straight ahead. The house seemed to have shrunk, and it had assuredly grown a whole lot shabbier as if, like its owner, it had opted out, stoically accepted the inevitability of decay. Frost had cracked bricks in the path, crumbled them into holes. The curtains at the front windows were partially drawn, and those in the dining-room were sagging from their hooks. The paint on the front door that had been kept snow-white and gleaming was blistered and dirt-streaked. Sight is a more potent sense than hearing. Confrontation with the house was a more eloquent and urgent message of what lay ahead of me than Tim's briefing. Walking up the path I felt as though I was sentenced to carry a crushing burden up a mountain.

When I put my hand on the rail, lifted my foot to reach the bottom step, the front door parted, and in the opening Aunt Edith looked down at me. My first reaction was blazing relief: she hadn't changed. Tim had painted too black a pitcure. Why, she was still wearing the navy dress with the white bob of lace in which I'd said goodbye to her.

I jumped the steps and with my arms around her, the tall strong-boned unyielding frame with its thin cover of flesh felt no different. I pressed my cheek to hers that was wrinkled and very dry and cool against my lips. 'Aunt Edith, oh it's so good to see you.'

'Come your ways in. You'll be worn out with all the traipsing about you've done.'

She and my father had been born and brought up in Derbyshire, and on the rare occasions when she was under a stress of emotions, she lapsed into the soft dialect of her native country. Like the door that had been opened before I'd had time to ring the bell, it bid me welcome. My spirit lifted, and I could have laughed aloud because she'd instantly set to rout the dreads that had put lead into my feet coming up the path.

At that moment it ceased to matter there was no love between us. What existed was a bond spliced with respcct, the incxplicable, compulsive claim of blood on blood, plus an exact knowledge of each other that was the result of sharing the same roof for twenty years. It added up to a good enough substitute for love.

I was smiling when she closed the door, stretched out her left hand to grasp the heavy stick propped against the hall-stand. To reach the sitting-room she had to limp through a brilliant shaft of March sunlight streaming down from the tall landing window. I felt the smile fading on my lips, the onset of a creeping dismay. She limped painfully, and the effort of taking each step thinned and tightened her mouth to a grimace. Even more shocking in a woman who had truly counted cleanliness and neatness next to Godliness, was a rip in the hem of her dress, and the black lace shoes that hadn't been cleaned for weeks. No, Tim hadn't exaggerated. Coupled with pity there was a shaming fear in me that I'd fail in the task he'd set me.

CHAPTER THREE

The kitchen door flew wide as Mrs Curtis scurried forward to present herself. Though she had grandchildren of my age, her proudest boast – with some justification – was that she'd kept her figure. To emphasize its youthfulness she wore a near-mini skirt and an orange polo-necked sweater. Her hair which I remembered as mousy-grey was a brassy gold.

Her shrewish brown eyes flittered over every inch of me as she pumped my hand. 'My, you're a sight for sore eyes. Had a good time in America, did you? My boy Arnie's eldest girl, Vanessa, was only saying last week that's where she's aiming to go. She's a qualified hairdresser now, first assistant at the Beauty Box in Helsby. You should look in and see her. Works miracles with hair, she does, miracles.' Her glance lifted meaningly, suggesting mine could do with one.

Aunt Edith's voice that still retained the penetrating quality of a teacher of small unruly children, cut through the skittish chat. 'Mrs Curtis, if you'll be good enough to bring in the tea-tray and kettle, we'll make tea when we are ready. And please remember to cover the bread and butter. It was too dry to be eatable yesterday.'

'Right you are,' Mrs Curtis murmured without deflecting her glance from me.

Aunt Edith's tone hardened to one of icy courtesy. 'That will be all, thank you, Mrs Curtis. I've left your money in an envelope on the dresser.'

As she limped into the sitting-room Mrs Curtis cast her eyes heavenwards in a plea for deliverance. 'Poor old soul, lives in the past, she does. Thinks five bob an hour a bloomin' fortune.' She darted a sly glance bright with threat at me. 'Now you're home you'll have to bring her ideas up to date. Half a day in the Supermarket in Helsby pays as much as a week's charing for her.' She aped virtue. 'Of course, I'd be the last to leave an old lady in the lurch, but now the Council's put the rent up, well your first duty's to yourself, that's what I always say. And with Harry taken . . .'

I edged firmly away. Harry Curtis had died when I was at school, and not even Tim could expect me to mend Mrs Curtis's manners the instant I crossed the threshold.

An electric fire had replaced the old coal one. To one side of it Aunt Edith, who had never allowed herself to be seduced by the comfort of soft upholstery, sat in a chair with a hide seat and back, wooden arms, ramrod straight, scorning even the Spartan support it offered her spine. She had been blessed with one beautiful feature, thick, lustrous hair that as long as I could remember had been snow-white. As though to belittle its quality, she dressed it with brutal severity, brushing it tight behind her ears from a centre-parting, discouraging it from softening the sharp contours of her high cheek bones, the over-prominent Roman nose, the mouth that set itself naturally in a stern, forbidding line.

As I went towards her, I thought: not so much entrenched as Tim had described, but a Stoic entombed within her own four walls. Had I brought her to this?

She rapped out: 'I'd better warn you that while you've been gone, I've grown as deaf as a post. You'll have to speak up, but I'd be obliged if you wouldn't shout.'

'I'll remember.' I pulled a stool into the centre of the hearthrug directly facing her. 'Apart from the deafness, how are you?

Her answer was uncompromising, prickly proud. 'A great deal better than young Tim Woodham would have you believe. He's a well-meaning lad with a kind heart but that doesn't give him the right to dictate to folks over twice his age. I don't take kindly to being bossed.'

She sounded so perky that I laughed. 'As if I didn't know!'

'Aye, you should.' Her eyes that had once been a bright china blue, had grown paler, but they were still capable of issuing a fearsome challenge. 'Christina, you didn't come home from New York on my account, did you?'

'Of course I didn't. I explained in my letter: my new job's in London, but I've got a month before I start and I wanted to spend part of it with you.'

She pondered, weighing my words for truth, before she nodded, gave me a pass mark. For a moment she was silent, looking over my head, then she queried sharply: 'Though it meant coming back to Berghmere?'

'Yes.' Now I was the stoic.

She lowered her gaze, subjected me to a deep, searching look before she awarded me one of her rare smiles that had the effect of putting a light behind her face that eased away the gauntness, erased a few of the myriad lines, then she sighed. 'You're a good girl. You always were. I never blamed you.'

Perhaps after all this time she believed she spoke the truth. Perhaps she'd forgotten. If so, I was prepared to forget too.

Glad to be done with sentiment, she raised her head higher, spoke with dry adamancy: 'As long as we've got one thing straight. You're here on holiday, not to nurse an old woman who's got no use for a nurse. Now, away you go and unpack your suitcase, get the creases out of your clothes. I've had your room made ready.'

All the rooms in South View were square, like a series of cubes set on top of one another. By 'readying' a room Aunt Edith meant cleaning, dusting, airing the mattress, making up the bed with fresh linen. Supplying heat, even at the bitter tail-end of winter, would never have crossed her mind, even if the means to provide it had existed, which they didn't. The degree of cold made me catch my breath, and a smell of fustiness, presumably coming from a patch of green-grey mould on the ceiling near the fireplace, settled unpleasantly in my nostrils.

I hadn't expected any changes or additions, consequently the room's abysmal cheerlessness was no surprise. Possessing perfectly adequate furniture, it never occurred to Aunt Edith to waste good money buying pieces that were more pleasing or comfortable. Wryly I lifted the corner of the washed-out Indian cotton bedspread that had been in use since I'd graduated from a child's cot. Wispy thin, but no actual holes, so why discard it!

If it had been the only bedroom I'd known, probably in my teens, I'd have rebelled against its darkness and miserable discomfort, but it had never been more to me than a dormitory. Without warning I began to shiver violently, not only from the physical cold that assaulted my flesh, but from an inner chill of appalling desolation at my banishment for ever from the house where my heart had found its home: Sweetcrab.

But there was no one to see me looking at it.

Immediately below the window was the back garden, its neatness proof that Tom Adkins, who dug and mowed, was still on the job. Deliberately postponing the pleasure or pain that lay waiting to pounce. I lengthened and slowed my glance, sliding it over the gate into the orchard, down the water-meadow, over the banks of reed the winter frosts had bleached honey-coloured until it reached the mere.

It was sickle-shaped, a curving half-mile of land-locked water. According to local legend it was bottomless, and no one to my knowledge had tried to plumb its depths – certainly not Magnus Leighton. Such rumours, serving to discourage trespassers either on foot or afloat, acted as an additional guard to his private property. On old maps it was marked as a decoy where wild fowl had been lured by tame duck decoys into a pipe terminating in a bow-net to be slaughtered at leisure. Magnus, a keen ornithologist, had on inheriting Sweetcrab, given orders for the pipe to be demolished.

When, at last, my glance dived timorously to find the mere, it was not there to see. A vaporous white cloud covered the steely-black water, out of which the tallest branches of the trees on the banks formed motionless skeletal patterns against a background of colourless sky. I opened the window, leaned out into the freezing air, and visible as a faint blur I could just define – or imagined I could – the tall chimneys of Sweetcrab. Even as I stared they grew fainter and more unsubstantial like a detail in a dream landscape, fading, dying.

Was Sweetcrab, robbed of its benevolent tyrant-master whose pride and enduring pleasure it had been, reduced to a mourning shadow of itself? I could not know. The vacuum left by Magnus's death shattered me anew. I literally could not imagine Sweetcrab without his quasi-despotic paternalism that made a warmth in the air so long as his lightest wish remained unquestioned.

I saw more clearly now than I had done in his lifetime that he was a curious survival from an earlier age: beneath the top-sheen of benevolence, the undisputed lord, master and dictator of his household, complete with eccentricities we'd counted as normal because they were his. He'd paid with his life for one: the loaded revolver that, since early in his marriage when Sweetcrab had been burgled and the culprits never apprehended, he'd kept in his desk drawer by day and under his pillow by night. The drawer unlocked in order that no second should be lost in seizing it. Another was the chamois-leather bag of diamonds hoarded in the safe as insurance against the horrors of inflation that could reduce his wealth to worthless stacks of paper, bringing his family to starvation. Mere idiosyncrasies of character, deep-seated obsessions, the seeds of megalomania? All questions that had never asked themselves until now, when it was too late to find the answers.

As I pulled the window inwards I was aware of the milk-white mist shifting and thinning, swathes of it lifting on a light rising wind, leaving eye-holes of space. One framed the Bird Hut, its structure cleared of mist so that it appeared to be suspended in the sky, cut free from the solid earth of its foundations thirty feet above the mere.

It was a substantial cabin erected by Magnus before I was born in handsome imported redwood, sited on a relatively high promontory that except where it dipped inwards to circle the gardens at Sweetcrab was the only projection in the mere's smooth circumference. Almost the whole of the south wall was an unbroken sheet of glass through which Magnus could focus his powerful binoculars on the wild fowl, bitterns, shearwaters and Marsh Harriers – and once an avocet – that frequented the reaches of the mere, the surrounding marshes and reed beds.

His personal, permanent hide, to which visitors were only admitted by invitation and of which he held the sole key – or had until that day two Septembers ago when Cary had made me a present ofa duplicate to provide us with shelter from the rain that had fallen incessantly during the two weeks I'd been home. Our most desperate need had been for shelter and privacy. Cary, who had spent his holiday in the Chelsea flat with Sue and me, vainly pressing Eric and Nathan to extend the deadline, was tied to Works hours. I was no longer welcome at Sweetcrab; there was no welcome for Cary at South View. A couple of outcasts, we were wearied to death of spending evenings in steamed-up cars, of pubs and hotels, of streaming macintoshes and damp feet.

At the sight of the key of the Bird Hut, I'd cried with incredulous delight: 'But how on earth did you coax it out of your father?'

'I helped myself to it for three hours while he was in London yesterday, long enough to have a duplicate struck in Helsby. Provided we sweep up the crumbs we can picnic there; I've checked the oil level in the lamps and the gas cylinder for the cooker. Okay. Draw the curtains tight and we'll be snug and warm, and alone. Heaven for two on a plate!'

We'd played it safe, made our separate ways on foot instead of taking our dinghies from their moorings at opposite ends of the mere to the dock Magnus had built below the sheer drop of the Bird Hut. We'd had six nights there before that last one. Recalling them was like looking back into a sequence of alternating dreams and nightmares. The intoxication of love and its sweet, drowsy aftermath. Cary's despair that ground deeper day by passing day, until it became a black cave into which he retreated beyond a point where I could reach him.

On the last night when I walked, chilled with dread, through the door of the Bird Hut, I'd found a Cary I had not seen for months: reborn, the icy bounds of crippling misery broken, tossed behind him, forgotten. His sea-blue eyes were as shadowless as a child's; physically he was remade, buoyant with restored confidence, the landscape of his mind cloudless.

Before I could speak he held out his arms in a sweeping gesture of exultation. 'Christy, I've found it. All these months it's been staring me in the face but, like the fool I am, I never saw it, the trump card that will win me the game. It's God's truth. And tonight I'm going to play it. No more begging. An ultimatum: five thousand pounds or I walk out of Sweetcrab for ever, shake the dust of Leighton's from my feet. All I'll leave behind will be curses.'

I lay stiff against his shoulder, wondering for a moment if he were drunk. 'He could let you.'

He leaned his head back, crowed with laughter. 'Not a chance. Already there's one weak branch on the family tree that hurts Father's pride, cuts his heart. And the top one, Wellesley, though you'd never get him to admit it, he knows damn well in a crunch despite all his lip service, Wellesley is for Wellesley. He doesn't see himself as a back-bench M.P. He sees himself at No. 10. The one thing Father couldn't stomach is the world knowing I'd voluntarily walked out on him, despoiled his image as a loving, indulgent father-figure. The patriarch!' He shook his head, convinced past argument. 'He's been gambling on my caving in, meekly accepting his answer. It's never occurred to him that I have a choice. And, by God, I have.'

I leaned away from him, confused by his somersault into an analysis of his father's reactions I found debatable. 'You're saying you'd be prepared never to see your mother or Hester again?'

'They'd never see me again; that's another round of ammunition in my war of nerves. Father would have to cope with Hester's tears and tantrums, and Mother's recriminations, plus explaining to the world at large that his younger son would rather work for anyone but him. God, why didn't I see it before. If you beg you automatically concede that he's all-powerful; refuse to beg and you disarm him. It's as simple as that.'

'Without the money, are Nathan and Eric going to give you a partnership, even a job?'

'I'd be surprised if they don't. They're not above playing their own war of nerves. They want the money if they can get it by fair means or foul, but even without it, they'll give me a job all right. On the printing side I'm worth my weight in gold to them. And it'll be a man's job, not one for an office boy who can't get five bob out of the petty cash unless God Almighty signs the slip.' The bitterness swept back over him, and he swerved away from me. 'Every employee, down to my own secretary saying "yes, Mr Cary," "certainly, Mr Cary," and knowing if he chooses to countermand one of my orders he'll do so without taking the trouble to tell me.'

'I don't know,' I said helplessly. 'I'm not sure it will work.'

He turned round, made a fist and touched me on the chin, the bitterness gone, forgotten, the exultation back in his voice. 'You'll see. I'll be back before midnight to walk you home as the dawn comes up, the cheque in my pocket.'

He left the Bird Hut at ten o'clock. There were guests for dinner at Sweetcrab: Markham who'd left Ophelia in London to come down and deal with problems that had arisen on the estate, Hugo Trent and old Mrs Conway, a widow who was the Leightons' nearest neighbour. Soon after ten, Magnus, who liked to retire to the library for his final series of night-caps, would assume they were on the point of departure, and by so doing politely pressure them into taking their leave. By the time Cary reached Sweetcrab, his mother, Hester and Addy would be upstairs, and if Wellesley, as was sometimes the case, had joined his father, it wouldn't be many minutes before he was firmly bid good night.

When dawn broke and Cary hadn't come back. I'd walked home alone, tossed wide awake in my bed until the doorbell sounded at 8.15 in the morning. Cary! I flew down the stairs on wings. Instead of Cary it was Sergeant Benham, an unknown plainclothes detective at his elbow. When, he inquired, had I last seen Mr Cary Leighton?

I went downstairs, plugged in the electric kettle and made the tea. When I'd poured it, Aunt Edith said in the manner of one pandering to a weakling: 'Pull your chair nearer the fire. I daresay after all that central heating you'll feel the cold for a day or two, but your blood will soon adjust itself. All that molly-coddling's not healthy.'

'But cosy!'

She either did not hear, or did not choose to. Her pale blue glance fixed on me over her cup had suddenly turned as avid and excited as a child's when the moment of delivery of an anticipated present has arrived. 'I want to hear all about the places you've been to, and now is the best time while they are fresh in your mind.' She as good as rubbed her hands in anticipation. 'Postcards are well enough but you only get the cameraman's favourite view.' She encouraged me with one of her tartly ironical smiles. 'We've got as much time now as we're ever likely to have, so start at the beginning and please don't gabble.'

I'd forgotten her thirst for knowledge, though heaven knows the memory of her unremitting efforts to implant it in me were still vivid; her iron-hard determination that I should enjoy a privilege that had been denied to her: a place at Lady Margaret Hall or Girton. That it was a goal that didn't beckon me, she'd dismissed as a child's stubborn inability to judge what was good for it. The waste of God-given talent she counted a sin on a level with blasphemy, and her mingled grief and wrath when she'd lost the battle had turned South View into a prison-house of recrimination. Now, because I'd crossed the Rockies, visited an Indian Reservation, looked into the Grand Canyon and stepped over the border into Mexico, I'd partially redeemed myself.

By trial and error I discovered that if I spoke directly to her, pitched my voice one note higher and didn't switch subjects she could hear me. She listened without a single interruption, totally absorbed in a process that turned my words into pictures inside her head. But when I finished, all she said was: 'At least you haven't forgotten how to talk English. Your diction is as good as it always was.'

'I daren't have come home if it hadn't been.'

She gave a laugh that was dry, yet warm, and it seemed as good a moment as any to broach one of the problems that Tim had heaped on my shoulders. 'Tim was talking about a hearing-aid. He's so keen on the idea that he's made an appointment for you to see a specialist at Helsby General next Tuesday morning.'

'With Charlie Sessler. He's come up in the world since thirty years ago when I hammered his multiplication tables into his head, or tried to.'

'Where? In Macclesfield?'

'Dengate Road Primary School. His father, Cyril Sessler,

had a greengrocer's shop in Wilberforce Street.'

'Maybe he'll remember you.'

'I shouldn't wonder. I rapped his knuckles often enough when he refused to apply what scant few brains he had for five minutes together.'

'He must have learnt to in the last thirty years.'

She gave a snort of doubt. 'Old Mrs Harris had one of his contraptions. She'd have been better off with an ear-trumpet.'

'If you feel that when you've tried it out, you can tell him so.'

'I shall,' she promised with relish.

After I'd washed up the tea things in cold water which ran out of the hot tap, I went to see Joe about hiring a car.

He came sauntering up to me wiping his hands on an oily rag that was his personal trade mark, in key with his image of himself as an embryo Lord Nuffield, even Henry Ford: the backyard genius who ended up a millionaire. He was in his late thirties, with a wife and four children, short, balding and tubby, but his leery roving eye optimistically courted every female in sight. I had to suffer ten minutes' flattering patter before I could break in. 'Joe, Dr Woodham said you had a Ford Anglia I could hire. Could I see it?'

He'd got it waiting, waxed that morning with his own hands. If I was thinking of buying I couldn't do better. One owner, middle-aged spinster who'd never driven it over forty, serviced regular as clockwork. Seeing that I was an old friend, he was prepared to cut his profit.

I told him firmly I was hiring, not buying. Since I only needed a car for taxi-ing about, I wasn't too fussy. With a proviso that if it crocked up, he'd lend me another while it was in for repair, we clinched the deal.

While he was in his shed-office collecting the forms, I wandered round the yard looking over the wrecks and a few relatively new cars in for servicing. There was one eye-catcher: a silver-grey Mercedes 3.5 coupé over which I stood covetously.

'Very handsome,' I remarked, when Joe came back. 'Not

yours?' You never knew with Joe; for six weeks he'd once owned a Rolls.

'No such luck. Mrs Leighton's. Serviced in Norwich, but as she was in a hurry for a quick polish, her ladyship deigned to trust it to me, on condition I didn't open the bonnet.'

His glance was directly angled to catch my reaction to the name. You couldn't, in fairness, blame him. I'd been interrogated by the police half a dozen times, been publicly ostracized by the Leightons, and before Magnus had been in his grave a month skipped the country.

Driving off in the Anglia, I had to run against the grain of my imagination to see Esmée Leighton at the wheel of that gorgeous car instead of in her normal form of daily transport: a run of the mill estate car. Cary's mother, dressed in a uniform of rubbed sheepskin jacket in winter, shirt-waist cottons and woolly cardigans all summer, was an almost classic figure of upper-class country wife with no more use for ostentatious display of wealth than her husband who had abhorred it except when his comfort was in question.

For a moment as I turned into the High Street I had a queer feeling of displacement, as though behind my back a woman I'd known since I was five years old had not only turned into a different person, but had never been that person. I'd not been so naïve as to imagine I could spend three weeks in Berghmere without a public confrontation with Mrs Leighton – not unless she happened to be away from Sweetcrab which, according to Joe, she wasn't. The likeliest venue was the street, in Berghmere or in the nearby market town of Helsby.

In the eyes of Cary's mother, I'd played the rôle of her younger son's evil genius. He had met Nathan and Eric at a party Sue and I had given at the flat. But for my enthusiasm for the partnership scheme, he would never have been mesmerized into entertaining a criminally irresponsible pipe-dream that jeopardized his future. Not only that, I'd been guilty of sowing discord in a united family to whom I owed a debt of gratitude in return for the privileges and affection lavished on me.

And later, when Magnus was dead, her terrible silent indictment had been written on my memory for life: but for me she would not have been robbed of her husband, her daughter of a father, and her younger son would not have been a hunted criminal.

I'd calculated that if we passed in a street she would drop a blind over her eyes, pretend I wasn't there, unless Hester were by her side. Then she'd have to. Or would she? Even the name spoken in my thoughts made my heart move, though I'd learned that to brood on Hester was to open an old wound that still throbbed on the nights when I couldn't sleep. I'd written her three times from New York, but she had not answered. Had the letters been confiscated before they reached her hands? Had she been indoctrinated to hate and revile her old loved and loving companion? How, I wondered endlessly, had they explained to her that fatal explosion of death in the library? What answers could they give her when she asked where her father and Cary had gone? I dropped a shutter on such futile speculations. To seek answers was to enter a mental maze and emerge no wiser than I'd gone in.

I drove the length of the High Street, getting the feel of the car, the right-hand drive. Berghmere was a typical East Anglian village, possessing loads to charm the eye, plus a few down-at-heel corners, and some miserably shoddy flanks. The High Street was the main target for tourists' cameras, its solid houses set flush with the pavement, some black and white, some colour-washed, one or two still thatched in Norfolk reed. Except that there were a couple more tea-shops, a new snack-bar, and a sign with an arrow pointing down Tomb Lane to 'Public Conveniences' I couldn't spot any radical changes.

Around the Swan extra moorings had been provided for yachts and motor cruisers, and a field on the far side of the river converted into a caravan park. Both served a warning that from Whitsuntide onwards Berghmere would be thronged with amateur sailors, but they would not concern me. By then I'd be settled in London, mentally and physically stretched to meet the demands of an exacting tireless old boss getting to grips with a new job, Berghmere a place I'd visit for a couple of nights every month or so to check up on Aunt Edith.

I made a detour round the square which was the main shopping centre. At half-past five, most of the shops were closed, and the wind had too icy an edge to encourage window-gazing. Among the dozen or so people about there was not one I recognized. By the time I was back in the High Street a sprinkle of rain was pattering on the wind-screen and I stopped crawling. I had come within fifty yards of the turn for South View when a young man emerged from a doorway, sprinted across the road in front of the car. I braked, pulled into the curb, the agonizingly familiar pattern of thudding heartbeats, swimming senses re-establishing itself. I fought against it as hard and relentlessly as though I were engaged in a death struggle with life itself at stake. And I won. Though the figure, the grace of movement, the briefly-glimpsed profile had a shadow resemblance to Cary, it was not Cary. I drew in my breath, turned on the ignition, and beneath the shakiness was conscious of a ripple of pride in myself: after being crippled for two and a half years, I'd learned to take my first firm steps. Those other times when I'd persuaded myself I'd been cured had been mirages of hope. This time I knew beyond the quiver of doubt that I'd suffered my last spasm of dementia that created a phantom picture of Cary's face and figure on the lens of my eye. So why were the tears sliding down my cheeks? Not, surely, because I'd said good-bye for ever to my beloved ghost.

CHAPTER FOUR

On Sunday morning I drove Aunt Edith – dressed in her ancient best that I'd sponged and pressed and stitched – to church. We left half an hour early to put the daffodils she'd ordered me pick from the garden on my parents' grave, ostensibly as a tribute to both, but more truthfully in loving memory of my father. Though she'd never spoken an ill word against my mother, I'd sensed since childhood that she'd counted her as a puny weakling with nothing to her credit but a pretty face and beguiling ways – the very type of female most likely to die in bearing her first child.

Berghmere Church and graveyard, built at the end of a rising lane leading away from the village, was an island of stone in a sea of farmland, and famous enough to merit a paragraph in most guidebooks on East Anglia. Built of flints, with a square tower topped by a glittering gilded-cock weather-vane, it was one of the last with a reed-thatched roof. In summer it was packed with visitors who surreptitiously gazed about during the service to identify the fifteenth-century marble font, the five-hundred-year-old brasses.

But spring was still tentative, capriciously bent on denying its arrival, and the congregation that barely filled a third of the pews was composed of locals. A few covert and some blatantly inquisitive glances were directed towards me. With my arrival heralded by Joe, and probably mentioned around by Tim, my presence could hardly be unexpected. Any qualms of discomfort I suffered were more than offset by Aunt Edith's palpable satisfaction. As nearly as she could bring herself to do in a sacred place she preened herself on what amounted to a public declaration that she was not totally abandoned by kith and kin, a charge on public sympathy.

Waiting for the choir of mixed boys and girls to process to their stalls, I was forcibly pulled back, held fast imprisoned in the memory of the last occasion I'd been inside Berghmere

Church: for Magnus's funeral. I fought hard against remembering that day of blackness, but the numbing shock and blind bewilderment seemed to have permeated the fabric of the church, from which it exuded now to half-stupefy me. I had a disembodied sense of past and present cohering into one time zone, with the present common-form service superimposed on the stronger etched scene wherein Magnus's coffin had rested on the bier before the altar, and behind it his veiled widow and bereaved family had behaved on that day and in the ones that followed as if I did not exist.

I stared at their empty pew, and then in a desperate effort to cut myself free, slid my glance across the aisle to the companion pew which every Sunday morning had been occupied by General Markham Drake, V.C., in school holidays accompanied by his grandson. Empty, too, which was no surprise. After Markham had outraged local opinion by not attending his grandfather's funeral, his appearances at church had become spasmodic. When the General died, Markham's marriage to Ophelia was a year old, and they'd been travelling in Asia, feasting eyes and senses on the temples of Thailand and Cambodia. The family lawyer had put out a diplomatic statement to the effect they had revised their itinerary without notifying him, and his cable breaking the news that General Drake was in a coma had not reached Markham until after his grandfather's funeral. But in the days of trans-world telephones and jet planes! Villagers had been openly sceptical, fixed the blame on the woman he'd picked for his wife, half-Argentinian, half-French, who had not spent more than four nights at Holland Court. The chronic disease of the born-rich, restlessness, the unrelenting battle to hold ennui at bay, had kept her journeying to exotic lands where every day provided a new sensation, and in village opinion Markham in choosing to indulge his bride, had neglected his bounden Christian duty to comfort his grandfather on his deathbed.

I reflected hazily that the common experience of the havoc left in the wake of violent death, its spectre-haunted after-existence should, in theory, have spun a bond of shared experience between us. I doubted whether in practice this would prove so. The Markham Drake I'd known had been a singularly self-sufficient young man. Beneath the blazing charm, the talent he exercised as naturally as breathing for relishing any company, he'd been as proud as a peacock – never a sharer.

After the service we were hemmed inside the porch by people proffering hands to shake, some in simple goodwill, others because it provided them with an opportunity to ask what questions were permissible in public while they examined me minutely for the marks of guilt or grief.

Mrs Wain kept close beside me on the path down to the lych-gate, whispering into my ear, 'You know, Christina, my husband and I would be only too glad to drive your aunt to church and back. We pass her door, so it would be no trouble. We've offered to do so, time and again.'

An offer that would be rejected out of hand on the grounds that Mr Wain was the local butcher. In this day and age Aunt Edith would not be seen accepting a favour from a tradesman! I made soothing noises to the effect that she never made up her mind until the last minute, that she didn't like to be bound by a definite commitment, but Mrs Wain remained unconvinced, hurt and offended that her kindness had been spurned – which it had.

As I eased Aunt Edith out of the car, I was in a mood to berate her for such preposterous snobbery, but she took the wind out of my sails by the rare warmth with which she thanked me. 'That was a great treat for me, Christina. It was good of you to take all that trouble.' Characteristically she couldn't deny herself the pleasure of injecting a sting in the tail. 'And it can't have done you any harm to go to church once in a month of Sundays! Not that the new parson is much of a preacher. I could have delivered a better sermon myself.'

After lunch I decided to go and see Liz. Half-way to the garage I paused, reversed my steps. The Mortimers' garden ran down to Lixen Broad, and the most direct route was by boat. If Harold Barnes, the owner of the Swan, was about, he'd hire me a dinghy. The decision made I was made light-hearted by the prospect of release from the treadmill of cars and roads into the space and freedom of inland waterways.

Peering through a porthole I located Harold in the galley of a six-berth cabin cruiser, fitting a cylinder of gas to a cooker. He was elderly, heavily built and slow-moving, but long years of practice had taught him to accommodate his bulk to restricted spaces.

'Why, if it isn't Miss Graham! I did hear you was coming home. Let me tighten this up and I'll be out in a jiffy.'

'Don't hurry for me. I'll enjoy having a look round. What a splendid fleet you've got, and every luxury on tap.'

'That's what the customers demand, all the mod. cons. they have at home, and no roughing it. Now they've got fridges, it'll be dishwashers next.'

When he joined me on the quay, he inquired: 'And you're keeping well, Miss Graham?'

Just that, not a single probing question, a sly glance. He had an inborn respect for other people's sensitivity that kept him from even inquiring how I'd enjoyed New York.

'I'm fine, on my way to see the Mortimers on Lixen Broad, and I thought, why not go by boat, as I used to. Could you hire me a dinghy with an outboard?'

'I can do better than that.' He led me to a narrower mooring channel, pointed a proud finger. '*Daybreak*. She's mine, what I use for answering S.O.S.'s from customers; you've no idea the pickles they land themselves in. But this afternoon, with only experienced hands out, I'm not likely to need her, and you're more than welcome, Miss Graham. She's got a canvas hood that'll keep you dry if it comes on to rain, and there's signs it will.'

Daybreak, with her midnight blue fibre-glass hull, snappy lines, looked to me like a scaled-down model of a power boat.

'She's a darling. Are you sure you trust me with her?'

He grinned. 'I reckon I'm not taking overmuch risk. She's got a six h.p. motor with wheel and cable steering. She'll not give you any trouble. Hop in and get the feel of her.'

I climbed into the cockpit, checked over the simple controls. 'I'll take good care of her,' I promised. 'And have her back by four-thiry.'

He insisted over and over again, it was a pleasure to lend

her to me and joked, as I headed her out of the mooring: 'You'll not be needing a map!'

Daybreak was bliss to handle and recaptured for me the sharp, cool delight of moving through unwinding stretches of limpid water. Cows placidly grazed where meadowland sloped down to the broad, and the monotonous, harsh cry of wild fowl broke over my head where reeds and marsh had established their private kingdoms. Emptiness was a balm that soothed fret and slackened my taut nerves. By the time I tied up at the Mortimers' boathouse, I'd decided that I'd collect Liz and we'd spend the next couple of hours in *Daybreak*. On the other side of an ocean I'd seen myself as a self-contained human until temporarily slotted into Berghmere to perform a single function: what Sue termed 'sorting out Aunt Edith'. But self-containment had mocked and eluded me. Quite genuinely, I longed to see Liz again, but I also wanted to use her as a sounding post. There were questions I could ask her that I could put to no one else.

Climbing the slope of the lawn I saw four figures clustered round a car outside the garage: Mr and Mrs Mortimer, Liz and a young man who was lifting a suitcase into the boot while Liz kissed her mother. They formed a self-explanatory tableau. Liz and the young man were on the point of departure. Unwilling to play the rôle of an unexpected caller who'd caused a hold-up, I dived quickly behind a group of shrubs, but not quickly enough: Liz had seen me. She came racing down the lawn, her face that Sue had once likened to that of a mournful Madonna alight with joy, though when she came within earshot her voice was a wail: 'Christy, oh, Christy, it's really you!' She grabbed my hand. 'Oh, hell and damnation . . .'

'Don't panic. I can see I've arrived at the wrong moment. It's all my fault, I should have telephoned. You're off somewhere, aren't you?'

'To stay with Tony's mother, and I can't get out of it.' She looked beside herself. 'You wrote and said you were coming home, but not when and for how long. Christy, you're not going back to London right away, are you?' Her great brown velvet eyes brimmed with anxiety – when it came to looks Sue and I were non-starters beside Liz. 'Oh, Christy, you can't.'

'Don't worry. I'm here for three weeks.' I caught the flash of light on her finger. 'Liz, you've gone and done it, got engaged to that doctor you mentioned in your letters.'

'At Easter, but he's the only son of a widowed mum, and she's convinced I'm out to steal her treasure . . . as if I would!'

'She's only got to see you and she'll love you.'

She gave a choky laugh. 'Like hell, she will. But I'm going to put everything I know into making her trust me for Tony's sake. He's got a terrific conscience about her.' She held out her hand. 'Come and meet him. If we're late, we can blame it on the Sunday traffic.'

'Not now, Liz. Phone me when you get home, I'll still be here.'

'But you can't rush away. Stay and have tea with Mummy and Daddy.'

I shook my head. Mrs Mortimer, an obsessively organized housewife who mapped out every minute of her day the moment she woke, was definitely not the type to open her arms to an unexpected visitor – certainly not to me with my smirched past! And I wasn't in the mood for one of her over-formal Sunday teas.

Liz expected to be home on Wednesday which gave us four days before she was due at her girls' boarding school in Gloucestershire. We arranged we'd meet on one of them.

Back in *Daybreak*, I checked the time: two whole hours before four-thirty tea at South View. I studied the sky: for once Harold Barnes's weather-lore had let him down. The clouds were on the run and a pastel sun was picking out notes of pale colour in the banks, rinsing the water with blue. It would have been more fun with Liz aboard, but even to be alone on the water afforded me more pleasure than had come my way in a long while.

I passed under the low hump-backed bridge from which they'd hung felons in the old days, and pondered on the alternative routes open to me. In the end I chose Riseby Cut, ruler-straight as a canal, that linked Lixen Broad with the river, a sluggish waterway narrowed to half its width by great mats of weeds. I joined the river where it divided to encircle a reach of speckled gold sand, and chose the left-hand loop that wound through farmland drained by a criss-cross of dykes and ditches that glinted like veins of silver threaded through the green-brown earth. A single cabin cruiser passed me, a Spartan sun-bather on the deck, otherwise the landscape was mine to share with coots and shovellers and a single heron which took off in a huff at being disturbed, trailing its stork-like legs.

I was looking for the old windmill, one of the hundreds that had operated the drainage pumps in the old days, now minus its sails, reduced to the stump of its brick tower. I found it behind a golden burst of pussy willow, and alongside it the signs planted at intervals along the river bank: PRIVATE – NO MOORING. Had they always been there? I couldn't remember. In any case, I didn't intend to trespass on Drake property, merely to pause and look for a while.

I hitched the painter round an alder root, clambered up the bank that was greasy with a top coating of mud and wet weed. Before my eyes lay a vast tranquil patchwork of fields, some greening with winter-sown wheat, some newly drilled and dense brown. Beyond, cloistered within a plantation of trees was Holland Court, or what remained of it after an enemy aircraft limping home to Berlin in 1944 had crashed on the West Wing. The General and the few aged staff left to him had been on fire-watch duty at the church; his son's wife, his grandson and nurse asleep on the opposite side of the house, and there'd been no casualties except for the crew who'd died in a funeral pyre of blazing stucco and slates.

When his son was demobilized the General planned to rebuild, but a week before peace in Europe was signed Captain Markham Drake was killed by a sniper's bullet, and the plans were abandoned, the rubble cleared and the foundations paved, left open to the sky. The rump of the house had provided ample space for one old man, a young widow and a five-year-old boy. When Clarissa Drake married Louis Trenet, a Free French pilot, and moved to Paris, there was only the old man and the little boy to house. Some said, devoid of natural feeling, Clarissa Drake had heartlessly abandoned her child in the heat of a new love; others that General Drake had done a deal, literally bought his grandson for a capital sum that had set Louis Trenet on the road to wealth and industrial prestige in his homeland.

Each summer Markham divided two months between the Trenets' Paris apartment and their villa in Rocquebrune. Though Clarissa Trenet bore no more children, suggesting she didn't yearn for offspring, as boy and adult Markham was devoted to his mother.

I leant against the rough-grained circular trunk of the windmill, watching pheasants picking at seeds, standing motionless so as not to put them to flight. In the interlude of absolute quiet truth welled, and after a momentary ripple of shock, I accepted it. I had not arrived at my destination by chance; sub-consciously I'd been making my way directly towards it since I'd left the Mortimers'.

In my inner ear the memory of Sue's voice berating me stirred. 'Come off it, Christy. Setting your cap at the Young Squire, being led down the garden path! If I hadn't seen it with my own eyes, I wouldn't have believed it.'

And my unrepentant retort: 'Suppose he's setting his cap at me.'

She'd made a rude noise. 'A few games of tennis, a little dalliance in the moonlight, taking you out to dinner once . . .'

'Twice.'

'Okay, twice. What's the odds? They're phantom wedding bells you've got ringing in your head. You must be out of your tiny mind to believe he seriously fancies you. He can have any girl for the asking; they literally throw themselves at his feet in shoals, begging to be seduced. To him you're one of the Sweetcrab mob, a kid at a secretarial school destined to be someone's typist, not Mrs Markham Drake. Christy, you know him, God's gift to women, not one woman, not for a long while yet, and then it won't be you.'

I hadn't believed her, but my pride had been scorched. As a result my awareness became keener, my perception deeper, and I'd had forced down my throat a truth that was as bitter as a devil's brew. I was not the only girl on Markham

Drake's list. With the monstrous arrogance of an eighteen-year-old wallowing in first love, I'd refused two dates, paraded myself before him escorted by a boy whose name I couldn't even recall. At night I'd dreamed he came to South View contrite, begging, mouthing every cliché in the book. Instead he went off on his annual visit to his mother, stayed away for a year with some vague idea that he might enter one of his stepfather's industrial concerns, and when he did return to Holland Court, he'd brought his bride with him.

If Sue could have seen me now she'd have been as brutally outspoken as she'd been all those years ago – to no purpose; I no longer had a heart to lose.

The field before me changed colour in the middle: wet chocolate in the shade, apricot where the afternoon sun had dried out the earth. In the far distance I could see a moving dot and a matchstick figure steadily descending the incline. Moments later the matchstick figure and dot defined themselves as a man with a dog at his heels walking down the path that followed the leafless boundary hedge. Not only a dog but a black labrador. Bonnie? How long did labradors live? Surely Bonnie had been an old lady when General Drake died!

But Bonnie or not, it was Markham. The rhythmic stride, the superbly co-ordinated physique could belong to no one else, and there, as final confirmation, was the glint of his chestnut hair as the sun struck it. His presence was so apt it was as though, to satisfy my dreaming nostalgia, I'd played a shameful trick on him, conjured him out of the thin air. The sheer unexpectedness of it, surely against all laws of average, induced a feeling of apprehension, as though meeting him posed a hazard. I turned my head, seeking a hidden place and found I had only to slide round the windmill stump, jump down the bank, and dive, head bent, back to the shelter of *Daybreak*.

But I dithered too long or his progress was quicker than I'd calculated. In the end there was less risk of embarrassment in standing my ground than in being caught ignominiously running away. Once committed I found myself absorbed in getting his face into clear vision, tantalized because he kept it either bent or turned sideways to inspect the hedge. Markham Drake, I marvelled, a farmer about a farmer's traditional Sunday afternoon chore of walking his land, checking on crops and livestock! To think I'd lived to see the day.

When man and dog were within twenty yards of me, I whistled. Bonnie froze and then bounded tail waving towards me, her soft grizzled muzzle seeking my hand. Markham did not vary his pace until we were separated by no more than ten feet of path, then he stopped dead. My first reaction was that heart-breaking grief had not diminished his spectacular looks. He was as tall, as straight-backed as his grandfather, with the same high cheekbones, piercing glance. His eyes, though, were a different blue, not exactly darker but deeper in tone, a curious blue like the ultramarine in my old paint box, and guarded by thick, dark lashes.

He maintained that motionless statue pose, not speaking, giving me a grave and definitely measuring look from which it was impossible to gauge whether what he saw pleased or displeased him.

To short-circuit the odd tension that gave no sign of easing, I laughed. 'Imagine Bonnie remembering me!'

'Maybe it's dogs not elephants who have the longest memories.' He snapped his fingers. 'Here, old girl.'

She abandoned me, went to heel, and he closed the space dividing us. There followed another short deflating silence, as though he needed to reflect before he committed himself to a greeting. When it came it was abysmally conventional. 'Hello, Christy. How are you?'

'Fine. I'd better confess I'm trespassing. I've got a boat tied up where it says No Mooring.'

'No matter. You're very welcome so long as you don't leave a trail of Coca-Cola tins and plastic bags behind you.'

'Cross my heart, no litter,' I promised, and thereafter was made stupidly tongue-tied by a quality in him that suggested extreme wariness of me and made him cling to the safety rails of small-talk. I looked ahead, up the field, where pheasants had returned to feed on the seed: the most socially adept man I knew was . . . well, what? The only word was scared! But he didn't scare easy, and what was there in me to scare anybody? It must have been half a minute before my eye corner caught the shift of his head, the weight of his gaze on my profile.

Again the approach was cautious, super-conventional. 'Your aunt said you were coming home for a while before you start a new job in London. How long do you expect to be here?'

'About three weeks. Tim mentioned that you go and see her. That's nice of you.'

'No. Not nice at all. A pleasure for me.' His denial, instant, forthright replaced a shadow man by one that was half-real. 'How did you find her?'

'Down but not out. Tim's made some suggestions that would ease life for her. I'm praying that I can coax her into going along with them, but it's tricky . . .' I glanced up at him, openly angling for a smile. 'Minding the business of my elders and betters!'

At last the smile came, its warmth melting some of the deadness between us. It was a wonderful heart-whole smile, shining in his eyes, curving his lips that were so clearly defined they seemed to be carved, revealing a glimpse of the bright spirit that normally glowed in him – though not today. 'You can't expect to move a mountain overnight. But then you always were an impatient girl, weren't you?'

I marvelled that he remembered. 'Could be. Sometimes.'

'Were you on your way to Holland Court?'

'No. I went to see Liz but she was driving off to visit her future mum-in-law and as Harold Barnes had lent me his midget power boat I was making full use of it.' I wasn't only impatient by nature, I liked personal relationships straight, free of mystifying crooks. 'When you came down the field, first saw me, you looked . . . well, not only dumbfounded but appalled. Were you?'

'No.' His reply was unequivocable enough, but somewhere there was a note of evasion. 'No, of course I wasn't appalled.'

'Then what?'

'I was inspecting the hedge, deciding whether or not it needed relaying. I happened to look up and there you were, Christina Graham materialized out of space, part of the landscape.' He shot me a quick exploratory look before he finished: 'Sheer surprise must have slowed up my reactions.'

His reactions were needle-sharp, and he'd known from Aunt Edith, that I was coming home. So why invent such a clumsy excuse? 'Also,' he went on, 'I was trying to discover how much you'd changed.'

'And have I, much?'

The dark blue eyes cleared, but his voice retained its undertone of reserve, suggesting I was still being held on some sort of trial. 'Happily, not much. Touched up a little at the edges.'

'But *you* have. Look at you, a farmer forsooth!'

'Don't forget I spent nearly two years at Cirencester learning to be a farmer.'

'And bowed out before you completed the course!'

He said with the confidence that came from strength, 'Those two years weren't wasted. I could reel off milk-records, sugar-beet tonnage to prove it.' He slid me a wry smile. 'But I won't bore you. I am a farmer; before many years are up, I hope to be a good one. Apparently that astounds you.'

'It takes some getting used to,' I admitted.

He said nothing, but looked away from me up the apricot and chocolate-brown field. It might be that he was absorbed in assessing the good heart of his land, or his eyes might have been turned inward following a stream of thought I could not define. Failure to establish even the minimum of communication between us, with no knowledge whether it bored or amused him to spend five minutes in my company, affected me like being jammed in pack-ice. My impulse was to break the jam by any means, even one that would be painful to him.

I blurted out: 'I'm sorry I never wrote to you when Ophelia was killed.' I'd written three letters, stilted copy-book essays of sympathy, and torn them up in disgust at their banality. 'I didn't know what to say that wasn't miserably inadequate.'

'No one ever does,' he said in a voice tuned to comfort me. 'I'm glad you didn't try.'

'But I wanted you to know how desperately sorry I was.'

The deep indigo glance touched my face, then flicked instantly away. 'Don't let it bother you. I understand.'

I'd seen Ophelia twice. Once at a party General Drake had

given to introduce his grandson's bride to his neighbours. It had been mid-winter, when fur stoles, satin and velvet cocktail dresses were *de rigueur*, jewel-boxes unlocked and plundered. Even Aunt Edith had bought a new dress, and Sue and Liz and I had spent a whole day preparing for what amounted to a presentation – to a wisp of a girl without visible make-up in a nun-plain white woollen sheath-dress, no jewellery except her wedding ring, and straight ash-blonde hair styled as simply as a child's. Ophelia Drake had been a nymphlike creature, ethereal, light as thistledown, with the inborn, effortlessly controlled poise of a princess, plus a simplicity of manner that charmed on sight and a lovely graciousness that came to her out of the air she breathed. Though time had proved Ophelia had no desire to acquire friends in Berghmere, she'd behaved as though it was her firm intention to spend the rest of her life among us. And she'd done her homework. She'd clasped my hand with its scarlet lacquered nails in her fragile one, with its nails buffed to shell pink, nursed it with affection. 'Dear Christina! Markham has talked to me about you. He's known you ever since you were a little girl, hasn't he? You're one of his friends I've been most looking forward to meeting.'

The second time had been when I'd hopped off a bus in Helsby. They'd been strolling, arms tightly linked, along the opposite pavement, rain streaming down their radiant laughing faces, as though to be out together in a storm was a marvellously exciting adventure. While I'd stood watching them a gust of wind had blown her Burberry apart, revealed its mink lining.

'I don't believe it,' Sue declared when I told her. 'A mink-lined mac!'

I glanced upwards at his profile and wondered, if you'd won and lost such an unearthly fairy creature what chance you had of finding another. I remembered, too, that he'd lost not only Ophelia but his unborn child. Simultaneously he turned his head, our eyes met and I felt a stab of surprise. I'd expected some visible sign of grief, or maybe resentment at my blundering reference to Ophelia. I could see none, only that strange, unaccountable reserve, a watchfulness suggesting he was exercising some sort of self-discipline.

'And you?' he asked. 'What about you and Cary?'

Shock tingled through me at the sound of his name being tossed off in casual inquiry, then anger as I caught a whiff of anticipation, as though he was holding his breath for my answer. 'Nothing. What could there be?'

I stared down at a clump of hardy short-stalked primroses that were huddled against the windmill stump, prayed he would leave it there. My prayer went unheard.

He said, speaking slowly to emphasize his incredulity: 'You don't know where he is? You've no idea at all?'

'No.' As I turned towards him in furious rejection at the suggestion, he gave me a look of total disbelief that in different circumstances would have been comic. 'Why should you imagine I would know? How could I? Why did you ask me?'

The rattle of questions left him unmoved, but the incredulity remained, dragging his voice. 'You're saying you didn't go to New York because it would be easier on the other side of the Atlantic for you two to keep in touch?'

'I went because I had to get away, from London as well as Berghmere. Sue was on the point of leaving for New York, and she set about handling the mechanics of getting a job for me.' I heard my heavy breathing and with an effort steadied it. 'I went to New York to earn my living not to get in touch with Cary.'

He said in the tone of one baffled past belief: 'You've never heard from him?'

'No.'

His disbelief was all the more intolerable because it was an echo of my own. There'd been a whole night before Magnus's body had been discovered spread-eagled across his desk in the library when Addy came downstairs at 7 o'clock, another half-hour before the police arrived. Time of death had been put at around midnight. Without contrary evidence it had been assumed that Cary had fled from Sweetcrab immediately after the shooting. His car had been parked in the drive, and all morning the police had concentrated on combing the immediate neighbourhood. It wasn't until mid-afternoon that they learned that a male passenger answering to Cary's description had been on a mid-morning plane to Dublin. Surely, I'd tortured myself ten thousand times, in the hours between his flight from Sweetcrab and boarding the plane, there'd been a margin of minutes in which he could have telephoned me, or contrived some means of sending a message without fear of it being intercepted by the police.

Slowly, with stealth, a new thought took root and expanded, one that evoked images that were excruciatingly painful. 'If you were so certain that I'd heard from Cary, been in touch with him, others must have the same idea. Your aunt, for instance? Wellesley?'

'I imagine it has crossed their minds.' There was no doubt about his evasiveness now. 'Wasn't it a reasonable logical assumption? You and Cary were in love, planning to marry. Wouldn't you have moved heaven and earth to see each other? Or if that was too hazardous an operation at least have contrived some means of communication?'

In a vacuum! 'Your imagination misfired. There's been no communication, as you put it, between us. None.'

Esmée Leighton was his second cousin. Her much older sister had been married to General Drake. When Clarissa Drake abandoned Markham at Holland Court, Mrs Leighton had tried to assume the rôle of foster-mother to the orphaned boy. Her ambition thwarted by the General, thereafter she'd been at pains to enclose Markham within the family circle at Sweetcrab. Blood, I thought, snapping my teeth on an old saw, was thicker than water. To all intents Markham Drake was a Leighton. On the night of Magnus's murder, it had been he who in the chaos of ultimate catastrophe had been summoned to Sweetcrab either by Wellesley or Mrs Leighton and had taken upon himself the duty of calling the police.

For a moment he said nothing; when he spoke he chose his words with fastidious care. 'Does Cary still matter to you? Is he a factor in your present and your future?' He laid his curious, seeking gaze on my face. 'Are you any longer concerned about where he is living, how he is ordering his life?'

The questions struck me as not only extraordinarily insensitive but outright cruel. Yet Markham Drake was not by nature either cruel or insensitive – or hadn't been. 'Of course

I care. I'll always care.'

'Yet,' he said, pressing harder for confirmation of a truth that, unaccountably, he found difficult to assimilate, 'you don't know where he is? You've never known since the morning he left Sweetcrab?'

'No.'

His voice hardened, became half a taunt: 'What future is there in loving a man on the run for murder?' There was a sudden shift in his expression; the seekingness stayed but now suspicion was added. 'Or maybe . . .' he paused, as though in half a mind not to continue, then went on: 'Maybe you're of the opinion that Cary wasn't responsible for Magnus's death?'

I'd woken on countless mornings and told myself: that's how it happened, or that way or that. There was nothing to be gained by raising ghostlike from the graves in which I'd buried them those shimmering essays in faith, or committing to words the pathetic few that had stood the test of daylight. I said stiltedly: 'He should have a chance to give his version of what happened at Sweetcrab the night Magnus was shot, not be condemned unheard.'

His eyes roved speculatively over me. 'So you have come back to plead his case, prove his innocence!'

I leaned against the rough crumbled bricks, freezing and faint with cold hating resentment. My brain was capable of framing a denunciation that would demolish the injustice of his accusation, but I could not assemble it on my tongue, force it through my lips. And to be pinned, dumb, unprotesting under that deadly blue gaze that disbelieved my word, condemned me, was not to be borne. I launched myself from the windmill stump, ran for the path and fell headlong on the slimy weed. Bonnie tumbling after me.

He hauled me to my feet, held me upright, chided me roundly. 'Christy, for heavens' sake! Why did you take off like that? Here, let me take a look at you. Are you hurt?'

Too shaken to speak I made a motion of denial with my head. I wasn't hurt but my hands, jersey and slacks were plastered with mud.

'I'm sorry if I upset you, but you can't deny it was . . .'

'A logical assumption. Only it happened to be dead wrong.' I looked up into his face on which there was a dark expression of complete bafflement. 'You can please yourself whether or not you believe me.'

'I *do* believe you, Christy.' On the turn of a second the reserve melted, and his smile was the old wondrous one that charmed and consoled, wrapped you up warm in his concern. Old ladies, I remembered wryly, had been bowled over with what they'd called his chivalry. All in vain; too late. It was beyond even Markham Drake's legendary charm to comfort and restore a girl who felt as if she'd been flayed alive. 'It doesn't matter.' I managed to shrug my shoulders. 'Let's leave it.'

'You going off in a huff! After all, I had . . .' He abandoned, as though putting a toe on dangerous ground, whatever he'd been going to say. 'Come on, Christy, we'll go back to the house, get you cleaned up and feed you one of Mrs Bengy's splendid Sunday teas. You remember her, don't you, the cowman's wife? She's "doing" for me.'

I was conscious of zest and purpose something like happiness rising in him, but it was a mood I could not match. As he moved to take my hand, I put it behind me. 'Thanks, but I have to get back to South View for tea, and I should return Harold Barnes's boat.'

His reply was crisp and confident. 'No problem there. You can telephone from the house.' He bent down to whisk a strand of weed from my knee. 'You're drenched. The sooner I get you indoors the better.'

'I'd rather go home.'

My refusal took him by surprise. He'd always assumed that what he wanted he'd get. He complained with mild affront: 'You never used to hold your grudges.'

'I'm not holding one now.'

'The only other explanation is that you've had enough of my company.' He angled his head, leaving me only his profile; even so, I sensed the uncertainty creeping back to repossess him. Of a sudden he sloughed it off and the look he gave me was candid and forthright. 'A whole circle of lives was thrown off balance when Magnus was murdered, out of joint for years, maybe to a degree for ever. And you, loving them both, were a victim twice over.' The gentlest of smiles touched his mouth, reached his eyes. 'What I'm saying proves that I'm about as inadequate at communicating sympathy as you believed yourself to be when Ophelia was killed.'

Compassion that, when it had been offered me, I'd resented, thrust away, coming from him did not, perversely, offend me.

I shook my head, looked up the rising parti-coloured field, wanting to be gone, yet not wanting to go.

He pleaded: 'If I've hurt you, will you forgive me?'

What would have been inconceivable ten minutes before was startlingly easy. 'You're forgiven.'

'Then prove it by coming back to the house and eating one of Mrs Bengy's Sunday teas. Please!'

I refused for a complexity of reasons I couldn't explain and one that needed no explanation. In all but name he was a Leighton, their loyalties his but not mine. 'Some other day.'

Without further protest, he followed at my heels, Bonnie at his heels; he held *Daybreak* steady until I was in the cockpit, and untied the painter for me. Before I gunned the engine, I glanced up at the bank. From that angle he looked theatrically magnificent, an almost unbelievably exact replica of the man for who, aeons ago, I would quite literally have died. I smiled not at him but at my lost foolish self. He did not smile back, but regarded me with a rueful slightly brooding expression. I was content to leave it there, lift my hand to say goodbye for me.

As I headed *Daybreak* into the main stream he shouted after me: 'Another day. That's a promise.' And then I heard him laugh, not once but twice, a double ring of sheer joy.

I remember the plum purple rain clouds gathering over my head, the river turning darker and silkier by the minute, and a rising wind bending and rustling the reeds. Most curious of all, I remember the sound of my voice singing, as if the memory of the initial wariness that was only a hair's breadth from hostility and my reaction to that cruelly stabbing accusation had been blotted out of mind, vaporized by the sound of his laughter ringing out across the fast darkening water.

CHAPTER FIVE

On Tuesday morning I left Aunt Edith at the Out-Patients Department of Helsby General Hospital, promising to pick her up in an hour. She'd made it plain she considered the consultation a waste of effort undertaken solely to humour me and put an end to Tim's badgering. Nonetheless I had a shrewd suspicion she was not wholly averse from a session with a hospital consultant whose knuckles she had once rapped.

While she was in the hospital I went into town, rented a colour television and arranged for it to be delivered and the aerial erected next day. To forestall a battle of wills when it arrived, I'd already broached the subject, explaining – with some truth – that after two and a half years abroad, I needed a course of indoctrination in current political and social trends, and to familiarize myself with what arguments, big and small, were in the forefront of public discussion.

Though she obviously scorned such a cheap and demeaning source of acquiring information, she hadn't actually forbidden me to have it brought into the house, merely remarking tartly that I'd be able to have it removed when I went to London, and that if the chimney suffered by having that unsightly scarecrow of wires fixed to it, she'd hold those who put it up responsible for the damage.

Renting the television had taken longer than I'd expected, and I looked like being late back at the hospital. I was leaping up the steps to the swing doors leading to Reception when they opened outward and I heard the ring of a familiar voice: 'Christina! So you've arrived. I heard you were coming back to Berghmere. I must say you look well.'

Mrs Leighton. To me she belonged in the wide, imprecise category of the middle-aged, lodged fast in that dreary doldrum where looks are a secondary if not a third consideration. Her grey-brown hair had been shampooed and set once a month and between whiles left to a comb; her face dabbed with powder and a smear of lipstick that had to last out the day. She had a common-form middle-aged pear-shaped figure, near flat chested with bulging hips she clothed in serviceable neutral shades. The woman looking down at me did not quite match up to the one I'd known. To begin with she'd lost a stone in weight. bringing hips into proportion with her bust measurement, and the resulting slenderness gave her added height, but no grace – she'd always been an ungainly woman. The melting away of flesh on her face defined its bone structure more sharply, subtly altered the play of expression. Her hair was expertly styled, make-up carefully applied and she was wearing what looked to me like a model suit in green and cobalt tweed. Though it did little for her and, disastrously, she'd added a tie of mink at the neck, it was a *volte face* from the man-tailored, wide-lapelled, nipped-waisted suits she'd worn as long as I could remember.

And, most astonishing of all, she was smiling at me. True, it was a visibly forced smile containing no warmth, but it was there, a parting of her square mouth that showed off her magnificent teeth. Apparently she'd either outlived or chosen to blot from memory the undying hate she'd beamed at me across Magnus's grave.

Her voice, at least, was unchanged: rather high, confident, inclined to be patronizing. 'I intended to telephone you, but I've been rushed off my feet since cook fell and fractured her thigh! It's very painful for her and most inconvenient for the rest of us. I've been visiting her. What are you doing here?'

I explained about Aunt Edith's hearing-aid.

She gave me a brisk nod of commendation. 'They do miracles with impaired hearing nowadays. It is very sensible of Miss Graham to consider an aid.'

She hurriedly consulted her watch. 'Dear me. I must be on my way. I was due to collect Hester and Anna from the hairdresser's ten minutes ago.' She paused fractionally, and I caught a definite nervous flicker in her protuberant hazel eyes before they met mine, as though she was having to force herself to fulfil a painful duty. 'But first we must arrange a day for you to come to Sweetcrab.'

Despite her act that I was no longer regarded as a pariah,

the invitation caught me off balance. Then the reason for it burst upon me. Hester! By now she'd have discovered I was home. An inveterate eavesdropper, peeper through key-holes, expert picker of locks, she also possessed an uncanny sixth sense for sniffing out any fact her parents wished to withhold from her. She'd have pestered her mother for permission to see me, and since what Hester wanted she'd means at her disposal to obtain, Mrs Leighton had been blackmailed into issuing the invitation. To have refused would have been to invite even greater risks and possibly public embarrassment. The fact that Hester wanted to see me made my heart lift, and I could feel myself smiling. 'How is Hester?'

'Very well.' Momentarily her plain face took on a glow of love that softened its new sharper angles. 'You'll hardly know her. Anna, her new companion, has opened up a wide new range of interests for her. She's so much happier, more fulfilled. Shall we say tomorrow?'

I should have refused. I hadn't the excuse of a shadow of doubt. For the short spell I was in Berghmere my salvation lay in keeping out of sight of Sweetcrab, ostracizing everyone who lived under its roof. To accept was a gratuitous act of self-punishment that risked wasting years of struggle to nail the past into the past. 'Thank you, I'd love to come.'

I looked over my shoulder as she hurried towards the hospital car park. From the back, except that her hips were narrower, she did not look all that different. I lingered, watching her as she got behind the wheel of the silver Mercedes and wondered if she'd always hankered after a fast, expensive foreign car, for less dowdy clothes – or were they no more than a part-compensation for widowhood? Simpler still, the natural perquisites of a woman now rich in her own right?

I started as Aunt Edith said at my shoulder: 'I saw you through the door and there seemed no point in sitting inside waiting.'

'I'm sorry I was late. I ran into Mrs Leighton.'

'Aye, so I saw,' she answered, refusing to evince any interest.

Fatigue was stamped on her face and her shoulders sagged.

'If you wait here, I'll bring the car and then you won't have to walk.'

Bone-hard pride, a determination not to be bossed in small matters no less than big, brought her limping in my wake. When I'd got her settled comfortably in the car, I asked: 'How did it go?'

'He played with his box of tricks and after a lot of fancy talk, he told me what I could have told him. It's nervous deafness, runs in the family. Your father would have been deaf if he'd lived, and both my parents were stone deaf before they were my age.'

'Hearing-aids weren't invented in their day. Can't Dr Sessler do anything for you?'

'He'd not be likely to admit it if he couldn't, would he?'

'Oh, I don't know. Did he remember you?'

'He remembered me right enough. He talked a lot about what he was pleased to call the good old days. By the looks of him I'd have thought his days were a good deal better now than when he spent his Saturday mornings humping round his father's greengrocery!' Having registered her protest, she was sufficiently mollified to add: 'There's no need for you to look so bothered, child. I promised to try one of his fiddly contrivances, but I warned him if it's no good, it'll go straight back to him.'

'Fair enough. When do you see him again?'

'The week after next. I've got a card with the date.'

'Tim will be pleased, and so will Markham.' On Sunday evening I'd told her that we'd met, without giving her a hint of the curious see-sawing quality of our meeting, of its inexplicable illusionary climax. Her gratification, the fossilized snobbery that induced it, had suddenly become comic, a little endearing, like a bit of genuine Victoriana. 'When does Markham usually come to see you?'

'Thursday evening.' She hesitated and then added – probably having decided I'd find out for myself: 'When he's in Helsby on market days he collects my tablets and embrocation from the chemist in the High Street.'

Not only district visitor but errand boy too! 'Why don't you get them from Tim?' I asked, knowing Tim did his own dispensing, then answered myself. She was dosing and rubbing herself with herbal remedies of which Tim either disapproved or counted as no more than placebos.

'He has too many patients already who could afford to buy their own aspirins and cotton wool instead of queueing up at his surgery door for cheap hand-outs. I'm not adding to it.'

I drove in silence for nearly a mile before I gathered up courage to say: 'Mrs Leighton asked me to go to Sweetcrab and have tea with Hester tomorrow.'

'What answer did you give her?'

'I said I'd go.'

She gave me a glance that whipped me with scorn. 'You should have known better. You've left all that behind you. What's the sense in turning back and picking it up again! They'll do you no good, none of them; they never have. Every single trouble you've had came from Sweetcrab.' She raised her voice to emphasize her bitter disappointment in me. 'I'd hoped you'd have learned your lesson by now, but it appears you haven't. More's the pity.'

I could be as obstinate as she was, but I'd no wish to embark on a fight when she was tired and probably in pain from stumping round hospital corridors. Instead I sought an answer to a small enigma that had been teasing me since I'd arrived at South View. 'What happened to Addy? Where did she go when she left Sweetcrab?'

'To keep house for her brother at Bloxstead. So far as I know she's still there.'

Adelaide Bray had come to Sweetcrab as Hester's nursery governess when Hester and I were five-year-olds. I worried around the terse snippet of information she'd grudgingly given me, before I said: 'I never understood why she left, at that particular time, when Hester must have needed her desperately.' Out of the corner of my eye I gave her a wary glance, querying whether I dare risk another question. 'Why did Addy leave Sweetcrab?'

'Mrs Leighton took Hester to London. They were there, oh, I forget how long, but I'd say for the best part of six months while Adelaide was at Bloxstead. When they returned to Sweetcrab either Adelaide Bray didn't choose to go back there or she wasn't invited.'

That I knew, from long experience of the nuances of her voice, was all that I'd get out of her, and I spent the last few miles summoning up my recollections of Addy's brother, Joe. He owned a small but quite famous boat-yard, and maybe half a dozen summer afternoons when we were of an age to be excited by such excursions, Addy had taken Hester and me to visit him. We'd gambolled in the shavings strewn about the lofty build-section where there was always a boat, more often more than one in the process of being hand-shaped by a craftsman. He was a big solid man, much older than Addy, so different in manner and appearance from his string-thin, brisk, quick-thinking sister, it was hard to credit they were close kin. Sometimes as a treat Addy had taken us to have tea in the cottage under the lea of the boat-yard where Joe, a bachelor, seemed content to do for himself. Downstairs there was a living-room kitchen and a prim Sunday-afternoon parlour, above them two bedrooms. Alongside the back door, inspected by us when Addy escorted us to the privy at the top of the garden, was a tin bath hung from a hook. With stabbing clarity I recalled Addy's extreme finickiness, her passion for fresh air, her long-legged strides that demanded space, and thought with an ache of pity: Addy penned in a workman's primitive cottage where, with small windows and half the light they admitted screened by the rearing sides of the build-section of the boat-yard, it had always seemed dusk.

'Doesn't she ever come back to Berghmere to visit anyone?'

'Not that I've heard.'

Bloxstead was only sixteen miles away. Addy had her own Mini. I found it hard to credit that she'd severed all connection with the girl she'd loved as devotedly and selflessly as if she'd been her own child. I marvelled scarcely less that in all this time I'd never suffered a pang of concern for her.

The shortest, most direct route to Sweetcrab was across the mere, but even if my dinghy hadn't been sold, on a day that threatened rain, with an ice-edged wind blowing grey and purple cushions of cloud across the sky, to have traversed the water-meadow with its patches of reed-sown marsh would have brought me to the door dishevelled and muddy-footed.

As an insulation against panicking nerves, I concentrated on deciding what to wear. My final choice was a caramel sleeveless wool dress with matching jacket that had been my last extravagant buy in New York, so cunningly simple it would hold its own against any competition. I'd shampooed and set my hair after breakfast, restrained its fly-away tendencies with spray. Taking a final look at myself, a part of me derided my efforts to arrive at Sweetcrab in peak form. As if Hester could care, and it *was* Hester I was going to see.

When I went to say goodbye to Aunt Edith, she was sitting bolt upright in her straight chair, wearing her most embattled air. She looked me over in silence before she delivered her verdict. 'Dressed in your best! Always your best for Sweetcrab. They've only to flick a finger and you start running. You never saw, and it seems you never will, that they used you, every one of them, and they're still using you.'

'I'm going to see Hester,' I stonewalled, refusing to be dragged backwards into old battlefields. 'It's perfectly natural that I should want to see her.'

'Hester is their responsibility not yours.' The faded blue eyes in her gaunt lined face were stone-hard and bitter with resentment that my heart's allegiance had not shifted. In the split second before she turned away to vent her derision on the grey-black tube of the television that had been installed that morning, I caught a shadow of mortal hurt. In the act of walking away I hesitated, conscience faintly stirred, then I went quickly out of the room. Hurt maybe, but in her pride, the old jealousies stirring in their graves. As I got into the car I fumed at the obstinate contrariness of her antiquated snobbery. In theory it should have worked in the Leightons' favour, but it never had. Magnus's authority even she hadn't disputed, Hester she'd tolerated, but all the others she'd viewed with disfavour next door to contempt.

By road Sweetcrab was three miles away. When I turned into the drive, the pink and silver house was waiting for me. It had been built in Elizabeth I's reign, a half-timbered substantial yeoman's house. Successive generations, plus the sheer destructive power of time had shorn it of its lands, rendered it half-derelict before it was bought by Magnus's father in the last year of the nineteenth century. It was he who had painstakingly restored it, colour-washed the plaster a blush rose pink, left its skeleton of beams the glimmering silver to which centuries of storm and tempest had weathered them. With the exception of the two russet brick chimneys no vertical or horizontal line remained true, and the top gables lurched so far forward they appeared to be in danger of toppling into the drive.

I parked the car in a space behind the garage block that had been extended to house four cars, and heard in my memory's ear Cary's protest when, coming home late, he'd been called to order next morning for boxing in his father's car. 'They each have a garage, but not me, oh, no! What am I supposed to do, leave it in the road, suspend it from the sky!' He'd heaved his exasperation out of his heart. 'Come the day, Christy, come the day!' He'd meant the day he'd leave Sweetcrab, become a junior partner in a London publishing house, be married to me. I'd dreamed along with him, though in my dream there'd been an important qualification: I'd seen us coming back to Sweetcrab, perhaps with a grandchild to win back Magnus's heart, entrance Hester.

Facing the oak door with its stout bands of iron, I saw infinitely clearer than the three giant beech trees that stood like sentinels over the house, the first short-stemmed Lent daffodils in the wild garden, their trumpets rocked by the wind, my diminutive self on that other spring day a month after my fifth birthday.

Stumbling out of the taxi, clutching Aunt Edith's hand, my movements contsricted by my clothes, every one of which was mint new, even the house slippers I carried in a linen bag on which Aunt Edith had embroidered my initials, and the kid gloves tethered to me by a length of string that ran down my coat sleeves.

I was being led like a lamb to slaughter to school, not a proper school, Aunt Edith had explained, that would come later, but to a private class with two other little girls, Elizabeth Mortimer and Susan Duncan who had been invited by Mrs Leighton to share her daughter's lessons with a governess whose name was Miss Bray. For weeks I had been brainwashed on how to behave: not to speak unless I was addressed; never to mumble, not to kick my heels against chair legs, to sip my morning milk – if it were offered – not gulp it, and to remember to wipe my mouth afterwards. As Aunt Edith reached to pull the bell, the hundred and one rules that must be obeyed or bring eternal shame on us both, flew out of my mind. A multiplicity of terrors, the most agonizing of which was that I should be sick on the step, turned me rigid as a pole, and at the moment the door opened tears burst from my eyes.

The tallest man I'd ever seen towered above me, and as I took my first craven, tear-blurred glance up into Magnus's face, I'd thought he looked like God. Before I'd known him a month I'd addressed him by his Christian name. He'd frowned and I'd shaken in my shoes, waiting for wrath to strike me down, yet summoning enough of my native childish cunning to stammer: 'It's such a beautiful name. No one else is called Magnus. Please, mayn't I?' For a moment he'd kept me on a knife-edge of suspense, then he'd laughed, and to the horror of his wife and Addy sanctioned the liberty.

A small girl had come running down the hall to peer at me under the protection of his arm. She had honey curls, and was dressed in a blue corduroy boiler suit that matched her eyes. Milk and cornflakes lined her pink mouth and there was a dab of marmalade on her nose.

'Hester, pet, this is Christina. Give her a big hug and welcome her to Sweetcrab.'

Hester kissed me, transferring half the cornflakes from her mouth to mine. 'You mustn't cry. I never do, do I, Daddy?'

For the first time I'd heard that rich bellow of laughter. 'Only when you don't get your own way.' He patted my shoulder. 'There, cheer up, little one, you're going to have lots of fun here. Hester, puss, take Christina along to Addy and introduce her.'

I never saw Aunt Edith go. From that moment she ceased to be the prime figure in my life. In a room where the unbelievably warm air was scented with bowls of hyacinths, I was fed a second breakfast before Sue and Liz arrived. The classes under Addy had continued until we were seven, when

Liz and Sue and I had gone to school. Not Hester. By then the doubts, the dread possibilities were established. To solace her, I'd spent every Saturday and Sunday at Sweetcrab, and in the holidays had lived there for weeks on end. Thus it came about that though South View was my official address, Sweetcrab was my home.

As I pulled the bell, a flash of hindsight suggested that the child I'd been had been seduced by central heating, by scones and cream cakes for tea every day, and by the petting and indulging of an adored daughter that had perforce overflowed on to me. Perhaps because I'd been first on the scene – Aunt Edith was so obsessively punctual she invariably arrived early at any destination – Hester's first allegiance had been given to me, leaving only crumbs for Liz and Sue.

Before the echo of the bell I'd rung had died, there came the sound of running footsteps, a high lilting voice demanding: 'Let me, let me. I want to open the door to Christy.'

Hearing it my heart moved under the old familiar wave of love and compassion, the unique blend of cherishing that Hester exacted, that was at once a burden and a joy. Would she. could she, have changed?

CHAPTER SIX

A fear that was banished by the sight of Hester's face. It was still the happiest face I knew, rounded, petal-skinned, framed by straying tendrils of soft butter-coloured curls, the plump small mouth widened in a smile of unflawed delight at the sight of me, brilliant sparks of excitement dancing in her hyacinth blue eyes.

Hester Mary Leighton, a month past her twenty-third birthday, with the I.Q. of a seven-year-old, and considerably less than that child's judgment, sense of responsibility, governed solely by unpredictable, uncontrollable impulses. The final diagnosis had categorized her as irremediably retarded.

She flung herself at me, gave me a bear-hug, and then breaking away, planted a smacking kiss on my mouth.

From behind her in the panelled hall her mother protested: 'Don't smother her, darling.' She held out her hand formally to me. 'Christina, how nice to see you. I'm sorry it's such a horrid day.'

Hester tugged at my arm. 'You've got to come and see my swimming pool. Now . . .'

Mrs Leighton's voice took on that unique note of indulgence that only Hester could evoke. 'Darling, you must let Christina have tea before you show her the pool.'

Her forehead corrugated into a glower, lips shaped up into an ugly pout – dire signals that Hester was not prepared to wait. This was the reverse side of the coin: the demon-child who flew into violent tantrums and fiend-like spells of screaming beyond the reach of reason, even love.

'I'm so cold I'm dying for some tea,' I lied and made my teeth chatter. Sometimes, in the initial stages, it was possible to coax her from the edge of the pit, sometimes not. Greed, as I'd calculated, proved my ally. She smiled, licked her lips. 'There's an extra cake for tea because you're here. Chocolate on top and inside.'

She snuggled against me as we by-passed doors leading off the hall into a series of rooms, until we reached the drawing-room that was larger than the others and higher-ceilinged. It had been added to the original structure by Magnus's 6 ft 2 in father who'd insisted on one room in which he could stretch his arms above his head and where daylight was not filtered by leaded windows.

On the threshold I had to make a conscious effort to subdue a cry of dismay for the loss of the soft blurred harmony of faded chintz and rubbed velvet. It had been 'done over' in a sophisticated colour scheme that blended every shade of green from chartreuse to dark olive. Another compensation for widowhood, or the fulfilment of a long-cherished ambition that Magnus had vetoed? Certainly he would not have countenanced any refurbishing of a room which suited him physically and temperamentally. I wondered if Mrs Leighton had dreamed long before he died of sweeping away the faded silk rugs that were unravelled at the corners, the sagging sofas and chairs, the collection of multi-coloured brocade cushions with ragged tassel fringes. It was a handsome, even elegant room now, but because of what it had displaced, it found no favour in my eyes.

Mrs Leighton called to a girl who rose from a writing desk, came forward. 'Christina, this is Hester's new companion, Anna Benet. Her home is in Geneva. Anna dear, may I introduce you to an old friend of Hester's, Christina Graham.'

A small cool hand firmly but briefly clasped mine, and a composed voice, with the merest inflexion of accent, murmured: 'How do you do, Miss Graham.' She was my height, as dark-haired as I was. Returning her greeting, I was tantalized by a feeling I'd seen her before, or someone closely resembling her.

Mrs Leighton divided a fond complacent smile between Hester and Anna. 'We hope Anna will stay with us for a long while, don't we, Hester?'

'Yes,' Hester answered absently, not taking her eyes off me.

'Mrs Leighton,' Anna Benet offered, 'would you like me to bring in the tea?'

'That would be sweet of you, Anna. Hester, would you go and help Anna by carrying one of the trays?'

Hester, feigning deafness, pulled me down beside her on the sofa. Her mother's voice coaxed more firmly: 'Darling, you know cook is in hospital and that Mrs Jones doesn't come in the afternoon, so that we are all doing our best to help. It isn't kind to leave all the work to Anna. If you go with her she'll have one less journey to make from the kitchen, and Christina won't have to wait so long for her tea.'

There was a strained silence charged with threat during which Hester mulishly deliberated and her mother and Anna tried to camouflage their anxiety, before with ill-grace Hester heaved herself to her feet. At the door she prodded a warning finger at me. 'You're not to go away. Christy, you're not to move one single step.'

'I won't. I promise.

When we were alone, Mrs Leighton spoke in the firm tone of one determined instantly to remove a tiresome misunderstanding. 'Hester and Anna are the greatest friends, practically inseparable. By widening her interests and encouraging her natural talents Anna has succeeded in undoing all the harm Addy did by over-protecting and frustrating her.' She darted a quick half-furtive glance at me to catch my reaction to the name, but as I'd none ready, it was wasted. 'They ride and swim together, and the three of us are going to stay in a chalet near Chamonix where she'll start learning to ski. Anna says her muscle co-ordination is exceptionally good, and as she's an athlete herself, she should be a sound judge.'

I started to make some suitable comment but she overrode it, her voice becoming more purposeful, racing a little to finish whatever she was determined to convey to me before we were interrupted. Her authority, though held subservient to Magnus's – a fact she'd not visibly resented – was in her own narrow domestic sphere equally autocratic: a minor planet to his sun.

'It was dear Markham who was instrumental in finding Anna. Clarissa is a friend of Madame Benet, and when Markham met Anna while he was staying with his mother, she happened to mention to him that she was anxious to spend some time in England, and he suggested she should write to me. At first I was doubtful whether a girl accustomed to a full and very varied social milieu would settle here, have sufficient congenial company of her own age.' Her eyes settled on me like one approaching the punch line. 'However, I needn't have worried, Markham takes care of that. They get on famously together, and she couldn't have a better escort, could she?'

I gave the answer she wanted. 'No, she couldn't.'

The task she'd taken upon herself completed, she heaved a sigh that to do her justice was probably heart-felt. 'He's such a dear boy. I endeavour not to indulge in wishful thinking, but I would be so thankful if he could put the tragedy of Ophelia behind him and marry again. Anna certainly has all the qualities to make him a perfect wife.'

Mrs Leighton might have updated her clothes, acquired a powerful foreign car, indulged a latent taste for interior decoration but in essentials she hadn't changed. She had always been a singularly tactless woman, and still was. Deliberately and with malice, she was warning me off. I should have found it amusing; I didn't altogether. I was saved the trouble of replying by the entry of Anna with Hester at her heels.

I looked hard at Anna Benet as she put the tea tray beside Mrs Leighton. Her back was half-turned, her eyes downcast, and beyond learning she had a prettily lifting eyebrow, a delicately drawn profile, and a natural grace of movement, I had to wait until she walked across the room and our two faces were reflected in a double portrait in a Regency mirror above the fireplace. Astnoishment hit me like a blow. The likeness was to myself – a likeness so remarkable we might have passed for twins. The only noticeable difference was in our eyes: hers were dark brown, mine blue-grey. As she moved to Mrs Leighton's side to take the filled cups, our glances crossed, and I saw that she, too, was conscious of the resemblance, resentful of it. In a way, so was I. It had a deflating effect, like rubbing shoulders at a party with a guest whose clothes-sense you deplore wearing an identical dress to your own.

While Anna and Hester handed the tea, scones and cakes, Mrs Leighton masterfully controlled the conversation, censoring the subjects, and directing it innocuously towards my experiences in the United States, Anna's home-life in Geneva. Hester ate stolidly from every plate within reach, not contributing a word. When a scene did not interest her, she opted out of it.

But even under her mother's determined stage-management there inevitably came a pause which I filled. 'You've re-done this room, haven't you?'

She said dismissively: 'Yes, some time ago now. Hugo was responsible for the all-over design.' To cut further comment from me, she turned to Anna. 'My dear, could you fetch me some more hot water?'

Hugo Trent, a bachelor in his forties, who ran an interior decorating shop in Helsby, lived alone in a chi-chi flat above. Whimsical, over-eager to please, I thought of him as a poseur, a pseudo-intellectual, and most certainly an incongruous habitué of Sweetcrab. But there'd been no denying the welcome he'd received from its mistress nor of his slavish devotion to her. Perhaps, I'd worked out, they fed a need in one another: he, a social climber if there ever was one, prized the solid understated prosperity of Sweetcrab, the friendship of a top-family which was of commercial value to him. And Mrs Leighton, I'd been driven to suppose, found his flattery, doting attention a pleasant contrast to her husband's habit of taking her for granted. It would never have occurred to Magnus to compliment his wife. She was his, therefore perfect, which rendered comment superfluous.

Neither Cary who referred to him disparagingly as Mum's platonic boy-friend nor I had been able to bear Hugo, but curiously Wellesley had never in my hearing objected to his limp, ever-smiling presence about the house; but then he flattered Wellesley too! Proof of the special relationship he enjoyed was that on the night Magnus was murdered, it was Hugo, along with Markham, to whom they'd turned spontaneously in the devastation of shock and grief. Both had been at Sweetcrab when the police arrived.

Hester said in her clear, ringing voice: 'I liked it best as it was before, and I want the picture back.' She pointed to the pretty Regency mirror above the fireplace. 'When is it coming back?'

I'd missed it too. It had been a composite portrait of the three Leighton children at five, eleven and seventeen. Though it had been stylized, derivative, the likenesses had been excellent, the design pleasing.

Mrs Leighton said with sweet patience: 'You know it had to go away to London to be cleaned and have a new frame because the old one was broken at one corner.'

'But it's been ages,' she complained petulantly. 'Why don't you tell the man in London we want it back?'

'Experts take a long time to do a job. Don't worry, it will be back soon.'

I wondered where it was: in a locked attic? Burnt? Had every other reminder of Cary been swept out of Sweetcrab in a scorched-earth policy?

Hester whined: 'But I want it back now. I want to look at . . .'

Her mother cut her off before the name she must have been indoctrinated into forgetting fell from her lips. 'Aren't you going to show Christina your swimming pool?'

The old ruse of distraction worked. 'Yes.' She was up, dragging at my hand. 'But first you've got to find it, and you never will. Never.'

When she'd fetched our coats, we went through the french window on to the terrace. Anna remained behind and began busying herself with collecting the tea-cups.

Beyond the terrace was a down-sweeping lawn enclosed by shrubberies and a rose-garden. I looked about but couldn't see a pool, and Hester giggled, clasped her hands. 'You can't see it, can you? You think we're making it up?'

To please her I said I did. When we reached the edge of the lawn and only the bog-garden separated us from the dark ice-still waters of the mere and there was still no swimming pool to be seen, her mother ordered: 'Hester, pet, you've teased Christina long enough, and we're all getting frozen in this wind. Now, please, straight here, no more games.'

She seized my hand, hugged it to her, and hurried me

along a path that had been cut at the top of the kitchen garden, screened by an overlap larch fence. 'You still can't guess, can you?'

I said no, but I could: the old barn. I should have realized that in East Anglia an out-door swimming pool would have been a pretty useless toy. They'd built an indoor one in the half-ruined barn which dated back to the time when Sweetcrab had been a farm, used to store winter fodder. It had been re-roofed with old tiles, its rotting doors replaced with sliding ones that glided apart at a touch.

'There!' Hester shouted, keeping a lynxlike watch on my face.

It couldn't have disappointed her. The sky-blue rectangle with its marble surround was approximately the size of Helsby's very modest public bath. The interior of the barn had been reduced to a shell and lined with pinewood and Spanish tiles. A wrought-iron twist of stairway erected behind the diving-board led up to a row of changing cabins.

'Hester, it's absolutely fabulous.' I sniffed the warm air. 'How long have you had it?'

Mrs Leighton answered. 'Just over a year.'

Hester dragged on my arm. 'You've got to come and swim with me. You've got to, Christy.'

'No swim suit.'

'There are lots of swim suits and bikinis.' Like a bird in flight she ran up the stairway, opened the door of a hot-air cupboard, showed off the swimming gear hanging there.

I still said no. I loathed swimming in a cap, and I didn't particularly wish to make my exit from Sweetcrab with my hair hanging in wet tails down my neck.

Opposition to what she wanted at a given moment and the desire to indulge her child's conceit in her new prowess did battle, put the pout back on her mouth, but conceit won.

As she disappeared into one of the cabins, her mother led me to a raised platform by a window set out with cushioned chaise-longues, low teak tables that overlooked the mere. As I sat down, I glanced at the boat-house. No boats were moored in the dock. If Cary's dinghy, or Magnus's day cruiser which he'd used as a ferry-boat to the Bird Hut hadn't been sold, they'd been padlocked in the boat-house, the key inaccessible to Hester's light seeking fingers. Ever since she'd sneaked away from Addy, taken the dinghy and nearly drowned, that had been the rule.

From the top diving board, Hester yelled: 'Christy, look at me.'

It was as near a perfect dive as made no difference but it did not satisfy her. She had to repeat it half a dozen times.

Her mother watched in silence, wrapped in the sweet content of seeing her handicapped child raised to equality with her peers. It was a mood that transformed her into an infinitely more appealing woman. When, conscious of my glance, she looked towards me, her smile was fiercely proud. When she did not speak, perhaps because she couldn't, I said: 'Hester's turned into a magnificent swimmer. What a wonderful, imaginative idea to give her an indoor pool. Was it yours?'

'Yes.' Some of the inward joy dissolved. Towards strangers, short-term acquaintances, she maintained a fiction that Hester, though admittedly a late-developer, immature for her age, was normal. But with me there could be no such face-saving pretence. I had shared the anguishing years, heard the last hope-dispelling verdict.

Visibly she braced herself to a task. When she spoke it was in the briskly authoritative voice she used to correct a servant, chide any child but her own daughter for misdemeanours. 'Christina, as we are alone this is an opportune moment for me to state my case, leave no margin for misunderstanding. You've seen fit to return to Berghmere, in my view unwisely and selfishly . . .' She paused, then conceded grudgingly: 'I suppose you have the right to do so, but . . .'

Nothing I'd done or she imagined I'd done, entitled her to take that high-handed manner with me. I interrupted. 'I most certainly had.'

The lines of her new thinner face tightened with a hard stubbornness. 'That's debatable, but it's pointless to discuss a *fait accompli*. You are here, which means I'm called upon to deal with a highly explosive situation. My sole concern is for Hester, to forestall any move on your part that might have a harmful effect on her health and well-being. To put it plainly,' she continued with stress on each word, 'I will not permit you to disturb or upset her.' Something in my face gave her pause, and I saw a muscle twitch at the corner of her mouth. She subdued it, continued with the harsh severity of a judge addressing a prisoner in a dock: 'It was my intention that Hester should be safely away from Sweetcrab during your visit to Berghmere. Unfortunately the chalet is let until the end of next week. Meanwhile though we endeavoured to keep the news from her, from some source Hester heard that you were coming home. As a result she worked herself into a dangerously excited state and insisted on seeing you; she would probably have made herself ill if I had withheld my permission.'

She stopped abruptly to gather her forces for a final attack. There was a pause during which I watched the resurgence of her undying hate for me. Her voice, when she did eventually speak, was low-toned but utterly remorseless. 'I've hoped and prayed, that we would be spared the intolerable ordeal of seeing you, and that Hester, if we were patient, would forget you. Though this was the only recompense within your power to make, you've seen fit to withhold that mercy from us. That being so, I have a moral right to insist that you give me your solemn word that after you leave Sweetcrab this afternoon, you will make no attempt to see or speak to Hester.'

'You mean,' I asked in a humiliatingly shaky voice, 'if I meet her in the street I'm to cut her dead?'

'During the few remaining days that we'll be at Sweetcrab, at no time will Hester leave the house unaccompanied by either Anna or myself. I will not permit her to talk to you about . . .' She stopped as abruptly as if caught in a trip-wire, her face contorted with either anguish or grief, then summoned every remnant of will to force the name through her lips. 'Cary. She hasn't spoken of him for eleven months but because you were there . . .' She stopped again, turned her bitter gaze on me. 'Christina, I'm waiting for your promise.'

Before I could speak, Hester bored without an audience, clambered half-way up the steps out of the pool, called: 'Christy, please come here, I want to talk to you.'

I stood up and had to steady my knees by gripping the arm of the chair before I called back: 'It's time I was going home, Hester. Goodbye.'

She scrambled out, wailed petulantly: 'But you can't go home, it's too early. I want you to dry my back.'

'Hester!' For once Mrs Leighton gave her daughter a direct order. 'Go and get dressed. Christina and I will wait for you.'

She dived into the pool, swam to the side nearest to us, clung to the rail and chanted in a sing-song: 'I'm not coming out until Christy promises to dry my back. I'll stay in the pool, swimming all night . . . all night.'

'You'd better go,' Mrs Leighton said to me in a choked voice. 'But if you have any affection for Hester, any concern for her well-being, you'll keep your word.'

That I hadn't given.

Hester clambered out of the pool, ran up the stairway and I followed. Once inside the changing cabin she slammed the door. She was aquiver with excitement from head to toe, practically gasping with it, her eyes brilliant with a frenzied light that frightened me. 'Christy, when's he coming? I know he's coming, but when?'

I stripped off her swim-suit, wrapped her in a warm towel, alarmed by the onset of one of her attacks of hysteria.

'Who?' I murmured hardly above a whisper.

'Cary,' she shouted at the top of her lungs in a fury at my obtuseness. 'Now that you've come home, he'll come too. But when's he coming?'

I laid two fingers gently on her lips. It was a private signal between us that she was to stop shouting and screaming and listen to me. Sometimes she heeded it, sometimes she didn't. This time her lips ceased quivering, but the light in her eyes was still too brilliant and wild. I knew that any distraction would only be momentary.

'Hester, lovey, listen to me. I've come home to spend a holiday with Aunt Edith before I start a new job in London. My coming back has nothing to do with Cary. I came to Berghmere to see you and Aunt Edith.'

She spat my fingers away in a rage of disappointment.

'You're making it up. You think I don't know, but I do. It's supposed to be a secret, but I know . . .'

The door opened inwards and Mrs Leighton said in an icy, tightly-controlled voice: 'There's not enough room in one cabin for two. Hester, please get dressed at once. Christina and I will wait for you by the pool. Christina, come with me.'

CHAPTER SEVEN

We returned to the house in single file: Hester leading, sullen and dumb now that by denying her fantasy hope I'd failed her; Mrs Leighton in the middle, a human wall to protect her daughter from contamination by me.

On the other side of the french window Anna was waiting. She'd changed her sweater and skirt for a grey cashmere dress and set out drinks. One swift intuitive look divided between the three of us alerted her to a crisis – on the possibility of which she'd probably been briefed by Mrs Leighton. She gave Hester a warm, friendly smile, coaxingly held out her hand. 'Come upstairs and I'll dry your hair with your new dryer.'

'Yes, darling, go with Anna and change your dress and shoes. Wellesley will be home soon.' Mrs Leighton angled her body in my direction but was careful to look over my head. 'Will you excuse me seeing you to your car? With cook in hospital I have to get ahead with preparations for dinner . . .'

Hester interrupted, remarking with gloating interest but no concern: 'Christy's got blood on her hand. It's running down her coat.'

I had only a vague recollection of scoring my hand against a bare rose-bush and stared blankly at blood dripping between my fingers, making splodges of scarlet on my white top coat. 'It's only a scratch,' I protested, searching in my pocket for a tissue that didn't appear to be there. A drop of blood falling on the carpet brought a gasp of exaggerated dismay from Mrs Leighton. She plucked a linen handkerchief from her sleeve, rammed it into my bleeding hand. 'Keep it wrapped up or it'll drip everywhere.' She sounded at breaking-point, as though by spotting the shadowy green-grey carpet I'd piled a final straw on the already intolerable burden I imposed on her. 'You'd better go and bathe your hand in the cloakroom. If you need it there's sticking plaster and a bandage in the cupboard above the basin.' Completely thrown off balance by this latest maddening delay in getting me out of the house, for once she dithered, changed her mind. 'Anna, perhaps you'd better go with Christina. Hester, come along. I'll dry your hair.'

She hustled Hester out of the room with a brusque peremptoriness she rarely displayed towards her daughter, with whom her patience was well nigh inexhaustible. And Hester, with a last gloating look at the darkening spot on the carpet, the blood seeping through her mother's handkerchief, departed without a word to me . . . her way of getting her own back!

Anna stood over me until the water from the tap under which I held my hand ran clear. 'It's only a scratch,' I insisted. 'It doesn't need a Band-aid.'

'It would be better for you to have one.' She applied it deftly, not speaking, scrupulously keeping contact between us at a minimum, never once glancing at our strangely similar faces in the mirror. Obeying orders but not garnishing them by a single friendly word, making it obvious she'd been warned by Mrs Leighton that I posed a threat to Hester's well-being which must at all costs be circumvented.

When she'd gone, I leaned against the basin. I had a curious feeling of mindlessly floating in a sort of chaos which I was powerless to reduce to order. Gradually Hester's words stopped their fire-cracker dance in my head, and I could begin, ponderously, clumsily, to separate sense from nonsense. I knew Hester too well to have my heart rent apart by the hysterical hope she'd hypnotized herself into believing was fact. Cary coming back to Berghmere . . . that was not possible. What had shaken me was not Hester's fantasy-story, but the pitiful revelation of love and loyalty, and faith kept alive in a child. It was not Mrs Leighton's vicious denunciation of me that plunged knives into my heart, but that she could persuade herself that I would willingly commit any act that would adversely affect Hester. All else I could forgive her, but not that.

As I stood upright without support, I heard the sound of cars arriving, the slamming of doors, followed by Mrs

Leighton's greeting to Wellesley before her voice broke into a near-shriek of pleasure. 'Markham! My dear boy, what a treat to see you! Anna will be delighted.'

'I'm not being a nuisance, am I? Wellesley and I ran into one another and he persuaded me to drop by for a drink on my way home.'

'Not only a drink but food. No, it's no good your protesting, I'm not going to listen to you.'

They went into the drawing-room, and the closed door brought my eavesdropping to an end.

I'd spent longer than I'd realized getting my mental breath; by now everyone would assume I was out of the house. I parted the cloakroom door a foot. The hall was empty and as far up the staircase as lay within my restricted vision. Should I creep silently away, make my final exit from Sweetcrab as furtive as a thief's? The thrust of pain I'd anticipated plunged deep, and then, unbelievably died. For a long moment I stood motionless, dazed by a revelation that defied credibility: it was over. The love-affair with a house that had begun on a doorstep when I was five years old had run its course, breathed its last bitter breath. I was free. Aunt Edith's eyes had been clearer than mine. They *had* used me as child, adolescent and woman, and I'd turned metaphorical somersaults to retain privileges that had only been leased to me so long as I served as companion and loving guardian to their darling and never presumed on rights that were no more than an act of grace. Oh, no, I decided, no creeping away.

With a firm step I walked through the lower hall. Though still not absolutely sure of the lasting power of my release, I maintained the tread until I was level with the drawing-room door. It opened and Wellesley said in the act of closing it behind him: 'Mother said you'd left, but knowing you I considered it advisable to verify you were no longer in the house.' He reached out, put his hand on my shoulder, made an effort to reverse me. 'As you are still here it provides us with an opportunity of discussing a matter of utmost concern to both of us.'

I resisted what amounted to a shove, stayed rooted where I was. I didn't like his touch, nor anything about Wellesley

Leighton. His only claim to good looks was his height, an impressive breadth that made his presence noticeable in any gathering. Raven-haired like his father, with curious very pale brown eyes, he had his mother's flattish, pallid countenance, except that his was coated in a sheen of self-importance, an aplomb that never cracked. He was, I'd decided long ago, a self-made man, made in his own image. He literally loved Wellesley Leighton.

'Your mother has already talked to me. There's nothing left for you to add.'

'There you're mistaken. Come with me.' He leaned past me, opened the door to the library. He was astute enough to have calculated on shock tactics to lower my physical resistance. They worked. As I looked into the room where Magnus had died the effect on me was racking grief, a black ache of despair. It was lined with his books, his Charles II desk was in the centre, the accoutrements of writing and reading set in the precise order he'd prescribed. His antique pistols were over the fireplace, and bolted into one wall was the green painted safe from which one day when it had been open, to divert a child, he'd heaped a pile of diamonds into my cupped palms.

Wellesley did not invite me to sit, neither did he take his father's massive wing arm-chair, but stood alongside it, behind the desk. 'Now,' he declaimed in his embryo politician's voice, 'shall we save time by getting down to the crux of this whole unsavoury business? Why have you returned to England, or, more precisely, to Berghmere?'

'I don't admit your right to ask that question, but as a favour I'll answer it. A job in London, an elderly, rather frail aunt in Berghmere.'

He threw me a thin smile of intense dislike. 'Not your cover story, if you please. The real one.' The square, well-fleshed face took on its most superior expression, practically Olympian. 'Even you must acknowledge that by its very nature you'll have to disclose it eventually. So let's waste no more of your time or mine.'

I looked at him, sensed that behind the imperturbability, the assumption of omnipotence, there breathed a ferocious, not quite controlled determination to force some admission out of me. But what? I hadn't a clue and, disliking him, I'd no inclination to expend effort on satisfying my curiosity. 'There is no other reason than the one I've given you.'

He thundered: 'Don't play games with me, Christina.'

'I'm not playing games,' I said, and turned my back on him.

For a heavy man he moved with extraordinary speed, was at my shoulder as I reached the door. 'You will wait until I've finished what I have to say to you. What is more important, you'll listen. I will phrase it simply and shortly so that you'll be able to memorize it. It won't take long. If, as I strongly suspect, you've come here as Cary's go-between, I warn you that your efforts are doomed to failure. Neither I nor my mother treat with blackmailers.'

Curiously the monstrous accusation had less effect on me than that Wellesley with his cool, contriving brain, thick insulation of suave all-knowingness, was disturbed to the marrow of his bones. Aunt Edith firmly believed that the Devil could enter into people and possess them. Wellesley, an ugly colour suffusing his pallid cheeks, his eyes aflame with concentrated hatred, looked such a man. 'It was you who brought my brother to ruin, who changed him into a blind, utterly reckless, ambition-maddened creature. It was you who made him a murderer. You who destroyed my father and my brother, who brought grief and desolation to this house. I'll suffer no more at your hands. And in no circumstances will I permit you to subject my mother to further torment. Be warned that we are not to be threatened or take the consequences.'

I thought simply: He's gone mad, and fumbled for the door handle, leaving him to rave at himself. Out in the hall I heard the outside bell ring, but it reached my ears as a distant sound from another world. I was passing the drawing-room door when it opened, and Markham cried out in blank astonishment: 'Christy! You're still here. Aunt Esmée said you'd gone.'

'I am not here,' I said, without slowing my pace. 'I'm on my way out.'

From behind me Wellesley said in his normal unctuous tone: 'Christina is just leaving. She's in a hurry, so we mustn't detain her.' He stepped ahead of me to open the front door, and I found my exit blocked by Hugo Trent.

His languid, effete form froze rigid at the sight of me. I was aware, though it caused me no concern, that he flung a wildly apprehensive glance at Wellesley over my head. He must have received some reassuring signal because a moment later he'd recaptured sufficient of his poise to hold out his boneless hand. 'Why, Christina! Back from foreign parts, I see, and looking as pretty and charming as ever.'

I ignored the proffered hand, determinedly shook off my shoulder a grasp that was probably Markham's, made my ears deaf to the sounds of speech about me. My final exit from Sweetcrab was in a white-hot incandescence of fury that had a gloriously cleansing effect. Not only had I left Sweetcrab for the last time, but I'd erased it from my life, along with the Leighton tribe, some of whom had different surnames like Drake and Trent.

Paradoxically the end of a day that had mauled me savagely brought me one small, homely triumph. As I opened the front door my eardrums were blasted by a television turned up to maximum sound. In the sitting-room, her back to me, Aunt Edith sat within two feet of the screen, the *Radio Times* balanced upon her knee, so absorbed in a documentary of an African Game Reserve that she was not aware of my presence. I left her watching a rhinoceros and its young wallowing in a mud bath, went to prepare supper. The reaction after the thumb-screw pressures of the afternoon, that final ugly scene in the library in which a man I'd known as impervious to self-doubt, sickeningly self-confident, had raged at me like a maniac, was a bubble of hysteria bursting in my throat. If I'd used my wits I should have been able to work out that for Aunt Edith the bait was not musical spectaculars, quiz games and Wild West epics but instructive and educational features that fed the mind, put before her eyes moving pictures of the far corners of the globe she now accepted she'd never see.

I did not call her until I heard the credit titles fading out.

She wore a look I'd never expected to see on her face: abashment at being caught red-handed in an act of playing with a toy she'd scorned.

During supper she was silent, neither referring to the film she'd watched nor my visit to Sweetcrab, but the memory of our parting hung darkly between us. Conscience dictated that she had a right to know the irrevocable decision that had made itself in me.

I feigned a light, uncaring tone. 'I saw Hester and she's fine. They've built her a magnificent swimming pool in the old barn and she's learned to swim like a fish, and dive. Apparently she rides too with the new companion they've got for her, a Swiss girl.'

'Is that so,' she murmured, eyes on her plate.

She left all the going to me – and the giving – but maybe I deserved it. 'Yes. And having seen for myself I'm satisfied. You don't have to worry, or lecture me, I shan't go back to Sweetcrab again. That chapter is finished.'

She laid down her knife and fork, gave me what I termed one of her 'iron' looks that bore down relentlessly on the heart of truth. 'Indeed!' she said inimically.

'This time,' I said, writhing under the scepticism she didn't bother to hide, 'I mean it. I haven't the slightest wish to go back. The spell's broken.'

'Spell,' she repeated after me. All at once she looked confused, set at a loss. When she did speak it was in a tone of wringing bitterness. 'I blame myself. If I hadn't taken you there when you were too young to judge, there'd never have been . . .'

I interrupted, shying violently away from seeing through her eyes pictures of people, places and scenes that had made up the main fabric of my life. 'That's nonsense. No one's to blame; certainly not you. Anyway, it's dead history. I've been to Sweetcrab for the last time. That's a promise, and I won't break it.'

I was in the kitchen making a chicken mousse when, next day, just before six, the bell rang. I heard Aunt Edith answer it, opened the door a crack to identify the caller, then silently closed it as he disappeared into the sitting-room with her. The Thursday messenger-boy with his pills and potions had arrived.

I'd had a long day of living with my resolution. It was rock-hard but with the shock-waves that had attended its birth still reverberating through my head, I was not yet in a state to rationalize it to anyone; certainly not Markham Drake.

I heard the click of the sitting-room door opening and his footsteps down the hall. As I could have confidently predicted, Aunt Edith had encouraged, probably ordered him to seek me out in the kitchen.

He paused on the threshold to survey the mess of bowls, mincer and a heap of greasy chicken bones spread across the table – and me. Though his splendid presence, his air of grandeur that to do him justice was unconscious, contrasted with the drab, slightly disgusting disorder made an impact on me, I was in no mood to acknowledge it. Without giving him a chance to speak, I asked: 'Do you think it's in her own interest to provide Aunt Edith with chemist's medicines? Wouldn't it be better for her to obtain all she needs on prescription from Tim?'

He came to the edge of the table, gave me an amused but pacifying smile. 'Oh, I don't know. They're harmless otherwise they wouldn't be off prescription. Anyway, what you've faith in often does you most good, especially if you've been addicted to it for half a century.' He laughed coaxingly. 'Don't be too hard on her.'

'Hard on her!'

'Yes.' He glanced at me sharply, the light teasing look gone. 'Christy, what's biting you?'

'Nothing.'

'No!' he mocked, then changed his tone, angling a letter he held slightly towards me. 'I've missed the post with a bid for a Frisian bull I'm determined to have, which means driving into Lowestoft and popping it through the auctioneer's letter-box. I've come to ask if you'd care to come with me. We could eat at the Crown; their food used to be passable. What do you say?'

'Thanks for the invitation, but no.'

As I passed to and fro collecting basins and mincer, piling them in the sink, I was aware of him studying me with a look that was so deeply considering it was near scheming, suggesting he was dangling alternatives before himself. The one he was most likely to choose, I decided, was a dignified withdrawal.

But he surprised me. From behind my back as I turned on a tap, he challenged: 'For heaven's sake, why not? Unless you've got something else on. Have you?'

'No.'

'Well, then, a meal out, in a public dining-room, doesn't commit you to anything. So I repeat why not?'

I turned off the tap, faced him. 'Because of your commitments. Your loyalties if you like. They're different from mine.'

Anger like thunder darkened his face, making him look haughty. 'Are you positive? Wouldn't it be a good idea to make sure that particular accusation sticks?'

'Oh, it'll stick all right.'

He looked down at the table, picked up a spoon and fiddled with it, his anger either swallowed or put into cold storage. 'Why did you go to Sweetcrab yesterday? You were not obliged to go, and yet you did. Wasn't that tantamount to an open invitation to trouble?'

'I had my reasons for going.'

'A flaming row with Wellesley!' He laughed but without amusement. 'Striding down the hall you looked like the wrath of God about to exact vengeance on anyone within reach.'

'I went to Sweetcrab to see Hester.'

'Ah, Hester!' Like everyone who loved her he spoke her name with a special note. 'And was Hester any happier when you left than when you arrived?' When I didn't answer, he lifted both his hands, held them up in appeal. 'Christy, I can't talk to you when you're flying round the kitchen armed with basins and lethal-looking mincing machines. I wouldn't put it past you to aim one at my head.'

'It's not funny. If you know, as you probably do, precisely what Wellesley said to me in the library, you should also know how unfunny that nasty little scene was.'

Before he could answer, Aunt Edith limped in, announced,

pleased as Punch with herself, 'There's no need for you to be bothering with those. I'm still capable of washing up a handful of spoons and forks. Away with you,' she ordered as though I were ten years old, 'and change your frock. It'll do you good to go out for an evening.'

The situation was so comic that if I hadn't laughed, I'd have been in danger of bursting into tears. As I swallowed the sound in my throat, I looked from one face to the other. On Aunt Edith's was prim satisfaction. At the end of her grim personal valley of grief and tribulation she spied, faint and far off, like the answer to her nightly prayers, the glimmer of a prize she'd coveted and given up for lost. No matter that to give it substance Ophelia had had to die, Cary to commit murder!

On Markham's? Nothing that I could positively identify. For the moment it was passive, waiting, as though he'd reached an emotional pause and was taking account of and weighing up factors that had, until then, never crossed his mind. If he'd urged me by one word, I'd have refused, but he stayed silent.

The dingy kitchen provided an incongruous background for a sudden sharp judgment I made on myself. For years I'd run too fast and too far – out of reach of truths I was certain now had been kept from me. What truths I couldn't imagine, but if I played my cards with skill and calculation I might be able to prise some of them out of Markham Drake.

'All right,' I said, 'give me five minutes.'

CHAPTER EIGHT

In the car and over a drink in the hotel bar, where we were boxed in by other customers, by unspoken agreement we declared an armistice, were at pains to raise no subject more controversial than Liz's engagement, my new job, Sue, and the latest sensation to hit the village: Mavis Rand's production of triplets.

The dining-room was of a size to accommodate the summer's high tide of holiday-makers. Out of season only a sprinkling of tables were occupied, mostly by what appeared to be commercial travellers eating enormous expense account meals at speed behind outspread evening newspapers. Visible through the panoramic windows that ran the length of the room was the deserted, wind-scored promenade and beyond it the North Sea tumbling grey and dispirited on to the famous sands. The fairy-lights that swung in dipping skeins between the dolphin lamp standards only served to emphasize the waste of desolation without and within.

When we'd ordered, Markham cast a dismayed look at the empty tables, the under-employed waiters, that reflected on his social expertise, remarked: 'Maybe this wasn't such a bright idea! I'm sorry.' I'd had enough of pussy-footing. To him I might or might not be more than a dinner-date, but to me the food we ate, the surroundings in which we ate it, were trifling incidentals unworthy of attention.

'Oh, I don't know. We seem to have ended up in what amounts to a private room. We could shout our heads off and no one would hear.' I ignored the bright warning flash in his glance, continued: 'I'd like to put one record straight. I didn't ask myself to Sweetcrab. I was expressly invited by Mrs Leighton, to see Hester. Though they'd done their utmost to keep the news of my arrival from her, she'd heard a whisper of it somehow, and was pestering to see me.'

'And in accepting the invitation you obviously tumbled

headlong into trouble.'

'Trouble, if that's the word, from Wellesley.' I kept a close guard on his expression, playing a guessing game with myself as to what it would reveal. 'He jumped clean out of his mind, man-handled me into the library, and accused me of being Cary's go-between, some sort of messenger girl hell-bent on blackmailing him and/or his mother!' He was looking as keenly at me as I was at him, but it was a narrowed, semi-blind look that told me nothing I wanted to know. I repeated: 'Wellesley actually accused me of coming home for the sole purpose of blackmailing him. On what grounds I can't imagine.'

His glance shifted so suddenly that I didn't catch the moment of its going. When he didn't speak, I prompted: 'If it weren't so ugly, it would be farcical. Don't you agree?'

He was shaken, but he wasn't prepared to let me see to what extent. It gave him a look of obstinacy with a dash of arrogance. 'If you've had no contact with Cary you could hardly play errand-girl for him, could you? Didn't you make that point plain to Wellesley?'

The 'if' jarred, but I let it pass. 'I explained my reasons for coming home. He rejected them out of hand. He wasn't in a mood to accept anything from me bar a confession of complicity in blackmail. Wellesley,' I stressed, 'cool-brained, self-possessed Wellesey, literally losing control of himself, taking off into orbit, ranting and raving, within a hair's-breadth of shaking me until my teeth rattled and the truth fell out. It was a fantastic scene. So what's got into him? What makes him positive I came home with one aim in mind, blackmail? And how did he suppose I intended to go about extorting money from him to keep covered up whatever he's got to hide? To be vulnerable to blackmail a skeleton rattling round in a cupboard is obligatory!'

He looked appalled, but two waiters bearing down on us with smoked salmon and a bottle of hock in an ice-bucket saved him from having to make an instant reply. When they were out of earshot, I asked: 'How would you explain Wellesley's reaction to a sight of me?'

He gave me a queer glance, both compassionate and angry. 'I can't explain it. I can't see inside Wellesley's mind.'

'But you must have discussed it, or me, after I'd gone.'

'No,' he said adamantly, 'we didn't. I was curious to know why you'd charged out of the house in a flaming temper, but with Hugo and Anna there, I didn't inquire. I was due to see my herdsman at the house at seven, so I'd only time for one drink.' His expression lightened, became wickedly sardonic. 'I assure you no one mentioned the word blackmail in my hearing. Or you.'

'And yet,' I suggested firmly, 'I must have been weighing heavily on their minds. Your aunt had delivered a few warning threats of her own during the afternoon. Anyway, Hugo and Anna don't come into the category of strangers. Hugo's an old family pet and my guess is that your aunt doesn't keep many secrets from Anna.'

'She's done a good job with Hester. I doubt in the circumstances if anyone could have done a better.'

'I'm sure,' I murmured, and a small uncommitted section of my mind registered his instant defence of her. 'But we aren't discussing Hugo and Anna. We were discussing the subject of blackmail, and what put that preposterous and quite horrible idea into Wellesley's head. You ought to be able to give me a clue . . . that is if you feel disposed to do so!'

He put down his fork, brought his deep indigo gaze up to mine. 'I haven't a clue to give you. What explanation is there but you both lost your tempers and in the heat of the moment, the shock of seeing you at Sweetcrab, Wellesley also lost his head?'

'I did not lose my temper.'

He lowered his gaze quickly and watching him I thought he had the look of a cornered man. It wasn't a rôle that he was accustomed to playing. It didn't suit him.

He said quietly, feeling his way: 'After the hell they've been through can you expect anyone at Sweetcrab to behave rationally, not to fly into sudden panics. suffer from nervestorms?' He paused, and I caught a shadow of something like apprehension surface in his eyes. 'Christy, how could it be otherwise? The sight of you revived all the horrors they want to forget, must forget if they are to survive.'

I said stiffly: 'They brought them back to me too.'

'I know,' he said, but he didn't sound as if he cared, he was too engrossed in arguing Wellesley's case. 'One of the fringe results of a sensational murder is the spate of anonymous letters written by cranks, the sick-minded, the criminally mischievous, even the odd clairvoyant after publicity, plus a minority of normal people who are genuinely convinced they have valuable information to contribute. In the early days they arrived by the sackful, now they've dwindled to a trickle, but they still come.'

'Do they?' It was an inevitable dirty aftermath to which I'd given no thought. I couldn't quite see its relevance now, then inspiration flashed, momentarily shook me. 'Are you suggesting that Wellesley received a tip-off in an anonymous letter that a dark-haired woman would shortly arrive on his doorstep as a messenger girl from his brother and proceed to blackmail him?'

'No.' He gave me a fiery, rebuking glance. 'I'm merely trying to put you in the picture, to explain, not condone or excuse Wellesley's extraordinary behaviour.'

He hadn't, I reflected wryly, done a very good job. All I'd sought from him were a few straight answers to a few simple questions. He hadn't chosen to give them to me.

To break the chilly silence of a stalemate that had settled between us, I said airily: 'Lots of changes at Sweetcrab, a swimming pool, a Mercedes 3.5 coupé, and a drawing-room straight out of *Homes and Gardens*! I imagine Wellesley is a rich man now? How did Magnus leave his money?'

He expressed his disapproval of the question by answering as factually as though he were reading from the will. 'A trust fund for Hester, Sweetcrab for life and a quarter of his estate to Aunt Esmée, half to Wellesley. The remaining quarter would have been Cary's if he hadn't forfeited it under the law which debars a murderer from profiting from the death of his victim.'

Grief, the unending futility of it all, wrenched at me, but

I held it at bay. 'And the richer you are the more vulnerable you are to blackmail.'

He said with heat: 'That word appears to obsess you.'

'It's a very emotive word. When it's applied to oneself it sticks in one's gullet and you can't get rid of it. Yet you seem to regard it as no more than a minor social misdemeanour on Wellesley's part!'

He ran a sombre glance over the ranks of empty white-starched tables, ridden by some grinding emotion he was striving to suppress. Yet when he brought it back to me it was candid, almost naked in its appeal. 'Christy, must you make a big issue out of it? Can't you take into account that by coming back to Berghmere inevitably you've brought Cary along with you, not in the flesh but his ghost? That's what Wellesley saw behind your shoulder, Cary. All right, I admit that his nerves aren't as steady as they used to be. Whose would be in his place! Memory dies hard in a thinly populated rural community, and it doesn't help that the police file is still open.' He paused for a response from me, and when I'd none to give him, he continued in a cooler, brisker tone: 'After all, the burden of proof lies with Wellesley. To qualify as a blackmailer you have to make an attempt to extort money. That means time will exonerate you.'

'Why, yes,' I cried softly, and looked at him, glad and grateful for a line of reasoning I hadn't been cool-witted enough to work out for myself.

But there was no answering gladness in his. I wanted to shout: 'What do you know that I don't?' But it wouldn't have brought me an answer. His loyalties were as immutable as mine. He wouldn't forsake them. If there were sides, he was on Wellesley's and his aunt's. At rock bottom the situation was simplicity itself. We distrusted each other and therefore nothing was straight between us; most probably never would be.

I lifted my glass. 'When I go back to London in a couple of weeks without passing on to anyone whatever message I'm supposed to have brought from Cary, the threat of blackmail will be lifted from Sweetcrab and all the Leightons will be able to sleep in their beds. You could spread the word around.' Before he could protest, I added: 'And here's to Farmer Drake of Holland Court!'

The switch of subject jolted him. For a moment he wore a distinctly wary look, before relief that I'd let him off the hook took its place. 'That's the answer,' he said with gratification, 'the only answer, Christy.'

The smile from the heart that put a glow on him that was barely resistible stayed while I drank his health. Then he laughed. 'Thanks. Farmer Drake, as you say, but not of Holland Court. Barker retired at Christmas and as soon as the builders have finished installing a modern heating system and added on a couple of extra rooms, I'll be moving into the Home Farm. It'll provide a more practical working base and with the programme of intense mixed farming I've mapped out, I prefer to be my own manager. Through no fault of Barker's, he was given no incentive or encouragement, the whole place, during the last years of Grandfather's life, was allowed to run down disastrously with the minimum of mechanization and wicked under-capitalization. Small wonder that about all I inherited was the land itself and most of that was in poor shape.'

His attention was so centred on giving me a progress report on drainage schemes, crop rotations, dairy herds and breeding lines that I doubt if he knew what he was eating or cared who was listening so long as he'd got a captive audience. I recalled from long-ago days his capacity for enormous and contagious enthusiasm that built a fire in him which irradiated his whole personality. The blaze was less fierce now, more controlled, as well it might be as it was pinned solidly to the earth itself. Maybe, after a lapse, his luck was holding in that, belatedly, he had found a career that satisfied his heart as well as his head. But I still marvelled, and half disbelieved, as I'd done when I'd watched him descend the field, Bonnie at his heels. Liz's prince, clothed in light and crowned with stars, holding forth on muck-spreading and drainage schemes. It took a lot of getting used to.

As I listened, more to the timbre of his voice than the subject matter, I was plunged into a ridiculous nostalgic yearning: that I was a girl he'd just met, that we were jointly testing each other out to discover whether it was a flash of casual liking or some infinitely more exciting sensual quality. A yearning so futile that I jeered at myself. We knew not too little about one another, but too much. There'd been Cary for me, Ophelia for him.

When the waiter brought the cheese and interrupted the outline of his plans for dramatically increasing the sugar-beet harvest, I asked: 'If you're not going to live at Holland Court, what's going to happen to it?'

A flicker of an emotion not quite sadness, but near enough, crossed his face, was instantly quenched. 'The plans for it can't be finalized until Ophelia's will is probated. As only two of the five executors are resident in Europe, one in Paris and the other in Zurich, it's a wretched long-drawn-out business, and I suspect they're dragging their feet. They're still arguing over the valuation of her estate in Argentina.'

I couldn't for the life of me see why Ophelia's will should affect any plan he might have for Holland Court which belonged to him. 'But what do you want to do with it?'

He gazed fixedly at the three stunted anemones arranged in an egg-cup-size vase in the centre of the table. 'She supported hundreds of charities but the one dearest to her was for the young incurably sick. I'd like to turn Holland Court over to them.' He looked across at me, his smile rueful. 'Sounds simple enough, but I assure you it isn't. We have to arrive not only at the sum required for a full-scale reconstruction of the building itself but the capital needed to maintain it in perpetuity. No charitable organization is going to say thank you for the gift of a rambling, spot-heated mansion unless it is handsomely endowed.' His gaze left me to beckon a waiter. 'Ophelia's will was drawn up when she was twenty-one, never altered when her first husband died or when we were married. Consequently, a dozen international lawyers are going to get comfortably rich before it's sorted out.'

While the waiter was pouring our second cups of coffee, a picture of the Home Farm jumped into my mind's eye. Mrs Barker before she died had been a friend of Aunt Edith's, and one day when she was ill we'd visited her, and I'd been ordered to sit mouse quiet in the window seat of the main bedroom out of earshot of their whispered sick-room confidences. From it I'd had a clear bird's-eye view of Holland Court. Why on earth should I recall that small, unnoteworthy picture? It served no purpose except to inform me that he'd have a view of Ophelia's memorial from his bedroom window. 'It sounds a marvellous idea,' I said. 'I hope you bring it off.'

'I will. I'm flying to Paris early next week to see Paquet, and I'm chivvying Schweizer who lives in Zurich to be there too. As soon as I've got them round a table I intend to put on some heavy pressure, get things moving.'

For the first time since he'd come into the kitchen we smiled at one another like a couple of old friends; no longer opponents sitting tight on opposite fences, bristling with mutual suspicion, but a man and a girl with old and proven insight into one another's strengths and weaknesses. I was impulsive, heedless and impatient; he, under the surface magnetism and grace, was as obstinate as the devil in pursuit of any subject on which he'd set his heart.

'Come on,' he said blithely, making a sweeping gesture that dismissed out of mind the hour behind us, 'let's get out of here, find ourselves somewhere less like a spread of baked meats at a funeral and have a drink.'

'I think I'd rather go home.' I didn't think, I was sure. I was too exhausted with the shadow-boxing in which we'd engaged to face another round.

He said good-humouredly: 'What a girl you are for wanting to go home!'

We walked to the car park in silence. As he unlocked the passenger door, he inquired: 'That's what you want, is it, to stop right here?'

'Yes.'

He went round to his side, sat back for a moment, then turned and looked straight at me. 'You are still in love with him, aren't you? Love embalmed for the rest of your life, is that it? Or does it satisfy you to sit beside a funeral pyre that never goes out? With no sight, no sound of him, emptiness and silence, it's got to be one or the other. Christy, can a woman stay loving for ever a man she's never likely to see again?'

There was, I discovered, no more fight left in me, only breath enough for one final statement of fact. 'I've never found out what kills love.'

Without another word he turned the ignition key. I watched hypnotically as the hedgerows sprang to life under the thrusting beams of the headlights. He drove fast by side roads he knew as well as if they'd been cut through his own land. We exchanged no word, perhaps we'd used them all up. Traffic was light, and as the miles flew by, I had an unreal sense of being sealed in a speeding capsule that brought a lulling illusion of safety. It seemed precious, and to retain it for as long as I could I closed my eyes.

When I woke the car was stationary facing the portico of Holland Court. It was such a startling setting in which to find myself that I thought I was dreaming until Markham said: 'It was the most comfortable spot I could think of to bring you for a night-cap. Do you mind?'

There was no choice, but if there'd been one I doubt whether, barely released from sleep, I would have been quick-witted enough to have suggested it. He only switched on one light in the main hall, which left huge shadowy areas, and except for the flesh-tones and the glint of medals, the portraits of the Drakes who'd lived to be old and honoured, or, like Markham's father, died young, were dim monochromes on the crimson damask wallpaper. Proud military men all of them, who wouldn't have relished any descendant of theirs turning working farmer. As he shepherded me, I wondered where he was taking me. All the ground-floor rooms were vast; were we about to be marooned in space for a second time that evening!

'The housekeeper's room,' he announced as he held open the green-baize door behind which I'd never penetrated. 'I use it for everything except sleeping. The only alternative on offer would involve us in removing half an acre of dust-sheets.'

It wasn't a large room by Holland Court standards, but

still sizeable. A residue of the old furniture remained, mostly pushed back haphazardly against the walls to accommodate a swivel chair and a desk on which piles of farming manuals and catalogues made a series of pyramids round a portable typewriter. Above it half a dozen charts with rising and falling graphs were drawing-pinned to the wall.

A round table covered in a crimson plush cloth with a bobble-fringe was pulled towards a damped-down fire that only needed a poke to stir it into a blaze.

'I'll move Flossie, then you can sit down.' The prying inquisitor of the car park had vanished from sight. In his place was a host whose sole concern was the comfort of his guest. He picked up a black and white Persian cat the size of a cushion from the only arm-chair, gave her a scratch behind the ear, settled her on the rug. 'She belonged to Mrs Cloves and she's determined to exercise squatter's rights to the end.' He gave the chair seat a perfunctory brush with his hand. 'I could wish she didn't live in a permanent state of moult.'

'What happened to Mrs Cloves?'

'Grandfather pensioned her off in his will, but she stayed on until last autumn waiting until she could move into a flat in Helsby. There was only one snag: no pets allowed. At the last moment she nearly refused to budge. Mrs Bengy and I had to call on our last reserves of persuasion. She has Flossie's weekly diet sheet taped to the kitchen wall and Mrs Cloves visits Flossie once a week to make sure I'm not ill-treating her. Now the sore point is that Flossie hasn't shown a sign of pining! What's it to be? Brandy?'

I said yes, and when he brought it he suggested: 'Try putting your feet on the fender, that way you won't feel the broken spring in the seat of the chair.'

It was polished steel, practically a museum piece. I propped my feet on its broad, solid top, felt a comforting warmth seep deeper into flesh I'd not realized was cold. As wary of speech as though it were a dangerous element – which indeed it was with us – we lifted our glasses in a silent toast.

The silence did not seem to bother him. He was relaxed; one would have said at peace with himself and his company

– only if you looked back at the words that had passed between us since we'd left South View, that could not be. The warmth, the brandy, the illusion of peace had a soporific effect on my brain, so that it operated in a state of drowsy bemusement: Markham and I contentedly sipping brandy in a back-stairs room at Holland Court, hugging the fire, a fat contented cat on the hearth! It was such a wild incongruity that it was barely believable. Time gone, I puzzled muzzily, drowned under a wastage of girl-tears; time to come when, perhaps, we'd both forget this strange out-of-place interlude. But in the immediate time-present curiously there was no astonishment, no unease.

Idly my eyes roved about the room until they connected with a framed colour photograph, probably an enlarged snapshot, in the centre of the mantelpiece, and there it stayed, pinned to an area of 6 x 4 ins. Markham and Ophelia under a vine-covered arbour, sitting close at a table, on which was set a great bowl of exotic fruit. He was leaning back, she forward, one of her hands resting on his arm. The shadows of the leaves overhead had the effect of merging him into the background and highlighting Ophelia's pale, straight hair, her delicate pencilled features and heart-touching fragility. The definition was so good that I could see the points of colour in her eyes that had been an extraordinary clear, pale green: sea-nymph's eyes.

Following my glance he said: 'It was taken in Lerici when we were staying there with her great-aunt Marthe. Ophelia loathed having her photograph taken and except Press pictures that's the only good one I've got.'

Something in me stiffened, then cringed. Did he want to talk about her? If he did, I'd have to listen. Surely you couldn't be jealous of the dead, of a woman who'd only been allotted a life-span of twenty-nine years! But you could, ah, you could indeed. For a moment I hated myself so hard it made me feel slightly sick.

He moved across the room, turned the swivel chair to face me, and sat down, seemingly totally absorbed in contemplating the golden liquid rocking gently in the glass cupped between his palms and the private thoughts that filled the channels of his mind. The firelight playing on his thick chestnut hair emphasized the incisiveness of his profile, the new lines seamed into his forehead, and, above all, the inner brooding, a containment in himself, a quietude that had not been there before.

I thought, is that how I look to Liz and Sue? Is that the wound that loss inflicts? Pain that had to be hidden because if anyone saw or spoke of it, it could not be endured?

He raised his head, caught me looking at him, said softly: 'Ophelia is dead.'

The flat statement hit me like a blow. A second later I doubted my hearing. Had I spoken those two words to myself, or had he actually said them? As though he could read my doubts, he repeated: 'Ophelia's dead. She's been dead for two years and three months. One morning she was gloriously alive, flying down the ski-trails, before sunset she was dead. Dead,' he repeated, his glance on mine so hypnotically compelling that I could not withdraw mine from its grasp.

His voice was quiet, unforced, but inexorable, audibly spelling out both a plea and a challenge. 'Christy, you can't follow your love into a grave. Neither can you split yourself in two, half of you living, half of you buried in the past. Oh, you long to . . .' A short harsh sound came from his throat. 'That is, when you've stopped wishing you'd died too. But if you do, how do you end up? I'll tell you, a live body that goes through the motions of living but is dead inside, a hollow man . . . or woman.'

I wanted to clap my hands over my ears, muffle his voice, but it went on remorselessly. 'Unfeeling and unfaithful, that's what you're saying, isn't it? But I'd want no one who'd loved me to sit by a grave and weep for me for ever, to spend thirty, forty years with a cold, uncomforted heart. I'd want them to fight a duel with death and grief, and when they'd won it grow once more into a whole human being, not half a one and that half hollow.'

When he stopped and there was no sound in the room but the hiss of flames in the grate, my mind emptied. I would not have believed that I was capable of speech, yet it was my voice that shattered the silence. 'Cary has no grave. He is not dead.'

Unable to meet his glance, even to look at him, I could feel, like a physical touch, his look at me that was both bleak and proud. Flossie stretched, settled herself more comfortably, and he bent, absently stroked her head.

When he did not speak, I cried: 'It's not the same. There's no parallel. Cary is not dead.' I paused and strove to lay my tongue to the simplest most explicit statement. 'He's still a part of me.' That was as near the truth as I could reach. A sense of being as possessed as that night he'd left me behind in the Bird Hut. I put down my glass, took my coat from the chair on which he'd thrown it.

He said nothing as he took it from me, held it out. That had been my intention, to leave no inch of room for argument, and I'd succeeded. When my arms were in the sleeves he turned me round, held me against him. I saw the kiss coming, felt no astonishment. He was young and, mourn as he might for his dead Ophelia, he needed sex. It could be that he genuinely desired an affair with me, short-lived with no strings, a part of the remedial process he called growing whole.

My body did not repulse him but my brain remained coolly alert and assessing. I saw the kiss, deep and seeking, as the first move in a planned exercise in seduction. Mrs Bengy would long ago have gone home to her cottage, leaving us an empty house in which there were no ears to hear, no eyes to pry. For no reason, I was sidetracked by a picture of Aunt Edith, sitting bolt upright in bed, her door ajar, watching for my return. Would she, I wondered, forswear her spinsterish Victorian code of decent behaviour for young women because my partner in sin was Markham Drake?

As I drew back, a tenderness brimmed in his eyes, curved his mouth, showing me the sweetest of all the different faces of love: the before face. For the flight of a second I thought: perhaps that's the way. Sated and honeyed with the act of love, maybe he'd tell me what he knew and I did not; the reason for the panic-fear that struck Wellesley and Mrs Leighton, and in a lesser degree himself at the sight of me.

Was the heart of it simply that I scared them all to death because they saw me as Cary's errand-girl? I didn't think so; that sixth sense of double dealing just out of sight was too strong.

Because, though I wasn't Cary's messenger-girl, I'd have given everything I possessed to be just that, I said: 'No. I'm still the girl who likes to go home.'

CHAPTER NINE

'I've got it!' Liz clicked her fingers. 'Mary Dennet. She'd be perfect.'

'Mary Dennet?' I queried. The morning had beaten a sudden retreat into mid-winter: puddles and pools iced over, and a coating of thick, furry frost on trees and twigs that had transformed the dried skeletons of cow parsley into fairy snow flowers. But at midday the sun had blazed through and on Liz's last free day we'd borrowed the Mortimers' small cruiser, gone picnicking on Hailsham Broad. Now we were crouched in thick sweaters and zipped up anoraks in the lea of a buffeting wind.

'She worked for Mother until she married a merchant seaman. She's a treasure and Mother would have her back like a shot, but there's the baby. He must be around three by now, and she has to bring him along. Mother's terrified he'll go berserk and wreck the place. How would your aunt react to a toddler?'

'It would depend on how well his mother kept him in order. If he's the explosive, rampaging type, she's not above disciplining him herself with a ruler! But anyone would be an improvement on Mrs Curtis. It's not the money, I could fix that by sending her extra, but that I don't trust her in an emergency, and, worse still, she treats Aunt Edith as though she were half-witted as well as deaf. I've made inquiries and so has Tim, but we haven't turned up anyone remotely suitable. Where does Mary Dennet live?'

'Quakers' Yard. We could call round and see her this afternoon, find out if she's fixed up. I know with her husband away for months at a stretch she wants daily work.'

'I can't engage her on the spot. Aunt Edith would have to okay her. It would be courting disaster to go over her head.'

'Of course. Any other problems?'

'Persuading the physiotherapist who got bawled out on the doorstep to call again – with Aunt Edith's permission. I'll have to organize some heat inside the house before next winter, but I'll probably hold my horses until the summer, combine it with essential repairs. Oh, and I've laid on Joe to taxi her to and from church.'

'Good for you. And, apart from Miss Graham, I mean . . .' She fluffed her question. She hadn't mentioned Cary, touched on any subject that might lead back on him. I hadn't told her of my visit to Sweetcrab, its mad-act climax. Liz shouldered more than her fair burden of other people's miseries, and now she had reassured her future mother-in-law she was as happy as a bird. Tony's appointment to a group practice in Birmingham had been confirmed, and the wedding set for the first Saturday after the end of the school term.

'No,' I lied. 'Everything's fine.'

She hugged her arms to protect herself against a sudden rise of wind that bent the dry stalks of the sea-lavender, stippled the sky-blue water. 'Christy, I don't think I could bear it if you were still . . .'

I couldn't let her finish. 'I'm not.'

She gave me a grieving look 'You're sure you're going to like this job in London.'

'I can't wait to get started.'

Still not wholly convinced, she asked: 'Who've you been seeing since you've been home?'

'Lots of people. I've had quite a welcome. Markham took me out to dinner last week.' My aim had been to erase any anxiety she felt about me that could smirch her richly deserved sheen of happiness, and I'd succeeded. Whereas Sue had jeered when my adolescent, love-hungry heart had lost itself to Markham Drake, Liz hadn't uttered a decrying word, but contented herself with silently beaming hope at me. Dear Liz born good, who would stay good until she died.

'Markham! Isn't it terrific, what he's accomplished in two years? All that drive, dedication to turn himself into an expert on soils, crops, stock, drainage, plus all the horribly complicated sums of modern farming. People laughed their heads off at first: you know, the big-headed seven-day wonder. Ah, they said, experience will teach him, bring him to his knees. Now he's proving them wrong. Barker, who was a pig-headed old man, was the chief stumbling block. With him gone, Markham's been able to build up a specialized team who're behind him all the way.' Suddenly the joy drained out of her voice, and she mourned: 'When I remember how he was when he came back to Holland Court after Ophelia was killed. Oh, Christy, it broke my heart. I suppose that was his only hope of salvation: work, grinding, dedicated work to build something.' She gave me a gentle tentative smile. 'Christy, good things do happen, but you have to believe, have faith that they will.'

Well, I thought, and for a moment loved her a little less. She and Sue had been getting together on the telephone, long confabs, on Christy's future, how to edge her tactfully but firmly in the right direction. Worse than Aunt Edith, with less excuse.

'Yes,' I admitted, 'good things happen.' Bad things too, like the sight of me striking fear into Mrs Leighton and Wellesley. Like Hester's doomed hope that Cary was coming home to Sweetcrab. Like Markham being physically attracted to a girl whom he didn't trust an inch.

To divert her thoughts and mine from channels that would lead us nowhere, I asked: 'What are you going to do about wedding presents? Have separate lists or a comprehensive one at somewhere like Harrods?'

She looked horrified. 'Asking for presents! If anyone wants to send us a present, Tony and I want what they choose.'

'You'll end up with six rolling pins, ten table lamps, and more waste-paper baskets than you'll wear out in fifty years of married life.' I laughed. 'Oh, I know, it's the thought that counts.'

'It is,' she said firmly.

We went back to Liz's for tea and then took the Anglia to Quakers' Yard. Mary Dennet was a sturdy young woman with a soft voice, a straight open glance, and a smile that suggested an easy-tempered nature. The child, absorbed in building a castle out of a pile of detergent cartons, appeared reasonably biddable for his age-group.

When Liz had covered the preliminaries, I explained: 'My aunt's elderly. She's a bit rigid in her ways and sometimes to a younger generation she seems unreasonably demanding.'

'I get on with old people, Miss. They like everything done as it's always been done. My granny was the same. But I'd not be prepared to have Gavin minded. Miss Graham would have to agree to my bringing him.'

We left it that I would sound Aunt Edith out and contact her. I drove Liz home, and it was only when she was getting out of the car that I remembered what I'd meant to ask her. 'Liz, do you ever see anything of Addy?'

'Not since she went to live at Bloxstead with her brother.' She hesitated, within an ace of self-reproach, then justified herself. 'I did think about contacting her, then I decided she might not like it. Why do you ask?'

'I wondered how she was.'

'You're not thinking of going to see her, are you? Christy, now she's cut free, my guess is that's how she wants to keep it. And you can't blame her, can you?'

She looked and sounded so worried that I said no and quickly changed the subject. 'I'll telephone and find out if any of your week-ends home coincide with mine. Don't take too long in deciding what Sue and I are going to wear. And, please, spare us the frills and rose-bud top-knots.'

'You can pick the style, have different ones if you like. All I care is that you'll both be walking behind me.' She laughed in happy amazement. 'Who'd ever have thought I'd be the first of us to get married?'

'Who ever would!' I mocked.

When I came out from garaging the car, the sun was setting in an extravaganza of crimson and orange, vermilion and gold. At the end of a day of all seasons the wind had died, and the air about me was soft as silk. I turned the corner by the garage and let my glance fall from the glory in the sky to the path that cut through the orchard to the water-meadow. Of their own volition my feet moved towards it.

The mere was almost black, too shadowed and hugged to itself to catch any reflection of the explosion of colour on the horizon. I walked a while, not allowing myself to think constructively until I reached my destination. Then my feet stopped moving and my eyes looked in a straight line across the water. The scrub surrounding the Bird Hut had not been cleared leaving the copse free to close in; two or three weedy saplings were splayed across the massive south-facing window. From a distance, perched on its miniature cliff, it looked like a garden chalet or a child's playhouse erected years ago and now abandoned.

As long as Aunt Edith lived I would see it distantly from my bedroom, but my heart had cried for a nearer view of the place where I'd loved my love and he'd loved me. As I gazed echoes of voices crowded and clouded my mind: Sue's charging me with living on two levels; Liz and her soft sweet talk of faith; Markham expounding a gospel of his own, offering me a tested product. And, suddenly, higher than the others, Sue's in the Chelsea flat: or *he's dead*. But that voice had no power to intimidate me. The dead have no means of hiring messenger-girls or striking terror into astute men of the world. Wellesley knew Cary was alive; more than likely where he was living.

I lingered until the last brush strokes of saffron and apricot had drained from the sky, and then I drew my gaze from the Bird Hut, pulled it back across the black, secret waters of the mere. In that final moment Cary seemed close, much nearer to me than when I'd run the breath out of my lungs to clamp my hold on a stranger.

The sense of nearness remained with me in the aftermath of sunset while the luminous indigo sky cast a light that faded before it touched the earth, so that my feet walked towards home in near darkness whereas my head was in the light.

The echo was so faint that at first, lost in myself, I disregarded it. But it was repeated, and half-way across the water-meadow I stood still, listening to the cadence of my name being called from far off, but coming nearer with each repetition until it was a cry of muffled anger.

Hester flung herself into my arms gasping and remonstrating. 'Why didn't you stop? I shouted and shouted but you went on walking away from me.'

It was pointless to inquire what she was doing alone by the mere after dusk. She'd either have lied or ignored the question. In any case the answer was obvious: she'd given her mother and Anna the slip, come secretly to find me. She had no coat, only a skirt and a wool sweater. I couldn't see her shoes but the chances were they were light-weight and her feet soaked. Even as I worked out her physical state for myself she began to shiver and sob convulsively.

'Don't leave me, Christy. Please don't run away from me.'

I hugged her. 'As if I would! But it's too cold and getting too dark to stay out here. Come on, let's hurry indoors where it'll be warm.'

She jerked away from me. 'I came to see you, not anybody else. Miss Graham will be there. Christy, please, let's stay outside where no one can see us.' She began to wail. 'I want to talk to you and they won't let me.'

I took one of her hands that was ice-cold, tucked it in the pocket of my anorak. 'There'll only be me,' I promised, with no idea whether I'd be able to make that promise good. 'We'll sit in the kitchen and talk as long as you want.' I'd used the word kitchen deliberately. Hester naturally gravitated towards it in any house in which she found herself, probably drawn by the promise or scent of food. 'I can't talk when I can't see you. Your face is just a smudge. Come on.'

She obeyed grudgingly, hiccoughly, holding my arm in a bear grip. When she got inside the kitchen, saw its emptiness, the sullenness left her, she giggled, and quick as a flash she flew to the door into the hall, turned the key.

'I don't like Miss Graham.' She eyed me under downcast lashes to see if she'd got away with it, and when I didn't reprove her, added with bravado, 'And I hate Mummy. I hate Anna.' She gave me a sly yet sweet smile. 'I hate everyone except you and Cary.'

'Do you?' I smiled as though she'd made a joke. Fortunately I'd done battle with the old coke boiler, got it to function reasonably well. I opened the doors, checked the draught, pulled up a stool and patted it invitingly. 'Let's get out of our wet shoes. Mine are soaked and so are yours.'

She sat down, allowed me to pull off her loafers. She wriggled her toes in the warmth until her nylons steamed, and then, with only the softest of sounds, she began to cry to herself.

I held her against my shoulder, the helpless inner weeping driving holes in my heart. 'Lovie, what is it?'

She wiped away the tears with the back of her hand. 'They're going to take me away, in the morning early, but I won't go. Christy, I can't go.' Without warning, she plunged forward as though some shock-wave had passed through her, and began to scream: 'I hate them. I wish they'd die. I want them to die.'

I pulled her face round, encased it in the palms of my hands, held it an inch away from my own. 'Hester, your mother loves you more than anyone else in the whole world. She loves you.' I intoned the words again and again. 'Hester, she loves you. Your mother loves you, and you can't hate someone who loves you, can you?'

She scowled but more out of principle than ill-temper, and I breathed easier, fairly confident that the spiral of uncontrollable hysteria was checked. As I withdrew my hands, she complained sourly: 'I only hate her sometimes, like now when she's going to take me away. I don't want to learn to ski. I want to stay at Sweetcrab and wait for Cary.' The scowl melted and in its place was her lovely child's smile. 'I know he's coming back, and when he does there will be Cary and you and me, just as it used to be.'

'Hester,' I said gently, 'Cary can't come home, not for a little while yet.'

She tossed her head in fury at being contradicted. 'But he is. I know . . .' She stopped suddenly, put her finger maddeningly on her lips. She loved to tease, even torment. 'It's a secret. They don't know I found out, but I did.'

I'm pretty sure that I would have shaken the truth out her if, at that moment, the telephone in the hall hadn't shrilled. She grabbed my hands, shaking with fright, whimpering: 'Don't make me go home, Christy, don't make me go.'

I soothed: 'It's only Sue. You remember Sue. She lives

in London now and when I start my new job I'm going to share a flat with her. She promised to ring me at half-past six and look, that's the time now.' I eased one hand free, pointed to the wall clock, prayed that Aunt Edith wouldn't hear the ringing, answer it.

She let me go, watched me unlock the door, frozen but all set to run like an animal scenting a trap as I closed the door behind me.

Markham said: 'Christy, is Hester with you?'

'Yes,' I whispered.

He spoke to someone at his shoulder before he continued: 'Thank God. She's been missing for two hours, and Anna's been worried sick, particularly as Aunt Esmée's in Norwich for the day. We'll drive over right away and collect her so that she's here safe and sound when her mother gets home. Christy, you'll keep her there until we arrive, won't you?'

'Yes, I'll keep her.' Anna sick with fright, summoning Markham.

As soon as I opened the door, Hester unleashed from fear, demanded: 'Did you give Sue my love? Did you tell her I was here?'

'I forgot. I will next time I speak to her.'

I stood beside her as with sleepy content she gazed into the orange-scarlet heart of the fire. She was made good, sweet-tempered, utterly amenable because she'd got what she wanted. When she knew I'd betrayed her she'd hate me, cast me out into darkness. I made her a mug of sweetened milk-coffee, found two Bourbon biscuits, and she munched and drank like the child she was. When she'd finished she said as though she were promising me a treat: 'When you and Cary are married I'm coming to live with you.' She took my affirmation for granted, and, mercifully, I did not have to speak.

She was so wrapped in dreaming content she did not hear the sound of the doorbell, Aunt Edith's voice, the double tread of footsteps on the linoleum in the hall. I kept my arms round her shoulders, shielding us both from the blow to come. When the door I'd left unlocked opened and she saw Anna and Markham, she gave me a single heart-breaking look of astounded disbelief at my treachery before her face went dead.

Anna, smiling, said in a cheerful unvexed tone: 'Hester, what a fright you gave me! One moment you were in your room and the next . . . you were nowhere to be found.' She took note of Hester's soaked loafers standing in a ring of water. 'And you've made yourself so muddy! I know, we'll exchange shoes. You can wear mine and I'll wear yours.' She kicked off her shoes, and I stepped back to let her put them on Hester's feet that were as unresisting and unresponsive as a wax dummy's. Upright, with difficulty forcing her feet into Hester's sodden shoes, Anna allowed herself one mild reproof. 'You know it is not polite to call on friends without first finding out if it will be convenient for them to entertain you.'

I said: 'Hester's always welcome.'

She answered without taking her eyes off Hester's wax dummy face. 'That's very kind of you, Miss Graham, but now we must go home or Mrs Leighton will arrive back and not know what's become of us.' She smiled, held out her hand. Hester could have screamed, shouted obscene words no one knew where she'd picked up, thrown any object within reach at our heads. Instead she pulled her cruellest trick: she turned her eyes sightless.

Markham who had remained on the threshold stepped into the room, eased Hester to her feet and laid the fleece-lined coat he'd been carrying over her shoulders, protectively, lovingly. She gave him no sign of recognition. Standing, she was as wooden-limbed as an automaton, totally absorbed either in convincing herself we were not there or willing us to drop dead. As she passed me I kissed her cheek. She did not notice. I left the trio to find their own way out, heard them talking briefly to Aunt Edith.

When the sound of the car had died away, Aunt Edith came into the kitchen, lectured me in her brisk, sensible fashion. 'Now what's the good of breaking your heart over something that can't be mended? She's got folks of her own to love and care for her. You did it for long enough, too long I'd have said if I'd had my way. You can't spend the rest of your life pandering to a child's whims and fancies. She's best left to her own.'

'But there's one of her own missing,' I pointed out. 'The one she loves best of all, Cary.'

'Aye,' she said, 'and is it likely to be to her good that you remind her of him?'

I was clearing away the supper dishes when I heard a car stop at the gate. I parted the dining-room curtains, certain it was Tim who was so driven by his working schedule that he often paid non-urgent visits late in the evening, but it was Markham who came striding up the path. Since he didn't ring the bell, he must have seen me.

He said, pushing against the door as I opened it: 'Christy, can we have a word alone? Where can we go?'

I went back into the dining-room and he followed at my heels. The old-fashioned ceiling light enclosed in a clear glass bell threw a hideous cold glare over a room that was without a single grace. I stood by the mass-produced fumed oak table and waited for him to speak first, conscious of the stress and tension in him but the memory of my betrayal still too near for me to feel concern for anyone but Hester.

He spoke with the urgent immediacy of one determined to hammer home his point in the shortest possible time. 'Christy, Hester is perfectly all right now. You've no reason to fret your heart out about her. That's why I came back, to let you know she's completely forgotten whatever upset her. Ten minutes after we got her home Aunt Esmée arrived with a new dress and some red ski-mitts for her. She tried them on, you know how she loves new clothes, prinked and pirouetted to give us a fashion show. Gay as a bird, laughing, not a care on her mind. Fortunately Anna does have a knack with her. At the start it was an enormous help her being like you. You must have noticed it.'

He stopped, smiled to coax me to smile, waiting for a comment, and when I made none, his eyes suddenly brimmed with amusement. 'And you didn't like it! Well, I suppose no girl does. But it's a mere superficial likeness, skin-deep. Anna is ruled by her head not her heart and is a very calm, very controlled person.'

'And I'm not.'

'Well, hardly! You must admit you're slightly addicted to taking leaps in the dark.'

There was an impulse in me to cry: I live in the dark. But I held my tongue.

'She's all right,' he insisted. 'I left her guzzling tomato juice still wearing her ski-mitts. And there's the excitement of the journey ahead, You know how she loves going places. I'm driving up to London airport in the morning to meet Paquet and Schweizer in Paris, so I'll be able to put the three of them on the plane to Geneva.'

'Out of harm's way! Naturally Hester's pleased to prink in a new dress. That's her nature. But tomorrow she'll be unhappy because she is being forcibly removed to Switzerland when she doesn't want to leave Sweetcrab.' I looked him straight in the eye. 'She's got it into her head that Cary's coming home, and she's determined to be there when he arrives.'

Shock drained and sharpened his gaze, and when he spoke his voice was angry. 'What gave her that extraordinary idea?'

'She plucked it out of the air, heard it through a keyhole, steamed open a letter, or simply dreamed it. Your guess is as good as mine.'

'Or maybe,' he said with biting innuendo, 'she heard it from you. Did she?'

I laughed in his face. 'It's years since I learnt it doesn't pay to lie to Hester. She's got a built-in truth-diviner. No, I didn't tell her. Maybe you should ask Wellesley.'

He made a gesture of furious rejection 'Contrary to what you believe, Wellesley and I don't live in one another's pockets. I don't automatically share his confidence, nor he mine. Agreed, there is a family relationship between us, and we have local interests in common, but I am not, I repeat not, answerable for his behaviour.'

He paused, his rage with me spent, the last few dregs for himself. After a long pause he came to my side and did an extraordinary thing. He took my hand and placed it against his cheek. It was no more than a touch, yet it penetrated through the ice in which I was enclosed, transmitted to me a yearning in him. For a fleeting moment I had a wondrous sense of a whole relationship pivoting, on the verge of re-forming itself, and then it was gone, like sheet lightning fading, and I was left mute, my hand hanging slack and cold at my side.

He said on a note of despair: 'Christy, I care about you, what happens to you. I can't explain it; you probably don't want me to, but try and keep safe and out of trouble while I'm gone. I should be back by Friday.'

I longed to recover that miraculous moment, to respond to his appeal but all I could see was Hester's face, her eyes made blind to the sight of me. 'Why should I fall into trouble?'

For a moment he didn't speak, then he tipped up my chin, and with none of the gentleness of the moment before looked down at me with savage intentness. 'Because you're a reckless young woman, and reckless young women are dangerous, not least to themselves.' He drew in his breath, exhaled it on an angry sigh. 'And by your own admission, you're possessed.'

'All women in love are.'

'By a ghost!'

'A living ghost. Cary's alive.'

For a moment the bitterness on his face chilled and frightened me: it was a look of hope lost, impossible to retrieve, and then he was gone, so fast that he seemed to be bent on speeding away from the sight of me.

CHAPTER TEN

Yet, perversely, the figure who dominated my dreams that night was neither Markham nor Hester but Addy. Or, more precisely, one recurring dream in which Addy was present as a mute elusive figure that slid out of sight over the rim of the dream before I could speak to her. I woke with a fixed determination, whether or not she welcomed me, to drive over to Bloxstead that afternoon and see her.

As I strained to keep my temper with Mrs Curtis's glittery-eyed threats, did the shopping and arranged with Mary Dennct to call and see Aunt Edith the next afternoon, a series of still pictures hung in my mind for a moment then abruptly switched off: snapshots of Addy in suspended motion.

Bent over Hester, directing a stitch on a piece of coarse canvas she was embroidering. Hester a small tyrant in a rage, a cup she'd flung at Addy frozen motionless in the air between them. Addy's hands buried in foam as she shampooed Hester's hair. On her feet, stiff with fright at having to reply to the toast at the twenty-first birthday party Magnus had given for her. She'd worn a dense blue belted shirt-waist dress, kind to her figure that was as flat as a boy's. On that summer day she'd been taller than anyone at Sweetcrab but Magnus, the flaming carrot hair coiled in a bun on the top of her head, her small amber-gold eyes glazed with terror at the ordeal of a formal speech ahead of her. In the last snapshot to unveil itself she was not physically present. Cary and I were sailing on Hailsham Broad in the last Easter holidays we'd spent together. Her name must have come up, and I'd teased him: 'You know, I think Addy fancies you.' The snapshot was of the two of us laughing at the joke I'd cracked, before he'd said: 'But one thing's for sure, she worships the ground Father walks on.'

Addy had been one of the linchpins that held Sweetcrab

together. To Hester she was a permanent stabilizing nanny-figure. To Mrs Leighton her most highly valued employee. To Magnus she was a dear, sweet girl whom he'd cherished fondly because she foresaw and fulfilled his every need before he put it into words. To Cary she was an able pair of hands that could be cajoled into performing a diversity of small services when he ran out of time. To Wellesley she was a domestic with an above-average domestic's intelligence. I knew full well in what different degrees of regard each Leighton had held Addy. What I didn't know was, behind her superlative efficiency, her never-failing obligingness, what places they had separately held in her heart.

Bloxstead straddled the river just above its junction with Bloxstead Broad. Though the season was weeks away, its slip-ways and mooring channels, packed with every conceivable type of craft, made a solid multi-coloured patchwork over the water courses. The old flint-stone cottage in which Joe and Addy had been born was outside the main stream of activity. I had to skirt the main moorings, then track back-wards to reach their boat-yard which fronted on to a small tributary that after a couple of loops flowed into the yacht basin. It still looked like a child's primitive drawing of a house: four squares for windows, an oblong for a door, but as I might have guessed, now that it was Addy's permanent home, its walls were freshly white-washed, its paintwork mint new. The pocket-sized lawns on either side of the path were clipped short and the borders under the downstairs windows weeded.

I banged on the knocker, waited with anticipation that was half pleasure, half apprehension for Addy's quick step. When it did not come, I knocked again and opened the letter box to peer through the flap. Continuing silence and the empty cube of entrance lobby, the steep ramp of the ladder-staircase told me as loud as words that Addy was not at home.

I picked my way across the boat-yard. As I entered the great shed of the build-section, the smell of wood and tar was less pungent than the one I'd known, and I wondered how reluctantly Joe had taken to fibre glass. Even so, the racing yacht on which he was working was in timber. Standing on the deck, he was far above me, and I had to look up as I called hello and smiled. When he did not smile back I assumed from that height he had not recognized me. 'Joe, you remember me, Christina Graham.'

He wiped his hands on his blue overalls, came backwards down the ladder, and only when we were on the same level, answered: 'I remember you, Miss Graham.'

The forelock of bright yellow hair, the smooth, high-coloured face, the thick but not fat body, and the strong hands that treated all wood as if it were alive and sensitive to touch had not changed. What had was that he didn't give me that shy slow-dawning smile that expressed his pleasure in the sight of any friend, no matter how busy he was.

'Joe, I came to see Addy. I've been to the cottage but she's not there.' I caught the clink of china behind a boarded-off corner that served as a makeshift kitchen and glanced towards it expectantly. 'Is she here?'

'That's my new apprentice, Jack Forster.' In confirmation a boy's face, framed in shoulder-length bleached hair, appeared round a partition. Joe said: 'You get on with your brewing up, me lad. There's nothing going on here to concern you.'

When the head disappeared I waited for Joe to answer my question. When he didn't, I repeated: 'Joe, I want to see Addy.'

'I can see that, Miss Graham, but maybe you'd best not.' He touched his lips with his tongue and I saw a bead of perspiration break on his baby-smooth brow. 'Leave things be, Miss Graham. That'd be my advice to you.' At last he smiled, but unsurely, the smile of a simple man way out of his depth. I was sorry to plague him, but my determination to see Addy did not weaken.

'Suppose,' I suggested, 'I go and have a cup of tea and then go back to the cottage. Is she likely to be home then?'

'She won't be home till the evening and then she'll be tired out, not wanting company.' He repeated: 'You'd best be leaving her alone, Miss Graham. After a mountain of trouble she's settled now, and she's happy in her own way.'

'But, Joe, I'm not going to unsettle her, make her unhappy.

I only want to see her.' When he showed no sign of relenting, I added: 'If you won't tell me where she is, I'll have to find someone who will.'

I turned towards the door, had nearly reached it when he said grudgingly: 'You'll find her at the shop.'

Addy working in a shop – for an instant I was startled, then I realized Addy would have to do a job. Four rooms, meals for two wouldn't begin to sap her near-inexhaustible energy. I turned my head. 'Which shop? In Bloxstead?'

'The Boatman, down on the Hard.' The conflict resolved, he allowed himself a footnote of pride. 'Her own shop that's taken a deal of hard work and contriving. It means the world to her, and well it may, there's not a finer shop in Bloxstead. I'd be obliged if you'd remember that, Miss Graham. It would be downright cruel to go upsetting her.'

'I won't, Joe,' I answered and wondered as I closed the door behind me what I'd promised and if, given a choice, I'd keep that promise.

After I'd parked the car, I'd passed The Boatman, given it a nostalgic glance. One window was crammed with a gorgeous, tempting conglomeration of tackle and bait, sheath knives, gas cylinders, plastic containers and every navigational aid; the other hung with a gaudy array of garments designed to be worn on water by both sexes.

The store operated on a self-service system. Customers prowled around, either went out empty-handed or presented their purchases at a cash-desk by the door tended by a youth in a nautical striped sweater. There was no sign of Addy. I was nearly at the bottom of ranks of packed shelves that acted as a divider separating the shop into two aisles, when I heard her firm, no-nonsense voice. 'If you keep your word and the life-jackets are delivered by the 20th, I'll accept them. If they aren't here by that date you must consider the order cancelled and I shall obtain them elsewhere.'

A harassed-looking young man, presumably a traveller, emerged from an office at the rear of the shop, practically bowing from the waist. 'Of course, Miss Bray. I quite understand. Before the 20th. You have my word.'

Before she could retreat into the office, I stepped forward, called her name.

The sound of my voice stiffened every muscle in her pole-thin body. The first thing I noticed was that she'd cropped her hair short and in the cutting it had lost some but not all its glowing depth of colour. She'd always been neat, finicky about the fit and quality of her clothes rather than the style, and the severe navy-blue slacks, matching jersey with a white polo-collar suited her. She'd never worn make-up and wore none now but she'd had the good sense to darken her light eyelashes. All told, I thought with relief, Addy looked in excellent shape.

She addressed me in the same brisk fashion she'd used on the commercial traveller. 'What do you want?'

'To see you. I went to the cottage and when you weren't there to the boat-yard. Joe told me where to find you.' To escape her impassive yet intense regard, I looked around me, congratulated her. 'This is a super shop, Addy. It's got everything.'

She ignored the compliment. 'Why did you want to see me?'

'Addy!' I exclaimed. 'I'm back in Berghmere for a week or two. Of course, I wanted to see you.' There was a girl within a couple of feet of me trying on oilskins for size, and on the other side two small boys playing whirligigs with a revolving sweet stand. 'Addy, please, can't we go into your office?'

She shrugged her shoulders. 'If you insist, but I must warn you that in ten minutes I'm due to relieve Victor at the cash-desk while he goes for tea.'

Her office was no more than an enlarged cupboard, but it was as expertly and economically stowed as a ship's cabin: shelves to the ceiling, two filing cabinets, a sturdy table behind which she sat and a bentwood chair for callers towards which she waved a not particularly welcoming invitation for me to be seated.

She looked at me with a regard in which there was not a flicker of curiosity, even of interest. When she did not speak, show any intention of doing so, I said: 'Addy, I came to find out how you were. No one in Berghmere seemed to know anything about you.'

'Or didn't choose to tell you. I wonder why!' she mocked drily. Then she gave a curious self-satisfied smile. 'I left Berghmere behind a long time ago. Come to that, so did you. You didn't exactly allow the grass to grow under your feet, did you! In the end we both proved highly expendable.'

'You could never have been that, not to Hester, most of all not at that particular time.'

I could catch no reaction to the name of the girl she'd loved and about whom her life had revolved for fifteen years. Mentally she seemed to be shrugging her shoulders. 'Children have short memories. Give them a new set of toys, a new playmate, and they're perfectly content. That's what Hester is and always will be, a child. You should know.'

She was referring to the swimming pool and the riding lessons, to Anna who was a replacement for the two of us; all the furnishings of the present, not admitting that Hester's present was built on the ruins of a calamitous past. Her total disinterest in me, suggesting that the sight of me sitting in her office was a tedious bore, drove me to say: 'She hadn't forgotten me, and she hasn't forgotten Cary.'

'Ah,' she said with a snap of sardonic relish, 'so that's why you've come to see me, is it, to talk about Cary.'

'Primarily I came to see you, to find out how you were.'

She spread her hands to show off the diminutive office. 'Well, here I am. No complaints. No grievances, no hankering after the past.' A flash of fierce pride broke cover. 'Self-employed. A successful shop-keeper. A free woman!'

Addy's world had been Sweetcrab. It was she who'd taken the full brunt of the initial shock-wave; Addy who, coming downstairs at seven o'clock and finding lights burning, had walked into the scene of bloody murder, whose appalling, atrocious duty it had been to awaken and reveal Magnus's death to his wife and son. Later, it had been Addy on whom the coroner's questions – perhaps out of a kindly wish to protect as far as it lay within his power the family who were his personal friends – had pressed hardest. How had it come about that no one had heard the shot? How was it that Mrs Leighton had slept the night through unaware that her husband hadn't come to bed? Why was it that they had summoned Mr Drake and Mr Trent to the house before they'd telephoned the police?

It had been Addy, calm, collected, a figure of unquestionable truth and trustworthiness, who'd explained the thickness and tight fit of the old, hand-hewn doors, the double lined curtains drawn across all windows, and the fact that the two rooms immediately above the library were unused guest rooms. She who had confirmed Mrs Leighton's testimony that it was not unusual for her, accustomed to her husband coming late to bed, to fall asleep and not waken when he entered their bedroom from his dressing-room. Addy, who had made logical and acceptable the fact that in the storm of grief and crazing shock, with no sure ground beneath their feet, desperately needing support, Mrs Leighton had telephoned her relative, Markham Drake, and a close family friend, Hugo Trent. Her intention, so far as it could be clarified after the event, had been to mount a search for her missing younger son. The idea that he might commit suicide had been in her mind.

Addy had been an exemplary witness, her testimony crucial. Now the terror that must have seized her by the throat was expunged from memory with no more effort than wiping scribbles of chalk from a slate. To me it was an act beyond the normal human being's capability.

'But can you,' I burst out, 'forget people you've loved, behave not only as if they didn't exist any more, but as if they never have?'

'What a sentimental little goose you are!' Her patronizing glance skimmed over me. 'Haven't you learned by now that you can forget whatever you have a mind to forget! It was in everyone's interests that a clean sweep was made at Sweetcrab, a new régime introduced. And I assure you I was more than ready to change my status from that of a perennial nursery-governess for one where at least I am my own boss.' Her voice took on a lecturing tone. 'It's what you should have done: re-thought and re-planned your life. You're young, pretty, sharp-witted, you've got a career, and presumably if you get tired of working for your living you can marry some suitable young man. I'm surprised you haven't.'

The hot jet of anger that spurted was not solely directed against Addy, but at a list of people two and half years' long containing all those who'd preached, or patently wanted to preach cold common sense to me. Cut your losses, start again, you're young with all your life before you . . .

'I was going to marry Cary, not some young man. The man you're going to spend the rest of your life with kisses you goodbye, walks through a door, and you never see him again. You don't know where he is living, how he is living, whether he's in want, starving, any single fact about him. All you have is a huge blank sheet on which you keep drawing pictures . . . guessing pictures until you run out of guesses.'

My outburst had the effect of breaking through her composure to the extent that she no longer looked at me as though I were a piece of furniture but rather as a person she found weak and contemptible. 'Perhaps that was your penance!'

'Penance for what?'

'For being a spoiled and privileged brat, practically an adopted daughter, the bright one! For deluding yourself that you could eat your cake and have it: incite Cary to rebel against his father, involve him in a Palace Revolution, and then whisk him away to London to fame and fortune without forfeiting Sweetcrab, Magnus's regard. A couple of months and you saw yourself playing a dear little dove of peace that he wouldn't be able to resist.' Her eyes glinted with amusement. 'You certainly fooled yourself. And now what are you? A poor, innocent child thrown out into the snow! What you are, Christina, is plain stupid. If it hadn't been for your scheming interference, your smart London ideas of getting to the top in double-quick time, Magnus Leighton would be alive and Cary . . .'

She caught her breath as sharply as if pain had struck her, had to strive to pull her ruined calm back in place. The blood had drained from her face, leaving it a milk-white mask out of which two eyes as cold as stones stared at me. What she said simply wasn't true; mind or hindsight had distorted her judgment. But there was no impulse in me to justify myself.

I was intent on a certainty building up inside me. The gasp of pain, the stony hating glance had given away her secret. The reason she disliked me, held me in contempt was so old and threadbare it had become a cliché: the man she'd loved had been in love with me. Sensible, super-efficient Adelaide Bray had fallen in love with a man six years her junior who'd laughed his head off at the idea.

I said, as much to myself as to her: 'You were in love with Cary, weren't you?'

'Love!' She gave a high, scoffing laugh. 'Love is for sentimental little girls like you.' An expression of utter weariness closed on her face. 'Oh, for heaven's sake go and cry on someone else's shoulder. I've better and more productive things to do with my time than dry your tears.'

As if on cue, the door behind my back clicked open and she spoke over my head in her brisk shop-keeper's voice. 'I'll be along to take over from you in a minute, Victor. My caller is just leaving.'

When the door had shut, she stood up. 'Goodbye, Christina. The only advice I can give you is to go far away from Berghmere and find a suitable young man to marry you.'

But I wasn't ready to go.

'What happened at Sweetcrab the night Magnus was murdered? Was it exactly as you told the police and the coroner?'

She raised an eyebrow, inquired, unoffended, almost offhandedly: 'Are you suggesting we lied, perjured ourselves?'

'I wanted to be sure.'

'Then you can be,' she said in the same careless tone. 'Now if you don't mind . . .'

'I'll go when you've answered one more question.' It turned into three.

'Has Cary ever written to you? Have you ever known where he is? Or where he is now?'

'No,' she said so blandly and carelessly it was like the flick of a whip.

For a moment we stared at one another across the square deal table. Very slowly a sly, triumphant little smile grew on her face keeping pace with a spiralling conviction in me. She'd lied. She knew where Cary was, but if I went down on my knees and grovelled, she wouldn't tell me. And through the space of three long years I heard the echo of wild young laughter for which, though she'd never heard it, she was taking a revenge that was as sweet as nectar to her.

With her head in the air, an efficient rather formidable shop-keeper about her business of shop-keeping, she strode out of the cupboard-office and left me to find my own way out.

In the car I drove in a black rage at her power to hold me imprisoned in an impenetrable darkness from which she could have released me. But as the miles flew by, out of sight of that sly lick of a smile my conviction that she'd lied faltered. Suppose it had been a double-bluff: truth deliberately tossed off so casually that it had a false ring? To succeed she'd only to make me believe she'd lied. She'd called me stupid, and somewhere there'd been an inference that had my eyes been clearer, my wits keener-edged, I would not have been stumbling through foggy labyrinths debating with myself what was true and what falsehood.

As I drove up to the garage that is what I felt: stupid. I was either that or a lot of people had been at pains to blindfold me.

I'd left the doors open, and was within a few feet of driving in, when Hugo Trent stepped from behind the shelter of the right hand one. I stopped with a jerk, as he walked towards the car, waited until I lowered the window.

'Your aunt informed me you were out. As what I have to say must be said in private, I waited here for you to come back.' His light grey eyes hung on me with a deeply penetrating gaze that was at odds with his affected cooing voice, his lank, stooping form.

I couldn't imagine why he should have put himself to the discomfort of hanging about in the cold tail-end of the afternoon to see me, waited for him to tell me.

'Let me see, how long have you been home? Ten days? A fortnight? Long enough surely for it to become plain to you that you're wasting your time and causing a great deal of misery to people who haven't deserved it.'

He was a man for whom I had scant respect. A hanger-on, a licker of boots, a weak nonentity. I shrugged my shoulders, said lightly: 'Really, Hugo, I don't know what you're on about, I've a perfect right to come back to my own home, visit my aunt.'

'And as a friend of the Leightons, I have the right to protect them by every means within my power. You've already driven Esmée and Hester from Sweetcrab. You've caused Wellesley untold distress. How much longer are you going to torment them? If you persist, it's not Wellesley and Esmée who will suffer most but you and Cary. It's you two who will have to live with your consciences.'

He stopped, as drained as if he'd put forth a mighty effort, needed time to recoup his nervous energy. All his affectations of languor, pretensions to be what he wasn't seeped out of him. It was as though he'd stripped himself naked. His bottom lip quivered and he had to steady it before he could speak. 'Christina, I beg you, please go away.'

Gazing into his pathetic, desperate face, I puzzled what monstrous misjudgment of me bedevilled him and all the Leightons to induce Hugo metaphorically to go down on his knees to me; to set Wellesley shaking in his beautiful hand-made shoes, to put Mrs Leighton to flight, Markham treading a tight-rope between trust and suspicion, and Addy either to lie to me or pretend she was lying.

His plight was so pitiful that I made my voice as amiable as I could. 'Hugo, I've not come back to Berghmere to threaten anyone. On that my conscience is clear.'

'Go away,' he screeched in a spasm of mindless rage, and as he turned, I saw tears gush from his eyes.

Go away, I repeated to myself. That's what they all wanted: for me to go away.

CHAPTER ELEVEN

Tuesday was raw with squally showers. To save Mary Dennet having to push the pram to South View, I fetched and took her back in the car. Despite Aunt Edith's formidable manner – a combination of *grande dame* and headmistress – the meeting between them augured well.

On the drive home Mary Dennet said: 'I've settled with your auntie, Miss. I'm sure, once I've got used to her ways, we'll get on a treat. I've explained that I can't oblige her until the week after next on account of my next door neighbour being in hospital and I'm cooking for her husband and children. She understands, Miss.'

As long as she was installed as a daily help at South View before I went to London, the starting date was up to her. In any case, until she was paid off, there was still Mrs Curtis underfoot.

I dropped Mary Dennet and Gavin at their door half-way down Quakers' Yard. It was a narrow one-way street, the top exit of which, after a couple of right-hand turns, rejoined the High Street. But when I got there I found my way right blocked by a head-on crash between a couple of heavy lorries. On my heels came police cars with Accident Signs and in the distance there was the shrill warning of an ambulance siren.

Probably, with police authority, I could have edged my way through but I decided it was simpler to turn left on to what was known locally as the Back Road, the one that skirted the north shore of the mere. It involved a fifteen minutes' detour but at least I shouldn't risk blocking an ambulance or heavy lifting-gear. I'd gone about a mile when through the windscreen wipers I saw ahead of me on my nearside a man coming at a steady plod, shoulders bent forward under the weight of a heavy pack. In sheeting rain his plight was so dismal that, although we were going in opposite directions, I automatically slowed down. The Back Road, after by-passing the village proper, which on foot he could surely have reached quicker via the High Street, led to the hamlet of Gannet Ford, and that was a good six miles away.

I had almost stopped when he lifted his head, and for a dreamlike interval we stared at one another before he sharply dipped it, frantically, furtively, to shield his face and stepped deeper on to the sodden grass verge. Simultaneously. I put my foot on the accelerator. I continued for a couple of hundred yards and then I stopped dead. I half fell out of the car, stood bareheaded in the deluge. Though he'd disappeared, I didn't have to guess where. He'd taken the only turning on that side of the road, a few yards beyond the point at which we'd exchanged that cataleptic stare through the windscreen: the slippery, corkscrew path that led up from the road to the Bird Hut.

The attacks of hallucination I could no longer count had never yielded more than a figure outline, a particular walk, a rear view of a head, or the fleeting glimpse of a profile. Now I'd seen him full face head on, separated by feet, not yards and, past belief, run not towards him, but driven away. I stood in the road, supporting myself against the car, rain soaking my head and feet, and could not make sense of my idiot self. It wasn't too late: I need only drive the car into the verge and walk back to what was no more than a gap in the hedge. But my feet would not take me. Cary had come back to Berghmere. Cary had seen me and deliberately stepped aside, hidden his face. I needed time to absorb two facts so shocking they wouldn't stay fixed in my skull.

After an evening during which Aunt Edith had pronounced herself, with certain inevitable reservations, as satisfied with Mary Dennet, we'd watched an old Chaplin film on television, and I achieved such a masterly feat of acting that even her needle-sharp eyes had not noticed anything amiss with me, at ten she went to bed.

I waited until the crack of light under her door flicked out, and then burrowed in the cupboard under the stairs for a pair of Wellingtons, an ancient Burberry that were stowed there. I'd decided against taking the car; to have parked it, side-lights on, in the narrow Back Road would have been to risk rousing the curiosity of a patrolling police car. I had reached a condition of mind wherein I was beyond speculation or constructive thought, but there was one requirement so blindingly obvious that even I assimilated it: absolute secrecy.

The rain had ceased and the wind at ground level was without force but up in the sky it intermittently swept cushions of charcoal clouds across the three-quarter moon, blanketing out its light. The mere when I reached it was still lapped by spuming little waves whipped up by the afternoon's turbulence. For a while, using my torch minimally, I could keep to the path by the water's edge. When it lifted I had to clamber up a track that had once been clearly defined but was now thick with saplings and brambles, infestations of reed that had seeded from the lower reaches by the mere. I had to thrust my body forward, kick and trample with my boots to force a passage. Half-way up, when I stopped for breath, the moon burst free of cloud, and I saw the Bird Hut. Midway between the drawn curtains over the big south window there was a hairline of light.

The path flattened out suddenly, swung behind the Bird Hut to join the one that corkscrewed up from the road. At the door, under the shelter of the jutting porch, I dowsed my torch, stood motionless in the darkness, willing myself to be the girl at Heathrow who'd been electrified by joy, stood in blinding sunlight when outside it had been night. A girl who'd been me, but whom I couldn't recapture.

I lifted my hand, gave the two double knocks with a pause between that had been our signal.

The door acted as a shield and I could not see him until I stepped over the threshold and closed it behind me. His vibrating whisper of exultation caught and spun my heart. 'Christy, I've been willing you to come.' He exhaled the breath of suspense he'd held. 'I heard someone scrambling up from below, and it had to be you. Oh, Christy, Christy, my love.'

A pressure lamp burned on the centre table but we stood outside its ring of brilliance. Our hands reached, touched, but that first contact was butterfly light, tentative, as though in the world of the senses great oceans of space divided us. We moved forward and when we stood within the bright circle to look at him required an act of courage. There were changes, but so minimal they brought an easement in tension. His ashy-brown hair was longer, shaped differently, his oval, delicately moulded face subtly but not radically changed by two and a half years, though its skin tones were darker. His clothes were rough, worn, the grey pullover sagging at the neck, a hole in the elbow that had been darned and was pulling away from the darn. I fancied the body flesh beneath was thinner but I couldn't be sure. He waited, his wide sea-blue eyes never leaving me until I had looked my fill, then he raised his arms, held them out.

As they closed round me, the icy dam broke. To be cradled against his shoulder, to feel his lips travelling over my hair, hear his voice softly chanting my name was like coming home after a life of exile. We clung, not with passion but with an emotion that was sweeter, purer, and unblemished by conflict. I was pre-emptied of any urgency to learn about past or future. The living moment was enough.

He guided me to Magnus's arm-chair, squatted before me on his haunches. 'Let me look at you. That's all I want to do for evermore, to look at you.' He laughed with rich exuberant joy. 'You see! miracles happen. You're here. I'm here. If that's not a miracle, I don't know what is.'

A little light-headed, I laughed with him. 'No miracle. A couple of lorries crashed at the top of Quakers' Yard, and I had to drive home along the Back Road.'

He leaned back, tugged off my Wellingtons, slid the Burberry from my shoulders and pulled the oil stove nearer under high beat of ecstatic excitement still motivated by his old loving concern. 'I know what will warm you. Hot chocolate. There's still a tin of Father's super brand in the kitchen cupboard, and half a cylinder of gas.' He stood up, kissed me lightly, cherishingly. 'Don't move.'

As the warmth penetrated my feet they began to tingle. Something of the same reaction shook my brain out of its blissful quiescent numbness. I looked bemusedly at the centre table spread with the tumbled-out contents of the rucksack:

packets of crispbread, silver triangles of wrapped cheese, a bottle of water, a rolled up ball of socks, a pair of steel-rimmed dark glasses, and hanging over a chair a scruffy green anorak, one sleeve a patchwork of foreign flags, some of which were hanging by threads. Provisions for what? A siege? The wolves of fear that had been driven from sight and sound, slunk back, crouched on the horizon of my mind.

Humming under his breath he emerged lithe and graceful as a cat from the kitchen, bearing between his hands a tray on which were set two of Magnus's Spode breakfast cups and a scarlet tin of his specially packed shortbread. As tenderly as though I'd been an invalid, he placed the saucer in my hand. 'No whipped cream but otherwise up to standard. Drink up, my pretty love.'

I sipped, scalded my lip, and put the cup and saucer on the floor. Hot chocolate, lavishly topped with whipped cream served in the Spode cups had been Magnus's sole culinary art, a party-piece he'd put on for children and adults when they'd been invited to the Bird Hut, and which had to be paid for with extravagant praise. Without actively looking, I'd absorbed the room through my skin: his desk, his books and bird engravings, the divan covered with a black mohair rug, and the powerful German binoculars on the window-sill. If ever a room was haunted, the Bird Hut was. Magnus had created it for himself, taking into account no taste or need but his own. Some essence of him would possess it until it fell apart, rotted into dust. That his name should be casually spoken within its circumference, the chocolate served in his cups without a quiver of emotion, seemed a blasphemy.

I raised my head, looked into his face, searching for a sign that he shared the memories that were sweeping over me like a rip tide. His narrow head was slightly tipped, his expression one of rapt adoration. I saw his lips part, but with a leap of urgency I spoke before the words had time to leave his mouth. 'Why are you here? How *can* you be here?'

The quality of his smile altered fractionally but it did not fade. 'In a nutshell, my darling, to collect overdue debts. Call me a debt-collector.' He gave me his old wayward grin, teased: 'As to how I can be here, isn't it enough that I am here? Do you want the dreary technical details? All that was required to get me here was a plan in essence so simple it was virtually foolproof, plus nerve.' He relished and repeated the last word: 'Nerve'll get you anywhere. I didn't even have to break in; all this time I've kept the key, our key. A talisman.' He bent and kissed me as naturally as though we'd been parted for no longer than a week.

A gust of wind must have penetrated the window-frame. As it blew the centre parting in the curtains wide, fear pierced me and in response I jumped to close the give-away band of light. As I overlapped them, weighted the hem with Magnus's binoculars, I caught sight of the yawning star-shaped crack across the smooth expanse of glass. When I turned and faced him across the room, with no warning to cushion its loss, the lovely interlude of not needing to know was so far behind me it was out of sight, and there were areas of cold around my heart as I heard my voice accuse: 'You didn't want to see me. You bent your head, hid your face. You were praying I wouldn't recognize you!'

His answer was desperately placating. 'Only because I couldn't afford to take a chance, not on the last lap, nearly home. Through the windscreen, in that deluge I couldn't be a hundred per cent sure it was you. Christy, I had no idea you were back in Berghmere. It was only later, when I began to rethink it, that I was positive. That's when I began to pray, that you'd been sure too, that you'd come, and you did. My God, I wanted you as I've never wanted anyone on this earth.'

My mind had subtracted one sentence, ignored the rest. 'Back from where?'

'New York. That's where you were, wasn't it?'

'Who told you I'd gone to America?'

For a split second he looked discomfited, then his sea-blue eyes cleared and his soft mobile mouth shaped a sweet knowing smile. 'For the moment, let's say I have my spies.'

'One spy,' I amended. 'Addy!'

I didn't expect him to admit it, and he didn't, but by by-passing the question, he'd jerked my memory. That was his habit: either to ignore an issue that threatened him, or side-track round it – a habit I'd forgotten. 'If you knew where I was, out of England, couldn't you have sent me a letter, a message . . . two words, enough to tell me you were alive?'

'Two words between us!' He shook his head with loving scorn. 'Two words and there wouldn't have been enough oceans in the world to keep us apart. And that wasn't to be. We couldn't be together. Not till now, when between us we made a miracle.' He patted the seat of Magnus's chair, held out his hand. 'Come back to me and drink your chocolate before it gets cold.'

When I obeyed, he replaced the cup and saucer in my hand before he drank his own, munched some of the shortbread that I refused. Now it was plain that the flesh on his temples was thinner, the lines from nostrils to wide, tenderly shaped mouth traced deeper, and somewhere sandwiched between the loving smile and the inward exultant joy were juddering nerves to which my own responded with huge beats of fear. I ran my fingers over his head, barely touching it. Rank after rank of questions reared themselves in my head. I chose the simplest. 'Where have you been hiding? How have you lived?'

A quiver akin to a spasm of physical pain crossed his face, but when he spoke his tone was laconically dismissive. 'In a variety of little hells.' As if he'd hurt me, he seized my hands in an act of loving contrition, held them to his lips. 'You want to know,' he said breathlessly, as though facing the inevitable and rushing headlong to get it behind him. 'Of course you do, and you shall when it's finished, the final reckoning made.' His eyes implored. 'But not here, not tonight, with nothing finished.' He looked harried, pressed beyond endurance. 'I can't do it, not even for you. But one day we'll lie in the sun, on a beach, with waves lapping over our feet and we'll talk until there is nothing I know that you don't.' He leaned forward, cupped my face in his hands, his greeny-blue gaze so fervent in promise that it half-hypnotized me. 'See it with me, peer over the horizon to the time when it will be happening. Because it will, Christy, and sooner than you think. It's there already waiting for us.'

I nodded submissively, but the nod was a lie. I could see nothing except the unrelieved blackness of the past and a present that could be no less a hell than the ones he'd experienced.

I said stiffly: 'You've come to collect what? Money?'

In his quick-silver way his mood switched and he eyed me with a gleam of boyish relish. 'Money and Father's insurance against inflation, the hydrogen bomb and Red Revolution with blood running in the gutters of Helsby. His diamonds. Inflation has about trebled their value.'

The diamonds! I saw Magnus, guarding each one, letting them fall into my cupped palms. Would the contents of that small chamois-leather bag provide him with a future so impregnably safe that he need never look over his shoulder again? Belief refused to be born.

It was then that I caught the flick of his wrist to expose his watch. He was measuring time, capable of calculating it, rationing out a portion of it to me. The wound to love and self-esteem was illogical, maybe childish, but it was real.

'And Wellesley's going to give you the diamonds. When?'

'Tonight. Actually he doesn't know it will be tonight. Our agreement stipulated one of five nights starting with tonight. A specific one would have provided him with a chance, if he'd been so disposed, of marshalling the clan.' He frowned in self-chagrin. 'I'd intended to let him sweat it out until the fifth night, but it worked out for tonight.'

'What clan?'

'Markham, Hugo . . .' His tone that was evasive suddenly turned alert. 'Mother's not home, is she?'

'No. She and Hester are in Switzerland with the companion who replaced Addy.'

He looked relieved. 'Good. That's one part of the bargain kept. The rest will be in the bag before daylight.'

A dialogue composed entirely of riddles both exasperated and frightened me. His assumption that he'd only to make a statement to transform it into hard fact, ran a cold finger down my spine. When I spoke my voice, rather horribly, reminded me of Aunt Edith's in her most intransigent mood. 'There's something you should know right away. Wellesley's got it fixed in his head that I was in the know about your coming home, that we've been working some sort of double-act to blackmail him. I went to Sweetcrab last week to see Hester. There was a scene, quite violent and rather nasty, which culminated in him practically throwing me out of the house. The actual word he used was go-between.'

'Go-between!' he mouthed after me. His look was one of frozen stupefaction before the rigor eased into honest bafflement. 'How the hell did he work that one out? In heaven's name how could we have got together when we've never seen one another? Blackmail!' A sudden blaze of indignation stained his cheeks. 'Didn't you deny it, put him wise?'

'I tried, but I didn't succeed.'

He mused to himself, then, thrusting anxiety behind him, said decisively: 'It must have been seeing you that put that weird idea into his head. Anyway, it's crazy. You, a blackmailer!' He laughed.

'I imagine the idea's still in his head.'

Suddenly he leapt to his feet convulsed by an explosion of white-hot passion. A darkness closed over his face as he shouted at me in anger as though I were his enemy. 'The world turns mad, blows up in your face. All you possess, everyone you love, they cease to exist, and however hard you try you can't rebuild your world, get back the people who love you. You wake up not believing it's happened, that it's a nightmare, but it's for real. Oh, it's for real all right. And you're a goner if you don't come to terms with it, capitalize on what's left for you.' He gave a clipped harsh laugh. 'And Wellesley has the gall to talk of blackmail! What's to be settled between us is a fair and final reckoning.' Suddenly his eyes went dead. For a moment, I knew I had ceased to exist for him, then he whispered: 'I was their salvation. And if you want salvation you must be prepared to pay the market price for it.'

'Salvation!' I shouted. 'Cary, whose salvation?'

Life flicked back into the dead eyes. 'I was talking to myself,' he said brusquely, 'forget it. It's dead history, or it will be by tomorrow morning.'

The passion of anger and self-justification had wrung him limp. He collapsed, buried his head in my lap. My fingers traced its familiar shape, but there was no feeling of reality, only one word that could mean anything or nothing beating in my skull, and on deeper level the cold knowledge that if I had not driven home along the Back Road I would have been asleep in my bed. He would have come and gone away again and I'd never have known . . . maybe I'd have died without knowing.

I said: 'What happened at Sweetcrab that night? Really happened?'

I felt his body grow rigid. When he raised his head it was slowly, as laboriously as though the movement cost him pain. Even the folds of flesh on his face were stiff with tension and the remoteness of inner deliberation. Then he gave a long, half-shuddering sigh, and when it was spent, smiled so gently, so lovingly at me that my heart of its own free-will forgave all there was to forgive.

'I made a promise.'

The naïve, guileless admission had the effect of numbing my brain, but only for a moment. 'A promise to whom? Who was there for you to make a promise to?' My voice rose with my need to know. 'You'd left Sweetcrab before any of them woke. A promise to whom?'

A transfixion of sheer fright darkened his eyes, his voice shook, suddenly he looked older, more cunning, utterly different from the Cary I'd known. 'Forget it. I tell you, forget it.'

'I can't. I won't.' We stared at one another, his gaze cold, adamant for a long, agonizing moment, then I demanded: 'Who killed Magnus?'

He answered in the laconic manner of a man who's been asked a stupid question. 'I did. Who else!'

My hands flew up to hide my face. An end, not only to the volcano of hope of a moment before, but years of life-saving dream-wishes on which I'd fed my starved heart. Whose salvation he'd wrought became of no account if he'd murdered his father. And a promise he'd made to someone was dust on the wind.

He dragged my hands away, lifted me to my feet. His kisses savaged my face, but the fires of passion did not kill the sense I had of existing only on the periphery of his mind.

I pulled away and staggered so that he had to steady me.

'Listen,' the violence and intensity now centred in his voice. 'I have to go to Wellesley with a clean conscience, proof that I've kept faith. But after tonight, when the future is in my pocket, I'll give it to you, and tell you how it got there. I swear I'll give it to you. Christy, take that look off your face. I saved them, the whole damned clan, and you shall know how, why, but not tonight.' Fatally, he looked at his watch for the second time.

He'd told me one fact: the promise had been made to Wellesley. Wellesley who had no schoolboy code of honour, who had called his brother a blind, reckless and half-mad murderer. Now fear padded so close it had a scent. I wondered how much time I'd got. Not enough to waste a word, expend it on a single question. I had to do a precision job, expose fact with such blazing clarity it would cut through the delusions that filled his head.

'You're wanted for murder. You're going to Sweetcrab to keep some pre-arranged rendezvous you've made with Wellesley, or he with you. You see him meekly handing you money and a bag of diamonds with his blessing. Shall I tell you what he'll do? He'll have a police officer waiting behind the door to arrest you.'

He shook his head in amused admonishment. 'And face a murder trial that would drag his name in the mud, resurrect ugly memories that are only just beginning to fade! Subject Mother to the ordeal of testifying against her own son! Is that likely or, more to the point, like Wellesley? No, he'll be waiting alone. That was the deal, and it's in his own interests to keep it.'

I shouted: 'It's some dirty double-cross, a trap, and you're walking right into it. By morning you'll be in gaol. Merely by being here, you're half-way there.'

He gave me a lofty, chiding look that revealed to me who knew him down to his bones that he had sailed way beyond the reach of logic. In my anguish I could have screamed at him.

'Any double-cross,' he said blandly, 'would rebound on Wellesley's head. I assure you, he's acting in his own interest as well as mine.' He laughed with unflawed assurance, so that he looked young and gay and, in my eyes, pitiful. 'My silly scared little love, I can read every one of your suspicions and a pretty morbid collection they are. What do you see? Me walking into the lion's den and never coming out alive! The victim of a diabolical plot to silence a man with a new name, for whom there's no evidence that he's even in the country. Pot-shotted off or quietly strangled, buried by night, or dropped into the mere with bricks tied to his feet. Come on, admit it?'

'You said it,' I whispered, 'I didn't.'

'But that's a fair summary?'

'Yes.'

'It couldn't happen, and I'll tell you why.' He lifted my hand and kissed the tip of each one of my fingers. 'Because, though I don't need one, I've won myself a Guardian Angel – by way of a miracle, our private miracle. Aren't you my witness that I'm going to Sweetcrab? Won't you be my witness that I've come out alive?'

I cried, terror thinning, 'I can come with you?'

Hhe instantly demolished that hope. 'No witnesses at Sweetcrab. Wellesley and I in an empty house. That's the deal we made and that's how it's going to be.' He mused, then gave me his wayward boyish look, older now, yet still potent. 'I've got it. I travelled over on the boat-train from Paris, the hard way because the cross-Channel steamers are packed to the gunwales with students and school parties returning from their Easter hols, plus the usual quota of hippies. Through customs and immigration I wedged myself in a sleazy gang on the way back from Istanbul. I got searched for pot, but like the clean-limbed Englishmen they are, the uniformed officials kept their eyes away from my filthy person. To play it safe I'll go back as far as Paris by the same route, and before I board the boat-train from Victoria at 10.30 tomorrow, I'll telephone you, chink diamonds in your ear, make you eat every single one of your dark bloodthirsty doubts.'

'Back to where you came from, a bolt-hole where you'll be a prisoner for the rest of your life!'

He smiled proudly. 'I'll bc no man's prisoner, Christy, and we won't live in a bolt-hole. We'll have a home.'

He spoke the last word with deep yearning, offering me what he most wanted for himself.

'A home where?'

'You shall choose. Anywhere out of England where the sun shines nine months of the year.'

He had a dazzling picture in his mind's eye of a glittering sun-soaked scene, but to me it was a mirage of spun glass. 'Where's the temporary home you left to catch the boat-train from the Gare du Nord?' I saw his recoil, and silently raged at the montsrous imbalance in him that tricked him into distrusting me, yet put his life in the hands of a man who'd proclaimed him a murderer and a blackmailer. As he turned his head away, the image in my mind changed and I saw my half-demented self pursuing a Will-of-the-wisp phantom lover in New York, New Orleans and at Heathrow airport, a recurring self-torture from which surely he could have saved me.

I said: 'A blank two and a half-years long. No daylight even now, just riddles and mysteries because you made a promise you won't break even to me. One name isn't much to ask.'

'There's no time . . .'

'There's one second to give me the name of a city or a country.'

He whispered it, as though we were hedged about with eavesdroppers: 'Malta.'

'Malta!' I echoed, horrified. 'It's crawling with English tax-dodgers and tourists. Sue's parents run a restaurant in Sliema. They could have passed you in the street, recognized you.'

He corrected himself. 'More precisely, Gozo, an off-shore island that is certainly not crawling with English tourists. Working in a boat-yard, I came on it last spring. It belongs to an old man whose son was killed in the war, and whose grandson was drowned last winter. Living quarters went with it. It served its purpose but now, thank God, that chapter of hard labour is finished. I'm only going back to pack.' Nervous excitement kept him motionless, put flecks of brilliance in his eyes, a lovely gay smile on his mouth. 'And then we'll be together. Where?' Like a present he offered me a dish of names. 'Athens, Tunis, Puerto Rico, Tahiti?'

But the name I repeated to myself was Gozo. Did it actually exist or was it a name he'd dreamed up?

When I picked none of the sugar plums he offered me, without faltering he ran on: 'I'll write and give you my address, and we'll play it by ear from there.' He was as transparently happy as Hester when she went into free flight, escaped the trammels of earthly doubt, spun ecstatically in space. Seeing my look, he teased: 'You're so chockful of doubt it's running out of your ears. What a doubting Thomas you are!'

Now it was I who was calculating time, not in minutes but split seconds. My mind raced, thrusting witlessly hither and thither to lay hold of any instrument of persuasion that would save him from his reckless congenital gullibility. I grasped his hands and pressed them hard to my breast. 'Listen, please, please listen. Wellesley isn't going to give you Magnus's diamonds. You haven't seen him for so long you've forgotten the kind of man he is, one who gives away nothing. Nothing. But I saw him last week. In his eyes you're a blackmailer. It makes no difference that you aren't, that's how he sees you, and that's how he'll react to you. No matter what's been said in letters between you, or on the telephone . . . or however you've communicated with each other, that's what you are to him. A blackmailer and a murderer. There's only one way you can beat him, by not going to Sweetcrab.' I gulped for breath, raced on. 'Go to London, stay a couple of nights in some boarding-house or small hotel, out of sight until I've drawn out all the money I have in the bank. It's not a lot, but it's a substantial sum. And in eighteen months I'll have what Father left me, and you can have that too, every penny of it. Cary, it's equivalent to putting your neck in a noose to go to Sweetcrab, to play Wellesley's nasty, evil game. He'll win.'

Firmly, with the aloofness of dignity mortally injured, he withdrew his hands from my grasp, walked to the table and keeping his back to me, began fiddling with the pile of foodstuffs. 'Thanks, but I'm not looking for hand-outs, only what is mine by right. What I've earned. Considering what they made out of the sale of Leighton's my demands are excessively modest. For a song I'm letting Wellesley and the rest of them off the hook. Wellesley knows and accepts that.'

I could have demanded what hook. Instead I stood looking numbly at the back of his head, hypnotized by a new sound: rain drumming on the roof. The same muted rhythm that had been an accompaniment to that other night. And suddenly I was imprisoned in a frantic sense of time sliding backwards, going into reverse.

I beseeched: 'Don't go, please Cary, don't go to Sweetcrab.'

He swung round, his temper snapped, crying in a voice of hate: 'Stop badgering me. You know nothing . . . no one does who wasn't there. So don't judge, don't preach. Let me alone.' Becoming conscious of his ugly tone, contrition stirred him, and he begged with an ache of love: 'Christy, please, just wait until tonight is over. Then you shall know. I'll make that one of the conditions . . . no secrets between us. There's less than twelve hours to go and at the end of it there's the world we always wanted and never got waiting for us. It'll be all right. I promise. I'll telephone you before half-past ten tomorrow morning. And soon, only a few weeks, we'll start and look for a home.'

He checked his watch for the third time, turned away, began stowing the rucksack at speed, eager to be gone, half of him already gone, to Sweetcrab to pick up a bag of diamonds. A man who believed in fairy-stories.

The sense of *déjà vu* became overpowering, so total that I lost all capacity to think straight. Now or then? This night or that other one buried under an eternity of days and weeks and months and years? A reel of time remorselessly spinning backwards. There was nothing I could do to stop him going to Sweetcrab; equally it was beyond me to endure a parting I'd already lived through once.

He was so engrossed in his packing that he did not hear me move. I had my feet in my Wellingtons, my arms in my Burberry before he realized what I was about. Even then, understanding was slow to dawn and though he moved after me to the door, his reactions were slowed-down by the bright mirror pictures in his head, and I was through it before he could reach me. I heard his voice shouting my name, but I did not halt my steps. I was fleeing from my flesh and blood love faster than I'd pursued his phantom down New York streets, across Heathrow airport.

I turned coward, forsook him when he had no one else.

CHAPTER TWELVE

I slept because I willed myself to sink below the level of subconsciousness, enclosed in a cylinder at the bottom of a silent, fathomless sea. I surfaced in slow motion inch by inch up through the cloudy depths of oblivion to the stark reality of morning.

The scene in the Bird Hut was as clear and detailed in my memory as a blown-up print. On tape in my mind was a record of a promise made to Wellesley, and kept, even from me, of a bag of diamonds to be handed over at midnight in an empty house in payment for someone's salvation, and of wildly spinning pipe-dreams of a home in the sun where all mystification would be unravelled.

But I did not glance at the print, listen to the tape. They were no more than dead leaves fluttering in the wind balanced against the horrific burden of guilt that had sprung to life in me while I slept. I cared for nothing in the wide world except that Cary should keep his promise to me: telephone me from the mundane safety of Victoria Station, crow over me that I'd been wrong.

When I was dressed I looked out of my window. In the new, fresh-washed morning air, not only was the Bird Hut etched firm into the sky above the dull-sheened waters of the mere, but I could see the shape of the chimneys of Sweetcrab against the great heads of the beeches. Guilt, I discovered, had a voice, a thin, unceasing scream in my head: You shouldn't have forsaken him. You should have dogged his heels every foot of the way to Sweetcrab and back. I covered my ears to deaden the voice, and when it refused to be stilled I literally prayed, as a child prays: 'Please God, let him be right, just this once.'

At half past seven I took Aunt Edith's tea. She was sitting upright, away from the pillows, decently covered from neck to wrists, reading the *Church Times*, a figure of strength and rectitude so in possession of herself that for a moment the weight of fear eased as I kissed her cheek, but not the guilt.

As I drew back, her glance pried. 'You look poorly. What's amiss with you?'

'Nothing. I'm all right.'

'You've got a fever by the looks of you. You'd best get back to bed and I'll take your temperature.'

I forced a laugh. 'You'll do nothing of the sort. Breakfast downstairs for both of us in three-quarters of an hour.'

She couldn't, thank heaven, force me back to bed. To prove that I was fit and healthy, I forced down two slices of toast and all the inside of a boiled egg she could see without actually peering into the shell.

A further threat was posed by the arrival between 9.30 and 10 of Mrs Curtis, who at the first ring sprinted to the telephone, grabbed the receiver and detained the caller with bright chat as long as she could before grudgingly relinquishing the receiver.

This morning she arrived a-bustle with belligerency, all set for an outright assault on me. As soon as she was out of her outdoor clothes, she cornered me against the kitchen sink.

'It's high time we had things out, Miss Graham. They can't go on like this, with you hopping back to London and leaving me with the sole responsibility for your old auntie. The pittance she pays me doesn't come anywhere near the rate for the job.'

I'd offered to dismiss Mrs Curtis, but Aunt Edith had smartly retorted she was perfectly capable of informing a domestic servant she had no further need of her services and paying her off in lieu of notice.

I wriggled out of the corner and flouncing with umbrage she allowed herself to be ushered into the sitting-room where Aunt Edith was waiting for her.

I checked the time. Five minutes to ten. I sat on the bottom step of the stairs, within a hand's reach of the telephone, past caring who saw me. At ten on the dot the bell rang. Relief bounded so high it silenced the high, thin scream in my head. But it was Tim's voice that spoke in my ear, saying he'd checked and Aunt Edith's hearing-aid would be ready next Tuesday and as Dr Sessler had promised personally to explain its mechanism to her, would I make sure she didn't duck out.

I promised so curtly that he inquired: 'You all right, Christina?'

'I'm fine. But I'm expecting an urgent call from London. Would you mind if I rang off?'

It was the last thing he'd be likely to do, and with a 'Bye,' he cleared the line.

I sat there until Mrs Curtis emerged literally shaking and incoherent with rage to berate me for the wicked ingratitude of folks who called themselves Christians! Naturally, she didn't choose to stay where she wasn't appreciated, but I should live to regret it, mark my words. When she'd banged the door, I went into the kitchen to check my watch by the wall clock. It was one minute past half-past ten.

I've no recollection of the petty time-wasting chores with which I filled the remaining hours of the morning and afternoon, only that at four o'clock I reached the limit of my capacity to wait.

I dialled the number of Sweetcrab, armoured myself against disappointment by a warning that, with the morning cleaner gone, the chances of the call being answered were nil. A stilted voice, articulating with care, replied: 'This is the Leighton residence,' and I thanked providence for one piece of luck that had come my way. The voice belonged to Emily Pitcher who, before she married had been trained by Mrs Leighton into a passable imitation of a parlourmaid. After her marriage, children and husband permitting, she occasionally returned to Sweetcrab to wait at dinner-parties. She'd obviously been called in to prepare Wellesley's meals.

'Emily, you remember me, don't you? Christina Graham?'

'Why, yes, Miss, I do.' The falsetto dropped and there was only a tinge of reserve in her natural voice. 'Mrs Leighton, Miss Hester and Mademoiselle Benet aren't here, Miss. They've gone to Switzerland. There's only Mr Wellesley, and he won't be home till later.'

'It was Mr Wellesley I wanted. It's a personal matter, so

I don't want to disturb him by ringing his office. He hates that, doesn't he?'

'He can't abide it, Miss. He gave me a ticking off about it only the day before yesterday.'

'But if you can give me an idea what time you expect him home, I can ring him when he gets home.'

'Well, not exactly, Miss. He's got some sort of political committee meeting after he leaves the office. I'm to lay him a cold supper, but he said not to wait, as he probably wouldn't be back until half past eight, but you never know with him, it might be ten.'

I thanked her, dutifully inquired after her husband, whose name I fortunately remembered and the sex and approximate ages of her children.

I parked the car well back in a field entrance where it was shielded from the road by a hedge, and walked the last hundred yards or so to Sweetcrab. If Wellesley wasn't home, I'd return to the car and wait until his passed me. Contrarily, if he was home, there'd be no sound of an engine to alert him to my arrival. Surprise was my only ally, and I didn't want to squander a fraction of it.

The outside lights were switched off; the garage doors closed. The only blur of radiance visible was in the small ground-floor panelled room on the left which meant the door was open and the hall light on. With all the signs pointing to Wellesley being indoors, I rang the bell, demanded admittance to a house I'd vowed never to enter again.

Wellesley opened the front door holding a white napkin in his hand. With his back to the light, I could not gauge the expression that came to his face at the sight of me on the doorstep, but his voice was brusque to the point of rudeness. 'My mother and Hester are abroad.'

'It's you I want to see.' Not trusting him not to use physical force to keep me out, I stepped smartly past him.

'It is not convenient for me to see you. I only arrived home ten minutes ago after a lengthy committee meeting, and I've a great deal of paper work to do before I go to bed. Also, I'm in the middle of a meal. Now, if you would be good enough to excuse me.'

I took a flying look down the hall. Only one door was open: into the room which, long ago, Addy had used as a schoolroom. In daylight its chief merit was its charming view from the french window, directly opposite the point where the mere looped to within fifty yards of Sweetcrab. In a hard winter we'd been able to coax the mallards and shovellers and moorhens to feed round our feet on the small plot of lawn. I had no means of knowing what its present function was, but it seemed pretty obvious that Wellesley was eating his supper there.

I walked briskly towards it as he barked a protest: 'Christina, I take the strongest exception to your behaviour. I find it unpardonable.'

There was a lot more to it, but I didn't listen, except to measure that his mood was as aggressively hostile as on the last occasion we'd met. Yet when we were inside the room that had been converted into a breakfast-room or maybe a small family dining-room, I could find no trace of guilt on his smooth countenance, only righteous boiling indignation. Either he was genuinely affronted by the interruption of his evening meal or he was putting on a very good act.

He nailed me with a glance of concentrated venom. 'You must surely have realized by now that you are not a welcome visitor to this house?'

'I'm hardly likely to forget it after the reception you gave me the last time I was here when you accused me of attempted blackmail, being in league with Cary to extort money either from you or your mother. By now, having seen Cary, you'll be better informed. Where is he?'

He answered with heavy irony: 'My dear Christina, you are more likely to be cognisant of his whereabouts than I. Suppose you tell me. As for saying I've seen him . . . that, I presume, is a joke, one in rather poor taste in my opinion.'

'No joke. You have seen him. When I left him in the Bird Hut last night soon after half past eleven, he was on the point of setting out for Sweetcrab to keep a date he'd made with you.'

The only weakness shock exposed in him was a need to sit down. He did so abruptly on a chair at the round table before the remnants of his meal. Without an invitation I took one opposite alongside what had been Addy's writing desk.

For a moment astonishment held him mute, then he said, separately enunciating every syllable: 'You met Cary in the Bird Hut? Your old lovers' nest!' He inhaled slowly, exhaled, his eyes never leaving my face. 'You astound me, to a degree, I must admit, that defies credibility.' A thin smile came to his lips. 'You have a very fertile imagination, Christina, but you can hardly expect me to give credence to your statement that you and Cary spent last night in the Bird Hut?'

'We spent approximately an hour together talking before he left to keep his appointment with you.'

'Cary!' The tone was firmer now, sceptical, brutally mocking. 'Cary hasn't got the guts to return to England, face a murder charge. No, no.' He feigned puzzlement. 'So why have you come to me with this preposterous story? Is it supposed to pose some threat to me? Are you about to ask me for money?'

I said, slowly, distinctly: 'I'm asking you where Cary is now. You made arrangements to . . .'

'What arrangements?' he interrupted. 'Are you suggesting he and I have been in communication? That letters have passed between us.' He paused, inquired with soft menace: 'Are you accusing me of inviting or condoning a visit from a man who is wanted by the police of this country on a charge of murder?'

'You've certainly been in contact with him. How else was the date made: one of five nights when he would come to meet you at Sweetcrab!'

'Christina, listen and mark what I am about to say. If Cary had, by some means beyond my conception, managed to return to Berghmere, contacted me, it would have been my duty to hand him over to Inspector Braithwaite of Helsby C.I.D., and I assure you that I would not have failed in that duty. If Cary is in England which, I repeat, I simply do not believe, he came nowhere near Sweetcrab last night or any other night.'

'Then why, immediately you saw me, did you assume that he and I had ganged up to blackmail you?'

His calm broke under the impact of a passion of incensement. 'Because I know you, Christina. You never acknowledge you're beaten, do you! You'd lost out, lost everything on which you'd set your ambitious little heart. That being so, it was obvious you'd take steps to recoup your losses, and somehow you and Cary would connive to get together. That was my opinion, and it still holds good, though I admit to being baffled by the means you are employing. Frankly, I'm beginning to find this whole business insufferably tedious. You really cannot expect me to believe that pathetic little tale of yours. You and Cary in the Bird Hut, talking for an hour, talking about what, may I ask?'

'Among other subjects a promise he made to you in return for salvation.'

'A promise!' he repeated pettishly. 'What promise? And salvation, what's that supposed to mean? Whose salvation?'

I couldn't tell him because I didn't know. 'There was to be a final settlement between you at Sweetcrab on Tuesday night.'

'A settlement,' he roared at me. 'What sort of settlement do you make with the cold-blooded, merciless killer of your father!' He sucked in his breath to calm his rage. 'What settlement?'

'A fair and final settlement between you. When it was made you were going to give him Magnus's diamonds.'

He stared at me with such unrelenting, coldly-calculated malice that my nerve-ends flashed a warning of an empty house, guarded without by great spaces where a cry for help would go unheard.

'Are you saying, Christina, what I take you to be saying, that by some means you take care not to specify, I connived to pervert the course of justice, exacted a promise from my father's murderer I did not reveal to the police? Is that what you are saying?'

'Yes.'

'That I saw and talked with Cary after he'd murdered Father?'

'There isn't any other answer.'

He got up, walked to the telephone extension that was on a shelf beside the fireplace. He lifted the receiver to his ear, extended a finger towards the dial. 'What you've said gives me no alternative but to call the police. The sooner they are present to take an official statement from you the better.'

'I'm here for one purpose only: to find out where Cary is.'

'If I knew that, I would pass the information to the police.'

He thought a moment, then put the receiver back on its rest, brought his chill, contemptuous gaze to me, walked back to his chair. 'You've made it up, haven't you? Every word of it. All this talk of a promise, of a conspiracy, if you like. Loose accusations about salvation, my father's diamonds! It's pathetic, childish nonsense. My father's diamonds are no longer a negotiable commodity; furthermore, not mine to dispose of. They were left to my mother and she, wisely, consigned them to her bank vault in London. I repeat, they are not mine to give away; they are not even in the house. And yet you suggest I have been engaged in some nefarious, illegal negotiations with Cary to hand them over to him!' He laughed. 'I'm at a loss to fathom the purpose behind this highly-coloured tissue of lies. Tell me, how did he enter the country? Obviously under an assumed name armed with a false passport. Nevertheless, it would, if it had happened, have been quite a feat. Did he confide in you how he brought it off? And where, precisely, had he travelled from?'

I could have answered one of his questions, but I wasn't disposed to do so. The name of the offshore island was my pitifully meagre ammunition against his big guns. Gozo, I kept saying to myself, terrified that I'd forget the unlikely-sounding name or that it wouldn't exist on a map. He'd been going back there, to a boat-yard that shouldn't take too much finding on a small island, even though he was known under a different name.

My silence had given him the assurance he needed. 'You don't know! Of course you don't. If Cary wishes to preserve his freedom, he can under no circumstances return to England. Your story is arrant nonsense from start to finish.' He lifted a radish from a side-plate, nibbled it. 'But if you continue to spread your malicious tissue of lies, I warn you that you will receive a call from the police.' He darted a venomous glance at me. 'That is no idle threat, Christina. In your own interests you'd do well to heed it.'

'They won't have any occasion to come to me. I'll go to them.'

He waved his hand towards the telephone. 'Go ahead. Ask Inspector Braithwaite for an appointment and pour your preposterous concoction of lies into his ears.' His smile was smooth as silk, utterly meaningless. 'But don't be disappointed if he doesn't leap into action. Like all good detectives he's something of a psychologist. He recognizes a liar on sight.' He gave me a shrug of dismissal. 'Now if you would permit me to finish my meal.'

'We both know Cary came to Sweetcrab. Only you know if he left. But I'm going to find out.'

He reached for his wine glass. 'If you find him, give him a message from me. Any word of communication he sends me will be handed over to Helsby C.I.D. And the same applies to you. If you make another attempt to pester me, I shall summon the police.'

What, I asked myself driving home, had I expected? A full confession, the effortless overthrow of a man superbly armoured from attack by self-love? I did not know, only that the thin, faint screaming inside my head had started up again.

To avoid that steely, needling glance that stripped me down to the bone of my shortcomings I sat in the car in the garage until it was well past Aunt Edith's ten o'clock deadline for bed. My wait had been vain. The sitting-room door was open, she had angled her chair towards it and turned herself into a watchdog. My desperate need to climb the stairs, lie on my bed in the dark and juggle a myriad unmatching pieces around in my head until they made a coherent pattern was doomed, but when she called me I obeyed, at least as far as the threshold of the room. 'I'm tired, Aunt Edith. I'm going straight to bed.'

'But by the looks of you not to sleep.' She wore her sternest martinet pose. 'I'm an old woman plagued with creaking joints and deaf ears but there's nothing wrong with my eyes and not overmuch with my wits. Child, what ails you?'

'I'm tired,' I repeated woodenly.

'Aye, bone-tired and sick at heart.' Her voice softened a tone. 'There's a limit to the time you can fool me. I know you, child.'

It was a two-way knowledge. Behind us were years of infighting, of battles we'd separately won and lost. I was her cross. She was the rock under whose shadow I'd grown up, and however hard-voiced her strictures, the condemnation dictated by her puritanical conscience I knew in the ultimate she'd be for me. In a moment of crisis and chaos the relationship between us evoked a response from my heart, jerked words from my lips that, if I'd hesitated a second, I'd never have spoken. 'Cary's come back. I was with him in the Bird Hut on Tuesday night. He's come back. I saw him.'

She was so deeply and unexpectedly shocked it was as though her spirit leaped within her in despair and denunciation of the truth. Her skin lost the shadow-colour it possessed, and the tinge of blue in her lips grew more marked. She looked as if she was about to cry to God for strength to bear this new thunderbolt of grief. Instead she heaved herself to her feet, said in a voice without a tremor: 'Sit down, near the fire. You look perished. I'll make a pot of tea.'

A bubble of hysteria broke inside me. Tea, the English panacea for shock and injury to flesh and heart! It was a process that took her ten minutes. She had to carry each cup separately. I was too appalled at the inquisition ahead, husbanding my mental resources to meet it, to rouse myself to help her. I cursed the weakness in me that had tricked me into a confession.

At her command I drank half a cup of the hot, sweetened syrup, and when I put it down was impaled by a gaze made bitter and stone-hard with accusation. She believed the meeting in the Bird Hut had been pre-arranged, that I'd cheated her, lied. 'No,' I shouted. 'I didn't know. I couldn't know.' I shut my eyes to screen out a face that was straight out of the Old Testament. 'I was driving along the Back

Road after taking Mary Dennet home . . . and he was walking in the rain, on his way to the Bird Hut. Last night I went there to find him. He hadn't come to see me; if I hadn't taken the Back Road, I'd never have known he was in the country.' For a split second I marvelled that I could make the admission without pain. I opened my eyes, raised my voice to make sure she heard. 'He came to see Wellesley. After I left the Bird Hut he was going to Sweetcrab. Now Wellesley denies he went there . . .'

As though I were an hysterical child, she made me start from the beginning. She listened without interrupting, her burning, anguished gaze never leaving my face to ensure if her ears deprived her of a word, she could snatch it from my lips.

When I came to the end, she relinquished her visual hold of me, spoke as impartially as a judge pronouncing sentence: 'Call it a settlement or any other fancy name you please, but blackmail's as good a word as any.' She brought her glance back to me, spoke with the bitter rancour of inward despair. 'Not that you'd admit it. For you Cary Leighton was a walking, breathing paragon. And still is, I don't doubt.'

I brushed aside what, for me, had become an irrelevancy. If she started to argue, I'd scream. I enunciated carefully: 'I have to make sure he's safe, that he got away from Sweetcrab unharmed and caught his boat-train to Paris. Safe,' I repeated.

'And you're frightened he's come to harm because he didn't telephone you. That's all that's worrying you! Maybe he ran short of time and had to choose between telephoning you and catching his train!'

'All right, he hadn't time, or he forgot. That's not the point. If he reached the station it meant he'd been to Sweetcrab, seen Wellesley. And Wellesley denies he saw him.'

She countered sharply: 'Would you expect him to admit it? Housing a felon wanted for murder! I don't doubt that a few lies sit easy on Wellesley Leighton's conscience.'

'Not only on his. If Cary made a promise to Wellesley they must have seen one another, talked, after Magnus was dead. What about the others who were there: Mrs Leighton,

Addy, Hugo Trent and Markham, what have they got on their consciences?'

As I might have guessed, she seized on the last name, rounded on me. 'Markham's not a man to commit perjury. I'll not believe he'd be a party to any dishonourable act, or that he'd break the law of the land. All you've got is the word of a man who was a past master at deceiving himself. A son who doesn't deny that he murdered his father. What did all his talk amount to? Not worth a row of pins. His talk never did.'

What I was incapable of explaining to her, barely to myself, was that my concern to disinter any secrets that had been buried at Sweetcrab the night of Magnus's murder, was of secondary importance. In twenty-four hours my world had shrunk to a size so small that it could not encompass more than the guilt that consumed me.

'By rights you should have reported his arrival to Helsby police station.'

'Even you couldn't expect me to do that! In the end I did something worse: I let him go to Sweetcrab alone to meet Wellesley.'

'A son who slew his own father!'

'Vengeance,' I said, 'is the Lord's, not Wellesley's.'

'Nor yours.'

She looked old and tired to her bones, and I longed for both our sakes for her to be peaceably in bed. I feigned a yawn. 'Let's leave it for tonight.'

'Leaving won't cure it. Come and gone in a night, and what's he left behind? Talk that makes no sense but's going to break your heart.' The unbelievable happened: a tear slid over her lower eyelid, ran down her creased cheek. 'You're my child,' she mourned with racking sadness. 'My child who suffered because of her silly head and one man's wickedness against God. And now . . .'

I put my arms round her. 'It's not the same.' I laughed gently in an effort to console her. 'In my case history doesn't repeat itself. I promise, I only want to be certain he's safe, and that's an end to it.' An end . . . such a little word to spell my whole world!

'And how,' she demanded, the tears gone, ashamed of her weakness, and impotently angry with me and my twenty-three years of irresponsibility and misjudgments, 'do you propose setting about that?'

'I'll think of a way. Not now. In the morning.'

There were at least two options open to me, one of which was to take a plane to Valetta and then whatever transport was on offer to an offshore island called Gozo. The other was to discover from Mrs Bengy the estimated time of Markham's arrival at Holland Court.

CHAPTER THIRTEEN

At nine next morning I telephoned Mrs Bengy to inquire if she had any idea when Mr Drake would be home.

'Why he's back, Miss Graham. It was after two o'clock when I heard his car. And up this morning at seven when Tom was worried about a sick heifer. Then the telephone ringing its head off. Right done up, he looked, and out again as soon as he'd swallowed a bite of breakfast.'

'I wanted to see him, Mrs Bengy. Urgently. Will he be in at lunchtime?'

'No, that he won't, Miss. He's meeting two gentlemen off the London train and taking them to lunch in Helsby and then bringing them here. I don't know what to say, Miss. It doesn't look as if he'll have time for anything until after they've gone back this evening.' For a placid woman she sounded distracted and edgy. 'I've to get a cold supper, a buffet he called it. Just soup, a cold chicken, salad and cheese. To my mind that doesn't make much of a meal for two gentlemen before a journey.'

'Don't worry, Mrs Bengy. I'll ring him tonight.'

In a state of general fret, suddenly she started to get agitated on my behalf. 'But you saying it's urgent, Miss, I've just had a thought. You could try the Abbey. You know, them old ruins just above the weir. I heard him make an appointment to meet some gentlemen from the Preservation Society at ten o'clock. It seems there's been complaints about the fencing and the stock getting in.'

Selwick Abbey was a ruin, a haphazardly disposed skeleton of stone, its roof the sky, its floor a grass sward, built nine hundred odd years ago for monks of the Order of St Benedict. The river swept round three sides of it and when you were inside it was easy to imagine you were on an island. The destruction Henry VIII began, time and vandalism had completed. Now, over-late in its history, although it was on

Holland Court land, a preservation order had been slapped on it, and periodically an official inspected it for damage inflicted by fence-crashing cows and picnickers who were prone to light fires on its altar stone.

Driving down the ruler-straight hard track I saw two vehicles parked in the turn-around: a Land-Rover and a serviceable family saloon. I pulled in to the near side and waited. Within five minutes two men appeared through the decapitated arch of the gateway, one short and tubby, hatted and muffled to the ears in a city coat, gesticulating with his gloved hands, and the other tall, russet-headed, who had difficulty in accommodating his stride to the short strut of his companion.

When the black saloon had passed me, I drove up to the turn. Markham with one foot in the Land-Rover, jumped down, came striding to open my car door. 'Christy!' His smile was joyous with surprise. 'How did you know I was here?'

'I telephoned Mrs Bengy.'

Something in my voice or expression blew the smile off his face. I saw the wariness that had imprisoned him that Sunday afternoon at the windmill creep back. It had baffled me then, but not now. In the air between us I caught a whiff of fear that he would never permit to surface on his disciplined face. I'd have bet that one of his early morning telephone calls had been from Wellesley. It was a guess that should have stiffened my resolve, but though it did not falter, what I had determined to do loomed as an infinitely more complex task than when I'd rehearsed it in the car.

His handsome face took on a look of exasperation and battened down apprehension, and when he spoke his tone was half-way to anger. 'What the hell's been going on since I left?'

The morning was bright, with pale cascades of sunshine falling over the meadowland, but the wind still blew from the east. I shivered involuntarily, and he immediately hugged my elbow in his hand. 'Before you tell me, let's see if we can find some shelter.'

We found it in an angle of stonework that reached no

higher than our heads, in which a hazel tree now hung with trembling yellow-green catkins had seeded. There was a slab set on two uprights that provided a seat and through a gap in the jagged wall I could see across to the farther bank of the river where two women, baskets on their hips, were walking the marshalled rows of daffodils, picking the buds. They called out to one another and laughed as they stooped and rose like clockwork.

He touched my hand. 'Christy, I'm waiting to hear what you've got to tell me.'

It had to be done all at once, between two breaths. 'Cary's come back. I saw him in the Bird Hut on Tuesday night.'

'What are you saying? Do you even know *what* you're saying? That you saw and talked to Cary . . . You couldn't . . . I don't believe it . . .'

It was the first time on which I'd known him bereft of coherent speech. He was literally stupefied with shock. It lasted for five or six seconds, then he demanded roughly: 'Christy, is this some wild story?'

'No. Cary came back to Berghmere on Tuesday. I met him in the Bird Hut on Tuesday night.'

'You met him in the Bird Hut?' He looked and sounded appalled. 'You had some sort of date!'

'Please listen, just listen. I had no warning that he was coming. He didn't know I was here. I suppose you might call it a coincidence that defies credibility, but it happened. I was driving along the Back Road in the rain, and I saw him, and guessed where he was going. I went to find him. He was there not to see me but to see Wellesley. That's why he'd come back, to see Wellesley, not me.' I paused, schooled myself to keep to the bare skeleton of fact, mind and manner temperate. Lose my temper and all was lost. 'Wellesley was expecting him. The arrangements for the meeting had been made either by letter or telephone – I don't know, but one of the conditions was that there was to be no one else in the house. Presumably that's why Wellesley had made sure his mother, Hester and Anna were out of the way. Quite what he'd have done if the cook hadn't broken her thigh, I can't think. Probably given her an extra paid holiday.'

His condemnation was inexorable, pitiless. 'If what you say is true, he must be out of his mind. What's he playing at, some lunatic game of tag with the police? What does he expect to gain by it?' He stopped suddenly, said sharply: 'Money, is that it?'

'Yes,' I said, 'hush money.'

Now he'd gone so still that he scarcely seemed to breathe. Then his lips moved. 'Go on.'

'In an empty house, with no witnesses, no one to see him arriving or leaving, Wellesley was going to give him Magnus's diamonds.'

I looked at him, and the eyes that looked back at me were loaded with a terrible anxiety and his flesh on his face was rigid with concern. But concern and anxiety for whom? 'Yesterday evening I went to Sweetcrab. Wellesley won't admit that he saw Cary, that he had any knowledge he was in the country. His angle was that I dreamed it up; either that or I was bent on spreading a malicious string of lies. He ended by threatening me with the police.'

Obliquely through a gap in the tottering walls I saw a sailing dinghy with a red sail, and in the second before it slid out of the window frame the man bent deep and recklessly to kiss a girl sitting on the broad stern seat. The first time Markham had kissed me had been in a sailing boat when we'd been becalmed on Bloxstead Broad. I'd been paralysed with fright in case I disappointed him, shy and terrified and at his mercy. Was he now at mine? When he didn't speak, I asked: 'Hush money for what, do you suppose?'

'Didn't Cary tell you?'

'No.'

'How long were you together?'

The nagging at an irrelevance exasperated me. 'An hour, about that.'

'In that case why didn't he tell you?'

'He was bound by a promise . . . to Wellesley. Until they'd arrived at what he described as a fair and final settlement he wasn't prepared to break it.' His glance did not flinch, but it was remote, unreadable. 'A promise,' I repeated, 'that could only have been made after Magnus was dead. And which you must either have been a party to, or a witness. You were there; so was Hugo. What did you do, lie about the time you arrived at Sweetcrab, spend half a night plotting, and then sign an oath with your blood?'

He said with no audible feeling, 'There'd been enough blood spilled. If there is anything you need to know about that night, if there is anything to tell, you should ask Cary. I imagine you know where to find him.'

That I'd failed so abysmally to make myself plain, wasted so much time without coming to the heart of what I needed to know, was bitter. 'You don't understand. You don't want to. When I left Cary in the Bird Hut on Tuesday night, he was leaving, within minutes, for Sweetcrab. Only Wellesley knows where he is now, and he's not saying.'

'Do you blame him?'

'Not if Cary left Sweetcrab alive, unharmed.'

I'd shocked him. It took him a moment to recover, but when he spoke it was judicially. 'Are you accusing Wellesley of harming him, physically?'

'He could have murdered him, and who'd have known! He rides people who get into his way into the ground, then tramples them to death.' I heard the stubbornness in my voice deepen. 'I want to know that Cary walked out of Sweetcrab alive.'

'Why do you assume he didn't? If there was some secret deal between Cary and Wellesley to meet – though I still find that hard to swallow – would you expect Wellesley to admit it to you? He stirred restlessly, then slanted his glance towards me. 'What did you talk about the hour you were together?'

'An act of salvation. His.'

'To save whom?'

'One of you or all of you. You tell me. He wouldn't.'

He looked away from me, stared at the rows of daffodils. 'But this business of leaving Sweetcrab, unharmed: what makes you doubt he didn't?'

'He promised to telephone me before he caught the boat-train from Victoria Station on Wednesday morning. He didn't.'

He looked back at me with a glimmer of sceptical amusement, said with a note of relief: 'It could have slipped his mind. By now he could be safely back where he came from. Did he tell you where that was?'

'Yes.'

He didn't ask where but looked away again and the silence was made heavy and choking with painful deliberations he was turning over and over. When he'd reached his decision, he said: 'Wherever he's living, he's never been in need, without money to support himself. Wellesley has made funds available to him. I imagine, though he's never actually said so, through a numbered bank account in Switzerland on which Cary under whatever name he has assumed, has been authorized to draw. But it could have been provided through other channels. What I'm saying is that Cary was under no economic compulsion to take the enormous risk of coming back to this country.'

'That's nice to know!'

His head turned, and his blue glance challenged mine. 'I'm glad it's news to you!'

I said slowly, with conviction: 'That Sunday afternoon at the windmill, you implied you knew nothing about Cary, but you did; for instance that he was Wellesley's remittance man. Even now you know a great deal more than you're prepared to admit.' I felt one strand of my temper give. 'Blood oaths,' I raged, 'between you and Wellesley. Blood brothers conspiring God knows what that was outside the law. Wellesley shaking in his shoes at the sight of me, calling me a blackmailer, Cary's go-between. It didn't make sense, but it does now. Wellesley had banked on Cary slipping unseen into Sweetcrab, to be caught in a trap he'd baited with diamonds. And no one ever knowing he'd been and gone, or not gone. Then I turned up, and his guilty conscience saw me as an accomplice planted in the wings, in the know! Couldn't you have warned me?'

'You weren't a blackmailer, so you didn't need warning off. I was aware, when Wellesley heard you were coming back to Berghmere that some notion of that kind crossed his mind. That's all I knew. Assuming he was guilty of encouraging Cary to risk a life-sentence he'd hardly have been likely to confide in me or anyone else that he was about to compound a felony.'

'And what notion crossed your mind when you heard I was coming to Berghmere?'

'I thought it probable you'd somehow been in touch with Cary, come back to argue his case, put in a plea for whatever cash payments he was receiving from Wellesley to be stepped up.'

'Which would amount to blackmail.' I looked away from him. 'Do you still think so?'

'You know I don't.'

The words came so sure and warm from his lips, they fired my hope. 'Then prove it by helping me to find him?'

'Find your love!' He laughed softly, almost sorrowfully, but when he went on his voice had a cutting edge. 'Who's prepared to risk plunging a family who've survived one hell into another! No, no, Christy. You love him, you find him.'

That was the cold stone with which I must learn to live. Love that had reached its heights in the Bird Hut had died there. Tears stung my lids. Love was so dead that I could hardly recall its images, remember its perfume that had kept me company for two and a half years of exile. I had a sense of foundering, and yet one obstinate spark of faith refused to be quenched. I compressed all my energy into one last appeal. 'It's so simple,' I entreated. 'In the whole world I'm the only one who cares whether Cary Leighton is dead or alive. I'm not asking you to break any promises, give away any secrets. No loyalties are involved. I only want to make certain that Cary is alive, that he did walk out of Sweetcrab early Wednesday morning.' I looked at him, and he looked back at me, and for a second, while hope flickered, I saw his resolution weaken, but it steadied.

'You'll find him.' His smile was bitter. 'You'll find him,' he repeated, 'without any help from me or anyone else.'

I bit hard on the pain of failure and stood up. I spoke as though the sole matter that concerned me was that I'd made him late for an appointment. 'Mrs Bengy mentioned you had to meet the eleven-fifty-five London train. You'll have to drive fast or you won't make it.'

'I'll make it. Paquet and Schweizer find the preliminary estimates of the capital sum required for the conversion and maintenance of Holland Court grossly inflated. They want, I suppose reasonably enough, to inspect the place for themselves, and as they are together, it seemed an opportunity not to be missed.' He gave me a look that was sharp with suspicion. 'Where are you going?'

'I might go and see Addy,' I replied carelessly. 'Women don't take blood-oaths as seriously as little boys.'

'In Addy's case, I wouldn't be too sure. She's no wrecker.'

Meaning I was! It was an ugly word to hear applied to oneself, but it was pointless to justify myself against the accusation. He was committed to his loyalties; I to mine, though the basis of mine was different from what he believed. No longer a passion of love, rather an obligation of love; maybe, I thought, akin to that a mother has for a child. But whether this was so or not, the stone of guilt hung round my neck, the thin scream in my head, condemned me of betrayal.

With no more words, all will to plead drained out of me, I turned away, walked through the broken archway towards the car. His footsteps dogged mine, but I assumed he was making for the Land-Rover and did not turn until I felt the hard pressure of his hands on my shoulders.

He towered above me, his lowered gaze one of brilliant burning intensity. 'I've hurt you and I've failed you. Given a free choice I'd have done neither. Equally, if you'd known what that choice involved, you might not have damned me.'

More mystifying that led me nowhere. I dumbly shook my head, tried to move out of his grasp, but he wouldn't let me go.

'Christy, must you do it, embark on a one-girl crusade, run the risk of breaking what's left of your heart? Christy, damn it, after all this time, can't you let go?'

For a second time I had a fleeting sensation of allegiances shifting, reforming, then it was gone.

'No,' I said, and walked towards the car.

I drove home via Bloxstead. At The Boatman Victor was at his post behind the cash register but there was no sign of Addy. 'Oh, dear!' he commiserated, 'you're never likely to find Miss Bray here on the first Thursday in the month. That's her day for going up to the London wholesalers. If you'd telephoned I could have saved you a journey.' He clucked sympathy, then consoled: 'But she'll be here to-morrow.'

My aim had been to shock the truth about that September night at Sweetcrab out of Addy by shooting at her the news of Cary's arrival in Berghmere. Now, because she wasn't there to shock, my assurance wavered. What if she'd had advance information and it was stale news? Because she hadn't run as far and as fast as I had, I was positive she'd been Cary's spy-on-the-spot. With Wellesley's sanction and contrivance or without it? I couldn't guess. But a revelation in myself preached comfort. Though love may perish, either in a dwindling death or by a spear-thrust to the heart by a man counting running seconds, solicitude lives on. If I cared, it followed that Addy must care.

Aunt Edith was aware I'd been to see Markham. As we sat down to lunch her patience snapped. 'Well, what did he have to say? What advice did he give you?'

'Advice,' I countered. 'I didn't go to ask his advice. I wanted his co-operation. I didn't get it. He wasn't prepared to admit anything.' Resentment allied to pain threatened my calm, and I only hung on to it by the skin of my teeth. It had been naïve of me to imagine he'd betray his kith and kin at my behest, yet naïve or not, I'd seen myself bursting through the fog of mystification into light. I'd seen him caring, but he hadn't, and my obstinate hope had turned into bitterness.

She preached: 'You'd do well to heed him.'

I was in no mood to listen to her eulogies of Markham Drake. 'All things to all men!' I said wearily. 'You and I see two different versions of Markham Drake.'

'If that's your belief you're even more foolish than I

thought.' She paused, her pale glance fiercely admonishing. 'Why do you suppose he's put himself to the trouble of coming to see an old woman once a week for the last year and a half?'

'To bring your pills and embrocation you'd have done better to get on prescription from Tim. And for the pleasure of your company! Hero worship is heady stuff, and he could never do a single thing wrong in your eyes.'

'He did once,' she said with a dour sadness. 'He married a girl without a heart.'

I stared, momentarily knocked off balance, before I corrected her. 'He married a fabulously beautiful girl from the jet set, with millions of dollars in her bank balance. A rare prize whom he worshipped. That they loved each other isn't open to doubt. What are you, some sort of Mother-Confessor to whom he opens his heart?'

She left the question unanswered. 'He came here once a week not to see me but to read your letters and postcards. To learn how you were faring and what was happening to you in America.'

Quite simply I didn't believe her. For once she was guilty of indulging to a fatuous degree in a dream of wish-fulfilment. 'Wouldn't it have been simpler,' I said lightly, 'if he'd made a note of my address, written to me?'

'I don't doubt he had a good reason for not doing so.'

A devious reason, I corrected silently as I got up to clear the first course. In imagination I heard telephone wires humming as Leightons and non-Leightons conspired to seal their secrets tighter away from me. Nerves twitching, hearts pounding, brains at full stretch – when all I wanted from them was an assurance that Cary had emerged from Sweetcrab, gone back to his offshore island where I would be no more than a fading nostalgic memory.

I thought: round them up in a bunch, hammer that fact into their heads? But they weren't there to round up: Markham was showing his brace of international lawyers round Holland Court, bullying them into releasing sufficient of Ophelia's fortune to transform it into a living Memorial to her; Addy was in London, Mrs Leighton in Switzerland, and until I was better armed, to approach Wellesley was to invite a repeat performance of Wednesday night. I was left with Hugo Trent. As a tied liegeman of Esmée Leighton I contemptuously dismissed him. Not an incriminating word would pass his lips without her permission.

Mentally I picked up the only card left to me. The police. I could spend my afternoon at Helsby police station. I had no difficulty in recalling the man who had interrogated me. Detective Chief-Inspector Braithwaite had a face best described as deadpan. It was impossible to imagine it reflecting emotion. His voice, even-toned and authoritative, matched, and his manner never deviated from impersonal courtesy. We'd parted company without my having the remotest idea whether or not he'd placed any credence in the statement I'd signed. If I'd had to hazard a guess, I'd have said that he'd kept an open mind as to whether by an awareness of a premeditation of violence in Cary when he left the Bird Hut, I'd been an accessory before the act of murder. But I didn't know, and he'd take good care I never did. The idea of laying before him a factual account of the hour I'd spent with Cary in the Bird Hut on Tuesday night both drew and repelled me.

The reason I didn't drive to Helsby police station that afternoon was due to the unannounced arrival on the doorstep of Miss Peabody. When I'd been in my early teens she'd been the spinster sister of the bachelor vicar, indefatigable in parish work. After her brother's demise, I hadn't a clue what had happened to her – probably because I'd never inquired. And there she was: wispy-thin, spry, cocky and as irrepressible as the sparrow she called to mind.

She clapped her kid-gloved hands together, carolled: 'Why, if it isn't little Christina!' and tripped past me into the hall, nodding her head so energetically that the birds' wings on her hat simulated flight. 'My faithful steed!' She pressed her hands together in a spasm of panic. 'It will be all right at the kerb? No one will steal it, will they?'

Her steed was an elderly Rover in mint condition. I wondered how many cushions she needed under her tiny frame to see over the wheel.

When I'd reassured her, she ran on with chirpy pride:

'I was sixty-two when I took my driving test, and passed the first time.' She paused for a round of applause, then rattled on: 'And where's your dear aunt? Oh the sad tales I've been hearing that she's failing! That's why I said to myself when I woke this morning: "Away with you, Emily, and cheer up the dear, sweet soul."'

Emily Peabody stayed to tea and on till after supper. She was both a compulsive talker and a super egotist who, embarked on her mission to cheer and entertain, did not spare herself. After her brother's death, she'd taken a post as secretary-companion to a widow in London with an itch for travel. There appeared to be no country in Europe and Northern Africa – except Andorra and that omission was shortly to be rectified – that the two intrepid old dears had not visited, no adventure or misadventure that hadn't befallen them. Now, on a fortnight's holiday while her employer had withdrawn into a Health Hydro, she'd come to gladden the hearts of old friends by a round of visits.

On any other occasion, I'd have found her gallant and amusing. On this particular afternoon my reaction to the unending flow of chat was sheer exhaustion. Being mobile and in full possession of sight and hearing, she had a tendency to patronize and pity Aunt Edith that reduced her hostess to curt monosyllables.

'I'll try and find time to come again,' she promised as I saw her into her car. 'I'm sure it did poor Edith a world of good to be taken out of herself.'

Made restless by the wasted afternoon and evening, exasperated because I couldn't be sure if Emily Peabody hadn't arrived I'd have used them to good effect, I prowled about my bedroom, hearing the familiar small sounds of Aunt Edith stirring in bed as she read her Bible. She'd have prayed for me – she always did, the cuckoo-child Fate had wished upon her. It was only half past ten and I was not yet acclimatized to early bed-time. Though there'd be plenty of lights sprinkled through the village, from the rear windows of South View the thick black velvet of the night was an unrelieved expanse of darkness.

No, there was a single pin-prick of light, like a grounded

star. Stationary at first, then moving side-ways in a zig-zag course and beginning, I thought, though at that distance I couldn't be sure, to move higher. A poacher, after wild duck or rabbits? Momentarily the star blinked out and when it re-appeared again it was quite definitely climbing steadily. Suspicion jumped, coalesced into certainty. It could only be the light from a torch being borne up the flight of steps that led from the mere to the Bird Hut.

Joy blazed, zooming me out of a dark pit into bright sun-light. I heard my extravagantly happy laugh of wondrous relief. Not dead. Alive, still hiding-out. Any one of five nights he'd said, and for some reason after I'd left – perhaps because in retrospect my pleas, my furious fears for him had made an impact – he'd decided not to use the first two.

In the few seconds I lingered by the window waiting for the light to die when it reached the Bird Hut, as it did, I experienced a lovely, unearthly sense of absolute tranquillity. Deadness, darkness, all the stains of the past were washed out of me. In my inner ear I heard the echo of a voice crying: 'Let go, Christy,' and the miracle was that I could. With Cary safe and alive, I could let go.

I'd been given a second chance.

CHAPTER FOURTEEN

My feet, made nimble as a goat's, did not skid or stumble; my muscles were tireless and my lungs did not complain at the breakneck speed of my progress. To gain a half-minute I took a diagonal short cut up the bank instead of going a few yards farther to the steps leading up from the quay. During a fleeting backward look my eye drew for me a rocking block of shadow the shape and size of Magnus's day cruiser moored at the far side of the dock. A few feet higher and it was gone; or more likely had never been there except in my imagination that had resurrected a sight that belonged to the past.

On the last upward lap no twig cracked beneath my feet, no bramble skimmed my cheek. The first sound I made was when I eased apart the latch of the door. The Bird Hut was dimmer than it had been on Tuesday night, the illumination provided, not by the pressure lamp but by the handsome old-fashioned funnel lamp with a cut-glass bowl of paraffin and a solid silver base that stood on the central table. I went deeper into the room, calling his name softly – for no logical reason, with the Bird Hut blacked out we could have let off sirens without anyone hearing us.

The door into the kitchenette was closed, but at floor-level there was a slit of light. I had nearly reached it when my foot kicked against the edge of the rug, and I stumbled. Automatically stooping to straighten it, I picked up a bright scrap of cloth that had been tucked under its edge: one of the tourist badges that had been plastered down the sleeve of Cary's anorak.

It was in my hand when the door opened. Wellesley stood framed in the brighter light from the pressure lamp in the kitchen, a towel pinned round his waist, a half-wrung, dripping cloth hanging from his hand, his appearance in such a garb as ludicrous as though he were decked out in fancy-dress. Behind him was a stack of cardboard cartons.

With the bounteous gift from a merciful providence snatched from me, disappointment was so killing that my mind seized up. I had lived through a lovely dream to wake and find myself pitched back into the void.

Wellesley was in little better shape, but he recovered quicker than I did. Eyeing me with hauteur and loathing, he pronounced: 'You're trespassing. You have no right to be here without my permission, which I do not give.'

I looked at the huge stack of cartons, proof that the cruiser was not a figment of imagination but necessary transport to convey them to the Bird Hut, the wet rag, the improvised apron. 'A grand spring-cleaning,' I speculated aloud, 'to wipe out of existence any fingerprints Cary left behind for the police to find.'

He came deeper into the room and in the golden glow his pallid cheeks had an unhealthy sheen of sweat. 'I'm in the process of stripping it bare. After I have sorted and packed my father's personal effects, they and the furniture will be collected by a haulage company and delivered to Sweetcrab. The windows and door will be boarded up to secure them from vandals and your old love-nest left to disintegrate at the whim of the elements. After Father's death it would have been a simpler and more effective operation to set fire to it, but my mother did not find that plan acceptable.'

The final destruction of what was to him polluted ground! He was savouring a wound to me which was not there. I cared nothing that board by board the Bird Hut would rot into dust.

I said: 'Are you prepared to give me an answer to the question I asked you last night: Where is Cary now?'

His stillness and silence were so total that a stranger might have judged him a deaf-mute who had not heard me, but I knew he was consulting the workings of the calculating machine in his head. When at last he did speak it was in his normal, suavely confident tone. 'If I understood you rightly your main concern was my brother's safety. At least that was what you professed. Well, I can set your mind at rest. Cary is safe.'

'Safe, or dead,' I queried softly and marvelled at the flat, passionless tone in which I spoke the most dreadful of all words. I unclasped my palm and smoothed out the fragment of cloth, on which was woven a flag and the name Istanbul. I wondered if in that long blank of time between us, Cary had been to Turkey, or whether he'd bought a second-hand anorak on which, when it was new, some travelling youth had proudly sewn the badges.

When he did not answer, I looked at it, then at him. 'On Tuesday night it was hanging by a thread from Cary's sleeve. It dropped off.'

He gave an unforced hearty laugh. 'You could have picked it up out of any gutter.'

'Maybe,' I conceded. 'But it'll be your word against mine.'

'I'm willing to settle for that.'

'It may not be so clear-cut. By the law of averages I can't have been the only one who saw him on Tuesday afternoon. The conductor on the train from London, ticket collectors at Liverpool Street and Helsby, waiters bringing round cups of coffee on the train, people sitting in the same carriage, one probably in the next seat to his. How many? Ten, twenty, thirty, but among them will certainly be one, maybe more than one, who will remember him even though he was disguised as a hippy, and wore dark glasses. I don't question that while you're sitting opposite him Chief Inspector Braithwaite will appear to accept your word, but once you're out of his office, he'll go to work. No stone unturned, no avenue unexplored. An undercover beaver-man, that's him.'

He smiled malice at me. 'The only fact he is likely to turn up under a stone is that Christina Graham picked up a hitch-hiker on the Back Road, directed him to the Bird Hut and made an assignation with him for later that night. Which, I may say, would surprise no one who knew her.'

'He's more likely to get in touch with the Malta police, forward them a photograph of Cary Leighton, ask them to investigate a rumour that until a week ago an Englishman answering to his description was employed by the owner of a small boat-yard in Gozo.'

He lifted his hand to strike me, but it was a purely reflex

action, and he dropped it, but the fury that contorted his face was more terrifying than the threat of physical assault. 'You lied.' For a moment he looked demented, words jamming in his throat that fought to get free but couldn't.

'I never said I didn't know where he'd been living. I merely didn't choose to tell you.' I scoffed: 'Who would!'

'Gozo!' His voice was so hoarse and ugly it was barely recognizable. 'He swore he'd spoken to no one, had not been recognized by anyone, had not divulged to a living soul that he was coming to Sweetcrab.' He closed his eyes to wipe out the noxious sight of me and to concentrate on a memory of deceit that was two nights old, recited: 'He stood and denied separately and categorically every question I asked him, was hurt to the quick when I accused him of planting you as his accomplice. He hadn't seen you; he had no wish to see you. If you met accidentally in the street he doubted whether you'd recognize one another. He'd long ago ceased to think of you.' His lids parted. 'Yet, he'd come straight to Sweetcrab from your arms. He'd either confided in you where he was living, or you already knew. It makes no difference which.' He gave a sudden laugh of mirthless relish. 'Your lover-boy disowned you. Why don't you follow his example? Dead or alive he's worthless to you or anyone else.'

Cary was dead. The last breath had been driven from his body during the interval between my craven flight from the Bird Hut and waking next morning in my bed with a deadweight of guilt built into my heart that had been his final communication to me.

I whispered: 'Why did you kill him?'

He shrugged his heavy shoulders callously. 'The short answer is that I was not prepared to exist for the remainder of my life with a blackmailer hung round my neck.' He adopted a tone of persuasive reasonableness. 'A blackmailer's appetite for money is like a cancer-growth that by its very nature increases in size. Cary left Sweetcrab with sufficient money to maintain him until he had procured a new passport, established his identity. That accomplished, I was to make further funds available to him at specified intervals. I honoured my promise until his demands became so exorbitant I was no longer prepared, even in a position, to meet them. Preposterous demands!' He went silent, absorbed in doing astronomical sums in his head.

'Why force him to come and beg in person? Did you want him arrested? Was that the prize you were playing for?'

'No.' His look was a scathing denunciation of my stupidity. 'I'd hardly welcome that. He had a small talent for acting, so that risk was minimal. The reason I was compelled to force him to come to Sweetcrab was that he never disclosed to me an address that wasn't obsolete by the time either I or anyone else could reach it. If, as you say, he's been living in Gozo, it's news to me. The letters I have received from him during the past two months have been posted in Rome, where he must have paid some petty accomplice, the address for reply one at which he warned me I wouldn't be able to find him. What he called a necessary precaution in case letters went astray or were intercepted. Gozo!' he jeered. 'More than likely he picked the name out of his head. A lie. That's his natural medium of communication, lies.' He banged the table with his fist. 'His sole aim was to bleed me white, live like a lord on my money.'

Cary had lied himself into his grave. An admission that one named person in Berghmere knew beyond doubt he'd gone to Sweetcrab that night and Wellesley's murder plan would have been laid in ruins. He'd chosen to lie; I'd chosen to run away, and so he'd died. Mindless, compulsive grief rolled over me in giant, thundering waves. For an interval they blotted out of sight a man who revolted me, and when my vision cleared, I saw that Wellesley's mouth was shaped in a horrible patronizing smile.

I said with loathing so intense it made me feel sick: 'You killed him in cold blood. And after he was dead, what did you do, dig a hole in the earth and bury him?'

'There was no need for any such physical exertion.' He crossed the room, pulled the curtains wide, so that the great star-shaped crack glimmered against the blackness. 'There was a grave ready and waiting: the mere.' He continued as though he honestly wished to reassure me, obscenely provide me with comfort: 'It was a simple, relatively painless operation. A blow to the skull with what the police term a blunt instrument when his back was turned and he was insensible to any fact but that I'd trebled his allowance and was about to hand over Father's diamonds. You could truthfully say, he died happy, as happy as he was ever likely to be.'

Cary's last journey from Sweetcrab had been short: carried or dragged through the french window of the morning-room in which Addy had taught four little girls to read and trace maps of England, down the strip of lawn to the stone steps, the lowest under water, tipped into one of the boats, dropped weighted into the mere. There was no room in me for hate or vengeance, only for overwhelming grief.

It was Wellesley's voice, adopting a high moral tone that called me back. 'It would be futile at this late stage to upset yourself. Anyone with your true welfare at heart would counsel that you are well rid of him. It was a singularly ill-fated relationship which brought out the worst in both of you. But for your reckless encouragement the family row that culminated in Father's tragic death would not have happened. However, that is not a point I wish to labour. You're still young enough to build a new life for yourself.'

Hate was a red mist in my head; I had to shout through it. 'It's not swept under the carpet yet. All right, Cary was putting on pressure for more money, the diamonds. Yes, blackmailing you, if you like. But what was his threat if you didn't pay up?' I had to pause to catch my breath. 'Six of you round your father's corpse, swearing an oath of silence, secretly conspiring during the dead of night. Conspiring what?'

'Somewhat melodramatically phrased, but a fair enough description. I presume you asked Cary that very same question. And from your behaviour last night and again to-night, it is obvious that he didn't confide in you. Didn't, in fact, trust you.'

He left the window, came with slow, ponderous deliberation to the table, gave me one of his bland glances that told me he counted all danger past. He spoke reasonably, like a man with an easy conscience. 'I'll barter my answer for your promise not to go to the police.'

'Make a bargain with the devil!' Someone laughed and it could only have been me.

He looked musingly at his well-manicured, plumpish hands that rested on the table, then directed at me one of his suave, tongue-in-the-cheek, boardroom glances. 'On further reflection there is no call for a bargain between us. I am prepared to admit that in a crisis we were guilty of an error of judgment. Hindsight suggests it would have been wiser, indeed safer, to have sealed seven pairs of lips instead of six. At the time Markham pleaded vehemently for that to be done, but my mother refused to countenance the idea. She argued that the nature of your relationship with Cary automatically rendered you suspect, untrustworthy. And naturally, with my father lying dead, her wishes were sacrosanct. Cary made some protest, but I don't recall that it was unduly prolonged. Then, when she heard you were returning to Berghmere, she became distraught. It was almost as if she had a premonition that you would ferret out the truth. Because none of us dare be certain that you and Cary hadn't been in touch, she counted you as the greatest danger to which we were exposed. Separately she begged, demanded would be a better word, each of us to renew our promise of silence. We gave it to her.' For a moment, while his thoughts had strayed backward in time, his glance had left me. Now it returned, brimming with relish at the knife-edged suspense in which he'd kept me. 'I propose to remedy the error of judgment we made the night my father was murdered. It wasn't Cary who fired the gun. It was Hester.'

Shocked through with cold, sickening dismay, I still managed to shout a protest: 'But he said . . .'

He cut me off with a peremptory gesture of his hand that commanded silence. 'I'd be obliged if you would not interrupt. I find it extremely painful to recount what happened that night. Hester woke, after Mother and Addy were in bed, overheard Father and Cary quarrelling violently in the library. She crept downstairs and after, presumably, listening at the door, she burst in. According to Cary, Father, who had his back to the door, was ordering him out of the house, forbidding him to return. Before either of them realized what she was about, Hester had wrenched open the drawer of Father's desk, snatched the revolver, was waving it wildly in his face, screaming that if he didn't stop being angry with Cary she'd shoot him.'

His voice stopped dead and his face went motionless under a tyranny of memory. 'Before they could wrest the gun from her, she'd somehow released the safety-catch. She fired it, and Father died instantly.'

With a visible effort, he shook off the trauma, continued in a curious stilted voice: 'We were immediately presented with a problem of mammoth proportions, one that must be solved before daylight. Cary was the instrument of Father's death. He never, to do him justice, sought to deny that. But it was Hester who had fired the gun. By seven o'clock, when Addy normally came downstairs, we had to decide who should pay the price for my father's murder. We stood, literally, on the edge of an abyss: one false step and we should all perish.

'The revolver had been fired at too long range to lend support to a theory of suicide. For a while, after Hester had been put under sedatives, we worked on the presumption that we could put into action the solution Cary proposed without soliciting help from outsiders. It soon became clear this was a false hope. None of us could risk being seen leaving the house. If the police were to be led to assume for even a short interval that Cary was still somewhere in the immediate neighbourhood, his car must remain in the garage. Yet to have a minimal chance of escaping from the country before the police mounted a full-scale murder hunt, it was essential that he should be clear of the country, well on his way to London airport before seven o'clock. Our first need was a car and a driver bound to secrecy. My mother's choice was Hugo. He came instantly in answer to her telephone call, and his behaviour throughout was magnificent, one of unfaltering loyalty. Ideally, Hugo should have driven Cary to London airport, but that involved a risk of Hugo being seen returning home by someone who might later recall that fact, report it to the police once their inquiries were publicized in the Press. My mother would not countenance Hugo taking such a risk. Ultimately it was decided that he should drive Cary to

Colchester where he could catch an early workmen's train to London. This would allow Hugo time to reach home, garage his car, before we called the police. Either he misunderstood, forgot what had been arranged or his anxiety for Mother was so tormenting that he could not restrain himself from returning to Sweetcrab. He arrived barely ten minutes ahead of Helsby police. However, it was a lapse on his part that had no unfortunate consequences.

'We had a second desperate need: a substantial sum of cash to cover Cary's initial requirements, more than we could muster, even pooling our resources.' He pursed his lips in sardonic amazement. 'Strange as it may seem, no one gave a thought to the diamonds! You must understand that we were all in a state of shock, under pressures that made rational judgment nigh impossible. We had to work out intricate calculations of time, weigh one risk against another, make decisions that we distrusted as soon as we'd taken them. There was no safe ground within our reach, no step we could take and be positive it wouldn't lead us to ruin. No one who wasn't there could conceive what we endured and suffered that night . . .'

I thought he was going to weep, but he stood there grey-faced and stricken, his eyes dry, cornered, a confession wrung from him that in a crisis he'd panicked and lost his head. He put his hand to his upper lip to steady it, went on: 'We called Markham, asked him for money, and he brought along all he had in the safe at Holland Court . . .' Nearing the end of the hideous memories he'd been compelled to resurrect, his voice dragged. 'After Cary had gone . . . there was the waiting . . . no surety . . . nothing . . . not a thread of hope that might not, when tested, fray and split. In that purgatory Markham was a comfort to my mother, who was terrified that, no matter what we did, the truth would be revealed.' He sighed, finished: 'He was her salvation.'

'Cary was your salvation, your mother's and Hester's. He saved you all.'

Force returned to his voice. 'From the consequences of a murder for which he alone was responsible. He was guilty of inciting a child to fire a gun, but a child who was twenty years old, who would almost certainly have been declared unfit to plead, would never have been charged, but just as certainly taken from home, examined by psychiatrists who might have advised treatment involving some form of restrictive custody. My father's murderer had to be named . . . she would have been branded for life. My mother would have preferred to see her dead.' His smile was tired, but untouched by penitence. 'Yes, Christina, there was a conspiracy of silence, a silence six of us solemnly swore never to break, but it was a conspiracy of love.'

'Cary's love for Hester.'

'What Cary did, he did voluntarily. He was put under no compulsion, no pressure of any kind. The suggestion came from him, and once offered and accepted he behaved as though he were setting out on some high adventure.' His smile turned sour. 'But then he had us on our knees, where he'd always wanted us. We were grateful to him. I imagine we showed and spoke our gratitude. But with no appreciative audience to extol his self-sacrifice, it began to pall. It was characteristic that he should delude himself that he'd received too meagre a return for his self-martyrdom, turn to blackmail.'

'He asked you for money you'd never have missed. You kept him on a shoe-string!'

'That's a matter of opinion. I've explained that I was not prepared, on the brink of a political career, to put myself at the mercy of a man who had proved himself dishonourable, ready, if I refused to pay his price, to break a solemn promise he'd made beside his father's dead body. That was the pressure he put on me, the threat he made. A threat not only to me but to my mother and sister. Neither of them was safe as long as he lived.'

'There's someone else who knew Cary was coming back to Sweetcrab. Hester.'

He made a dismissive gesture. 'A child's dream. Mercifully her sub-conscious blotted out all recent memories of Father . . . probably the effect of the treatment she underwent afterwards. She accepted with no visible distress that he was dead without recalling the manner of his death. When she talked of him it was in relation to incidents that had occurred years ago. No. she couldn't have known.'

'But she did. She told me on two different occasions that Cary was coming back. She must have eavesdropped or found a letter.'

'Eavesdropped! Impossible. I confided to no one that Cary was coming back to Sweetcrab. A letter . . .' A tremor of uncertainty struck his face. 'I burnt the letters I received from him.'

'All of them, immediately you'd read them?'

He frowned in concentration. 'I kept one, the last short one, which was locked in a drawer in my desk for a few hours.'

'She got busy with a hairpin or a nail file! Didn't you know Hester is an expert lock-picker? Even if he didn't sign his name she would have recognized the handwriting.'

'No matter,' he said shortly. 'She'll forget. Every scrap of evidence that Cary and I were ever in communication has been destroyed.' The black pages read and turned over, he set about delivering a terse epilogue. 'The best advice I can give you, Christina, now there are no more mysteries for you to solve, is to cease harrowing yourself with a tragedy that is now irrevocable. We have never, I think you will agree, had a high regard for one another. Nevertheless, I do you the justice of believing that you will not wilfully lay Hester's life and my mother's in ruins for no good purpose.'

A wrecker, Markham had called me on the turn-around by the Abbey ruins. Some straying wisp of mind that remained unnumbed calculated the difference it would have made if there had been seven conspirators instead of six. I would not have been lost for years in a limbo-land; I'd never have become a demented woman who pursued strange men round street corners; there'd have been no blank sheets in my head on which to draw guessing pictures; no black tormenting distrust when I came back to Berghmere.

I looked up but he'd been so confident of my co-operation that he hadn't waited for an answer. He'd gone into the kitchen to fetch newspaper and two cartons which with a businesslike air he put on the table and began to pack with small objects.

'Who else knew you were plotting to kill him?'

He answered with pompous dignity that on any other occasion would have been ludicrous. 'I neither sought nor required anyone's co-operation in protecting the well-being of my mother and sister. I involved no one in the measures I was forced to take. My mother can continue to believe that somewhere her younger son is living out his life in reasonable comfort, safe from arrest and a prison sentence. Addy, Markham, Hugo, each of them had borne enough. I had not the right, certainly not the wish, to ask more of them.'

I cried in savage outrage: 'Since the night Magnus died, you've cold-bloodedly planned Cary's death, been niggardly with money to drive him into a trap you baited with diamonds.'

Naked, shameless fury struck him, spread a terrible purplish colour over his pale cheeks, proclaimed him a man who'd lost not only his temper but his reason. 'You dare to sit in judgment on me, to threaten . . .' He lunged across the table to seize and shake me, but his hand in its violent thrashing toppled the lamp and in the flash of a second a curtain of fire roared up between us. He screamed, beat at it with his hands and in doing so bathed them in the spreading paraffin, setting fire to his fingers.

The explosion of leaping flame was so instantaneous it left no space for shock to strike. A single word of command flew from my brain to my hands: smother. I dragged frantically at the rug, but one side of it was wedged under the heavy hand-hewn table. A second passed, perhaps two, before I relinquished my hold, flung my body on the plunging, pain-maddened man on fire. I had forced him half-way to the floor before, with a giant's strength, he flicked me off, and lunging, turned over the table, and toppled the cartons and newspapers to fuel the galloping flames.

I grabbed the mohair rug from the divan, but it was too light, and as soon as I flung it round him, it burst into orange-red licking tongues of devouring fire. As I wrenched off my suède jacket, pools of flame were multiplying round my feet, clawing greedily towards the cedar walls. But the horror-creature I tried to capture fought me off with maniacal strength, threw me in a sprawling heap among the fast multiplying little fires. Disconnected snippets of fire-drill flew in and out of my mind. Deny it oxygen . . . but it was too late. Surely outside, where the earth was damp, lay the only hope of escape. Half-blinded by smoke, I jumped over the snaking orange rivulets to the door, flung it open, shouted, but the sound of his name was lost in the crackle and snap of wood, the high ceaseless screaming of the human torch who arms outstretched, had turned into a cross of fire, wreathed in flames that were devouring him alive. I was no more than a foot behind him when he flung himself through the window into the night sky. There was a thunder crack of glass bursting asunder, then a bell-like tinkle of small delicate fragments falling.

I clambered through the jagged hole, insensitive as though anaesthetized to the slashes on my hands and arms, fell against a sapling, and as I struggled, reeling to my feet, automatically with burnt fingers pinched out the candle flames that were eating into my jersey.

I tumbled, sometimes upright, sometimes on all fours like an animal, down the steps, calling his name. When I reached the dock there was no one there, either dead or alive, no flames, no screams, no sound but the screech of birds and duck in panic flight over the mere that was made as light as day from the monster bonfire of the Bird Hut.

CHAPTER FIFTEEN

Harris, the gardener from Sweetcrab, who had been alerted to action by the sight of tree-tops on fire, an unnatural night sunset-glow in the sky, came leaping down the steps to find me crouched on the edge of the dock, my hands dragging the water in a futile effort to reach the black body with milk-white hands and face that glimmered under four feet of water.

Through the salt of blood and tears on my tongue, I moaned: 'I can't lift him. I can't get him out.'

He whipped off his jacket, wrapped it round my shoulders, heaved me to my feet, and propped me up on the lowest step. 'You leave everything to me, Miss. The fire engine is on the way. They're quick off the mark those fellows and as soon as they get here they'll send out a radio call for the police and ambulance. Ah, that's them now. Anybody else up there besides you and Mr Wellesley?' I shook my head.

I sat, emptied of all feeling, even the elementary one of being alive, and watched as though I were a spectator from outer space the firemen lift Wellesley's body out of the mere, lay it dripping on the dock. Under powerful lamps they set about their work of resuscitation. When they failed they took a couple of clean, red groundsheets and reverently and tidily made him into a parcel.

Inspector Braithwaite firmly, but with no force, using the most effective grip to haul a shocked woman to her feet, set me upright.

'We're going to get you to hospital.' he said in a voice that rang as familiarly in my ear as though we'd talked the day before. 'But I'm afraid the ambulance can't get nearer than the road. Do you think, if you hold on to me, you can make it, or shall I get a couple of firemen to bring a stretcher?'

'I can make it. But I don't need to go to hospital. If you

could send me home in a car.'

'Hospital's better; it looks to me as though you may need a few stitches in that arm. Oh, don't worry about your aunt, I'll contact her, reassure her that you've suffered no serious injury.'

We climbed the steps and when we reached the top I saw the roof of the Bird Hut had fallen in. Two firemen were playing hoses on black bubbling uprights of timber, charred unrecognizable lumps that had once been furniture, and pockets of hot sparking ash. Wellesley's desire to see it fired, burned to the ground had been granted posthumously at the cost of his life.

In the Casualty Department of Helsby General they were having a slack night. They stitched my arm, bathed and bound up my superficial cuts and burns. A young nurse was outspokenly dismayed by my singed hair. 'What a mess,' she condoled, 'all frizzled. You'll have to have a big chunk cut off, but best leave it to the hairdresser, eh? Give you a chance to try a new style.'

When they'd finished their clean-up job, given me a cup of tea, the Casualty Officer, a ginger-haired, baby-faced young doctor, asked: 'Now, what to do with you? We can keep you here for the night, give you a couple of pills that will put you to sleep for eight hours and I can hand that prowling policeman outside his marching orders. Or, if you prefer it, you can see him for ten minutes before you hop into bed. It's up to you.'

'I'd rather see him, and then I'd like to go home . . .' Somewhere a long way off there was a singing echo of a voice exclaiming: 'What a girl you are for wanting to go home!'

He wrinkled his snub nose. 'Don't advise that. You've had a pretty severe shock; there could be a delayed reaction. Have you got somebody responsible to look after you? And I don't mean a girl-friend or a boy-friend for that matter. A nice, cosy mum?'

That he didn't know me, that I was just some girl who'd landed in Casualty cut about and scorched by a fire, sent a steadying current through my veins. At that moment in time it was comforting not to be known.

'I live with my aunt, and she's the soul of responsibility. But could I have a few minutes alone before I see Inspector Braithwaite?'

'Sure, all the time you want. Let Nurse Bates know when you're ready.' Going out of the cubicle he winked. Illogically, that helped too.

With a policeman in attendance to take down every word I said, Chief Inspector Braithwaite sat facing me across a table. His manner was precisely the same as on the other occasion when he'd interrogated me. He used no pressure when I faltered, corrected myself and had to backtrack. Patient as Justice itself, his theory was that you'd only to let anyone talk long enough and they'd get so tied up in deceit that the truth would fall out of their lips.

Well versed in his working methods, I wasn't surprised that he asked me no questions. 'Thank you, Miss Graham. I'm sorry to have had to detain you after the ordeal you've been through but, as I'm sure you appreciate, I had to get the basic facts on record as soon as possible. We can leave the rest till the morning. I hope you'll feel better after a night's rest.'

When he opened the door of the office-room that had been loaned to him, immediately facing me, I saw three figures spread out in a frieze along the wall. Aunt Edith sitting in a chair, with Markham standing on one side of her, Tim on the other: the people whom I'd promised the casualty officer would take care of me. As they would.

The mild sedation under which Tim kept me had the effect of reshaping emotional levels, repressing the deepest, emphasizing the superficial: I worried more about the extra work I caused Aunt Edith than what I'd put into my statement to Chief Inspector Braithwaite, my evidence at the inquest. Another effect was that in conversation I'd become a mental cripple. What I intended to say lost itself on the way from my brain to my tongue, and to be certain I would not limp into silence I had to resort to short, simple sentences.

Each evening Markham came to South View. I watched

for his arrival and when he'd gone waited for the next day when he'd come again, not anxiously or fretfully, the fact that he would be there as laid down in the pattern of events as sun-rise next morning.

It was on the evening of the sixth day that he said: 'There's someone waiting in the car outside who'd like to see you. Aunt Esmée. But you don't have to see her if you'd rather not. Say no if it would upset you. I've not committed you beyond promising to ask you if you would. She's flying back to Switzerland tomorrow, so she won't come again.' He repeated: 'You don't have to see her, Christy.'

'If she wants to see me, of course I'll see her.'

He brought her to the door, closed it on us.

The first thing that hit me was that instead of her smart new clothes she was wearing a coat I remembered, a black and white check tweed that must have been ten years old – she'd worn it one Saturday afternoon when she'd taken Hester and me to see *The Sound of Music* in Norwich. I was still incapable of any positive strong emotion, but a shadow of feeling stirred, and I was able to meet her glance that immediately veered away from me.

She looked more dead than alive, her face not white but a yellowy-grey, her lips compressed and marked as though she'd held them steady under her teeth for days, and her eyes sunk back deeper into her head. Quickly I pulled a chair nearer to her.

'Thank you, Christina, it is good of you to see me, but I'd prefer to stand. What I have to say won't take long. Also, I have a great many matters to arrange and settle before I leave Sweetcrab in the morning. I shan't be coming back. The house will be put up for sale.'

Since she stood, I had to stand too, and in the cramped room we were forced within a foot of one another. I saw her breast rise and fall, a pulse throb in her throat, and remembered a fact I should not have forgotten: Wellesley had been buried that afternoon. Divers and grab-hooks had failed to reclaim Cary's body from the bottomless depths of the mere.

She spoke stiffly, as one performing a cruel duty imposed

on her by fate, looking at me, but in a way that suggested visually she held me at a distance. 'I wish to thank you for protecting Hester. For not revealing to the police what we guarded with our lives, that technically Hester was guilty of murdering her father.'

I'd been under no compulsion to lie. Chief Inspector Braithwaite had concentrated all his formidable resources on the investigation of a current murder and an accidental death. Granted, both constituted a sequel to an earlier murder, but neither had led him to question his iron-hard, unchallenged belief that Cary, guilty of his father's murder, had flown the country.

He and the coroner had learned from me that Cary had travelled to Sweetcrab for the purpose of exacting from Wellesley money and a collection of diamonds that had belonged to their father. Wellesley had not been prepared to concede to his demands. There'd followed arguments, succeeded by violence which had culminated in Cary's death. I withheld no fact relating to any meeting with Cary on the Back Road, my two visits to the Bird Hut except one poignant truth: the name of the owner of the hand that had fired the bullet into Magnus's heart.

'It was an act of mercy that we . . .' she corrected herself: 'That I had no right to expect from you. I'm grateful.'

In my lame speech I stated the obvious. 'They were both dead. In different ways each of them died to protect her.'

She stared, slack-lipped, blank-eyed into space as though she were seeing the two hideous deaths that had been meted out to her sons, the news of which had been broken to her by Markham when he'd met her at Heathrow. I reached and found the only comfort it was within my power to offer her. 'Wellesley described it as a conspiracy of love.'

'Which Cary would have kept. He would never have withdrawn the gift he gave to Hester. Wellesley misjudged him.' She shook her head as though the anguish in her voice offended her, steadied it to stoical calm. 'But I did not come here to discuss any aspect of the past. That is irrevocable. But to thank you on Hester's behalf and my own.'

'How is she?'

'She's well.' A shadow of a shadow of that old look of love touched her face. 'She knows nothing. Nor ever will, I pray. I left her with Anna ski-ing on the nursery slopes. Naturally, we shall remain abroad, probably in Switzerland. I've recently heard of a specialist at a clinic in Geneva who has had considerable success in treating patients with her condition. After we leave the chalet, I shall take an apartment, and for the time being Anna has promised to remain with us.'

Her glance flicked against my face, left it. 'Thank you for seeing me. Now if you will excuse me . . . I have a great deal to do before the morning.'

She didn't hold out her hand in what would have been a meaningless formality. The right words to express compassion, understanding were in my head, but I couldn't get them on my tongue. In the second before she turned to the door, I leaned forward and so lightly that I barely touched it, I kissed her cheek.

She gave me a look that seemed to come from the other side of an abyss of sadness. 'You must hold me guilty for my lack of trust both when my husband was murdered and when you came back to Berghmere. But how could I be sure that, passionately in love with Cary, you would stay silent while he sacrificed himself and your life together for Hester? Rightly or wrongly I judged that the temptation to clear his name at the expense of hers would be irresistible.' She seemed to debate with herself for a moment and then she said something I'd never expected to hear from her lips, simply, her heart behind it: 'I wish you well, Christina. I hope happiness comes to you. Goodbye.'

It was three weeks later on the way back from London that I saw Addy at Norwich station waiting for the bus-train to Helsby. She was some way up the platform and hadn't seen me, so I was free to stare. She was dressed in a navy reefer jacket over a cream skirt, her glowing hair freshly set. Her self-confident carriage, severe elegance, plus her air of being a woman who not only knew exactly where she was going, but found the going and the destination to her liking, caught and held quite a few speculative glances.

I let her get in the train ahead of me, then on an impulse sat down beside her. Her glance contained so little surprise, that I suspected she had, after all, seen me first.

She looked me over with almost clinical detachment. 'I'm glad to see you're better. It was a mercy you weren't more seriously injured.' She cleared her throat. 'Markham came to see me the day after it happened. I suppose he told you?'

'Yes.' It had been my suggestion: a debt owing to her.

Spring was firmly established now, hedges pricking with green, and all the primroses you could wish to see crowding together on the railway embankments. For a while she appeared to concentrate on the scenery, then with a quick twist of the head, she faced me. 'You've a right to know that I lied to you the day you came to the shop. Cary did write to me, four letters, the replies to be sent to Christopher Lawton at four different addresses. I received the last six months ago.' Her glance was sardonic, but her bitterness had not endured beyond the grave. 'You've no reason to feel jealous. I was simply his window on Berghmere, a slit window with a limited view. They all begin "Dear Addy" and end, "Yours C." If you'd like to have them, I'll give them to you.'

I thanked her and refused the offer.

Her glance, uncharacteristically uncertain, flicked across my face. When she'd made her decision, it cleared and she lowered her voice to an undertone though the seats facing us were empty. 'Once, just once in a life-time, he was offered the part he'd always yearned to play: top dog, the rôle of hero in an epic of self-sacrifice. He rose to the occasion as naturally and as single-mindedly as if his whole life had been a preparation for that moment. His faults and weaknesses fell away and he was strong enough to scale a height better men than he would never have attempted.' She sighed. 'But he couldn't stay there. He was starved of tribute, of gratitude and love for the sacrifice he'd made, and to get them he had to come back to Sweetcrab. It wasn't diamonds and money that drew him but reassurance that they'd not forgotten what he'd given them.' She flashed me an inquiring look, finished in a voice roughened with embarrassment: 'I thought that might be a comfort to you.'

'It is,' I said, though I'd worked it out for myself.

She resumed her normal brisk tone. 'Ah, well, now Sweetcrab's up for sale and the Leighton era is at an end. But I suppose you know all about it?'

'Yes, Mrs Leighton came to see me before she left.'

There was a querying look in her eye, a question hovering on her tongue but with the tact of which she was sometimes capable she suppressed it.

For the rest of the short journey we talked about her shop, the plans she was working on for an extension. Before the end of the year she hoped to secure the lease of the adjoining premises and by next season open it as a coffee and sandwich bar. It was difficult to equate the energetic resourceful business woman with the secretly love-sick girl who had spent her days fitting into someone else's formula for living. Released now, finally and for ever . . . forging ahead with vigour, Addy coming out top. I thought how mysterious were other people's lives and joked that she'd end up as mayor of Bloxstead.

'Why not! They could do with a few more women on the council.'

She had lowered her guard, taken me into her confidence; it spelled a lack of warmth in me, even a discourtesy, that I could not reciprocate by confiding to her an outline of my future, but it was a shortcoming I could not remedy.

When we stepped out of the train she inquired if I was being met or if I'd like a lift in the car she had parked in the station yard. I told her I was being met.

'Good!' she said as if she meant it, and her smile before she hurried towards the barrier was somehow final, as though she never expected to see me again.

He was waiting for me. In the second before he found me in the crowd, I saw his doubt, a grinding anxiety that revealed weakness where I'd believed none existed. He'd not been certain I'd come back. I'd known that I should, but no fact beyond that. Despite my visit to London my future was still a book of blank pages.

In the car he said: 'The builders moved out yesterday. I thought maybe you'd like to see the house. I warned Miss

Graham that we might go there first so she won't be worried if we don't arrive on time. How do you feel?'

The unexpectedness of the proposal, bringing the moment of commitment nearer roused a dread that I should fail him, that we should before the day's close arrive at a dismal end – not because I did not know my own mind but because I could never fully disclose that mind to him.

'Yes, I'd love to see it. How is she?'

'In good form. Qualified praise for Mary Dennet and the child, decidedly less for the hearing-aid. But when I looked in last night at least she was wearing it, probably because Tim and Dr Sessler have made a concerted attack to extract a promise she'll give it a fair trial.'

The Home Farm that I remembered as a gaunt, dilapidated Victorian dwelling, hedged about by a conglomeration of assorted farm buildings was virtually unrecognizable. Sash windows replaced the mean little casements, the rickety porch over the door had been ripped out, a new wing added, and the farm buildings demolished to provide a courtyard and garages. The whole, with its harshly discordant range of bricks, had been painted a gleaming white.

'There's still the garden to be laid-out,' he said quickly, as though I'd be put off by the heaps of builders' rubble through which we had to pick our way to the front door. 'And there's a foul stink of paint inside.'

He was so anxious, keyed-up, that I smiled up at him. He did not smile back, but slanted his head so that I had no more than a glimpse of what could have been longing or a simple desire to have the decision made and behind him. 'Who's being impatient now! Wave a wand and not only a brand new house, but roses blooming and a velvet lawn. I know instant gardens aren't on the market if you don't!'

Slotting the key into the door, he said defensively, feeling himself on trial and not liking it: 'It's my first venture in house-building.'

It might have been a house in which no one had ever lived, sprung new from the ground, shadows and sunlight sharing the expanses of the clean empty walls. Each room was no more than a shape filled by space until we reached the kitchen.

I stood on the threshold and laughed aloud. 'What could you know about refrigerators, free-standing units, dish-washers and food-mixers?'

He laughed back, the lovely glow in him released, so that he stood magnificent by my side and I thought, until he was an old man women would covet him. 'Precisely nothing. And when you know nothing, you buy advice from an expert: David Mason, an architect. I drew a sketch on the back of an envelope and he took over from there, rubbing his hands with glee at having a kitchen to plan without a woman breathing down his neck.'

'He doesn't appear to have left much out. All you need to make it perfect is Flossie snoozing around the place. Will you bring her?'

'I will if you don't object.'

With a jolt we were where I didn't want to be. I walked ahead of him into the big living-room that ran through the length of the house. There was a built-in semi-circular window-seat overlooking the rear garden that was reduced to a waste of desolation by mounds of sand and bricks, assorted lengths of piping, and an abandoned concrete mixer.

He sat down beside me. 'I made a resolution not to ask you today, to give you time, all the time in the world. Do you want to wipe the slate clean, forget what I said?'

I shook my head, but I couldn't look at him. He needed me; I needed him. I knew that, what I didn't know was whether sheer need was enough. Was I being greedy, asking for the sun and the moon and the stars to drop into my lap, to have nothing left to wish for ever again?'

He asked with reserve: 'How did it go in London?'

'Very well. Sue's on the brink of getting engaged to Jerry, or I think she is. And I had lunch with Gordon; he's raring to go.'

But not without me to iron out the creases. He had been coldly and fearsomely incensed at the possibility of my defection. 'For God's sake, Christy, you must know one way or the other! I'll grant you one week, no more, to make up your mind.'

But it would be made up today. I'd come to the end of stalling.

As if to sit still was unbearable, he got to his feet, walked with powerful swift strides to the window at the other end of the long room. 'Is it too soon?'

'No.' Time had played tricks; it might have been a year since I'd spent that hour with Cary in the Bird Hut.

'Then what?' he insisted.

The ghost of a woman so pale and perfect that I lacked courage to compete against her. Aunt Edith had declared she'd had a cold heart – but she'd spoken from prejudice not proof. If Ophelia had possessed a flaw, I knew I'd never learn it from him. Loyalty was bred into his bones.

He'd come back to my side while my mind had been silently debating. 'Is it so impossible? Can't you believe I'll make you happy? But I will.' He caught his breath with a kind of fierceness. 'There are damned few things in this life of which you can be certain, back against all odds. They're rare, precious, not to be lost. It's in me, I swear it is, the power to make you happy; it's part of loving you.'

He was fighting a battle he'd no need to win. I was not concerned with my happiness, but with his. I was a woman whom he desired, whom it could cost him pain to lose. But a second choice. Looking into the ruined garden, I contemplated the long road I'd travelled to this place, this time, this man that joined together in an empty house ready to be transformed into a home, surrounded by derelict spoiled earth waiting to be planted with shrubs and flowers. If I'd been like Liz, uncomplicated and good, no greed in me, the decision would have been made.

He sat down on the window-seat, took both my hands into his. 'Christy, I must know. I've a right to know. Is marriage to me an act you can't bear to contemplate? Is it as simple as that?'

I gazed into his strong, powerful face, saw it strained, with a look of desolation and loss barely held beneath the surface. 'It's that you can't prove what doesn't yet exist . . . the future.'

He looked puzzled. 'Why should you want to? It's there, my love, waiting for us to discover, to live and to cherish.'

If fear and jealousy hounded me to renounce what he offered, if I became a victim of my demeaning little sins that were reverberations from the past, I wouldn't pay a farthing for a future that was as dry and colourless as a desert.

He lifted my chin, forced my eyes to meet him and I became aware of a new deep knowingness in his blue gaze. 'I could be bedevilled by doubts too; I could be afraid. But I'm not.' He gave a whisper of a laugh that mocked himself. 'Maybe I've too much self-conceit. Be that as it may, I am sure. I have been since the Sunday by the windmill. There you were, sprung out of the earth, waiting for me. Or, that's how it seemed: one of those ever-remembered moments when the world spins round, the dark side is hidden, and all is light and promise.' Wonderment and a surge of desire was a heat in his body so powerful that its transmission to me was instantaneous. 'I love you, Christy. That's the heart and the whole of it. I love you.'

His look was of such naked clarity, a true and total giving of himself that it cleansed me of my contemptible crawling fears. They were gone, made meaningless as, in the house where we would live, in sight of the garden we would make, he gathered me into his arms.